BARBED WIRE *and* DAISIES

CAROL STRAZER

outskirtspress
DENVER, COLORADO

Barbed Wire & Daisies
All Rights Reserved.
Copyright © 2012 Carol Strazer
v3.0 r1.1

Cover created by Launie Parry
Cover Photo © 2012 Daniel Bettinger. All rights reserved - used with permission.

Outskirts Press, Inc.
http://www.outskirtspress.com

ISBN: 978-1-4327-9380-7

Library of Congress Control Number: 2012910406

Outskirts Press and the "OP" logo are trademarks belonging to Outskirts Press, Inc.

PRINTED IN THE UNITED STATES OF AMERICA

For the Prussian refugees and all who suffered from World War II,
and for my patient, supportive husband Bob and our dear family.

Chapter 1

"*Mutter*, what's that screeching? It hurts my ears. Make it stop," Elisabet yells, her hands clasping her head.

"Sirens, air raid sirens," Marike shouts in their native German tongue. She hopes the young children can't hear her terror.

"*Flugzeug, bombenangriff.* Bombers! I can hear their engines. They're getting closer." Without regard for the danger, her son, Heinz, shoves aside the bedroom window's black-out curtain and studies the silvery shapes silhouetted against a dark, turbulent sky.

Why, why did we have to come to Danzig…only to die? Marike chides herself. *I shouldn't have listened to my sister.* No time to think about that now.

"Heinz, close the curtain. Children come, follow me downstairs." Five small bodies squirm off the bed.

"Where's your cousin?"

"Under the covers. He won't come out," says Elisabet.

Despite her fear, Marike smiles inwardly at her five-year-old daughter's sense of responsibility. In the flickering light, Marike feels the bed clothes until she finds her nephew's small shaking body.

"Shush." Marike hugs him quickly until he is still.

"Mutter, Mutter!" he cries.

"He wants our mutter," her niece shouts.

In her rush to gather the six young children, Marike barely acknowledges her niece's concern. The two-story row house shudders.

"*Schnell weitergehen, bitte,* the basement. Edel, Elisabet, Heinz, Helena, Julianna, Jakob, follow me." As she says each child's name, she touches them gently. Then, she leads them toward the narrow stairway to the ground floor and kitchen. The hall light flickers, goes on once more, and then is extinguished. Blackness swallows them. Two-year-old Edel, her youngest, and his small cousin cling to her legs.

"Hold hands and stay together," Marike reminds them as she hobbles toward the stairway. Moving like a large caterpillar, they descend to the kitchen.

In the dark, Marike gropes for the doorknob and guides the children down the stairs into the basement. *When we arrived this morning, it was good that Heinz found the basement. If only we had found some food; then my sister would still be here. Why didn't I try to talk her out of leaving? What if she dies? I can barely care for my own four; how will I ever manage her two little ones? Still, we're lucky the director of refugees sent us to this vacant row house.*

Stretching her hand along the basement's cold concrete wall and moving slowly, Marike's knee bumps something. With her right hand, she begins to explore the mysterious object. Lights flash through the far window. Now, she sees it is a rough bench leaning against the wall.

"Come, children, sit." Immediately, both Edel and his small cousin climb on Marike's lap. Marike's niece follows her. Elisabet squeezes between them.

"I get to sit with my mutter. She's my mutter. C'mon, Helena, sit here." Elisabet pulls her younger sister next to her.

"Look....fireworks." Marike's young niece points a shaky finger at the faraway lights sparkling in the basement's only window.

"Those aren't fireworks. They're bombs," says Heinz.

"Heinz, don't. Now, children no arguing. Elisabet, you must be nice to your cousins. Don't shove. You can take—"

A large explosion rocks the house. The bench vibrates. Dust falls and Heinz coughs.

"Quick, cover your mouths." Marike demonstrates as she places her open hand to her lips. Obediently, the children place their hands over their faces. With the next flash, the children turn wide eyes toward the window where large cracks appear. Creaking noises come from upstairs, and the sounds of glass shattering can be heard as windows break. Marike and the children freeze.

Heinz asks, "It's the Allies, isn't it? 'Cause we're Prussian? What did *we* do?"

"Never mind that. We're safe. Look at this strong wall." Marike knocks her fist against the wall. *I hope it will hold* she worries.

Heinz persists, "But Mutter, why are the Allies bombing us?"

On either side of her, Marike feels the older children shiver. She balances the two small boys on her lap. They press against her, while she tries to cover them with her coat against the March cold.

When another nearby outburst produces a brilliant light, she sees the children's white faces. Her heart, already pounding with fear, contracts with the knowledge of their suffering, and she swallows a scream. *It's not fair—they're innocent babes. What have they done to deserve this?* Taking a deep breath, she whispers, "Dear Jesus, protect us. Help us."

In the sudden quiet, Marike counts the seconds before another eruption. The bombers must be circling, she guesses. As they return, she hears the engines' droning grow louder. Far away, like a drum beat, sounds the relentless rat-a-tat-tat of Neufahrwasser Harbor's anti-aircraft guns.

All those ships in the harbor, loaded with so many Prussian refugees fleeing the war. Please protect them and us. What about the children?

Even if they survive this terrible night, will they be forever fearful? What can I do?

Pray. If only she could remember all those Bible verses she'd memorized. Instead, her thoughts seem like her father's chickens—running in circles at every thunder clap. *Only this isn't thunder.* Wrapping her arms ever more securely around the children, she begins humming her favorite Mennonite hymn.

Marike doesn't know if the children can hear her over the noise, but music has always helped calm her before, and it seems to help now. The children, still whimpering, become quiet.

"Mutter, are they trying to bomb our house?" asks Elisabet.

Elisabet, her precocious eldest daughter at five, is always asking questions. Even as Marike struggles with an answer that won't terrify the children, she feels a mother's pride.

"Well dear, they aren't exactly bombing us. They're bombing the Harbor of Neufahrwasser and maybe Danzig, too. Don't worry. We're safe here on the outer edges of the city." The children nod their heads, and Marike prays she is right.

The children's questions make Marike shudder as she recalls her morning's conversation with the woman on the Red Cross bus as they traveled to the city. At first, she hadn't recognized her. So many women had crowded aboard, all dressed similarly in long, dark coats and muddy galoshes. In their hands, they clutched bags filled with their dearest possessions.

Yet the friendly woman greeted Marike, reminding her that they belonged to the same Mennonite congregation.

Icy fear smothers her as she recalls the woman's stern warning. "You'd better get those children out of Danzig, quick. The Russians are on the edges of Danzig and Gotenhafen. You've heard what they'll do to us Prussians."

As her four children, all under the age of seven, listened, Marike interrupted her. She didn't want her children frightened. The sharp-nosed woman pulled Marike near her and whispered shocking stories of grisly acts the Russian troops committed—raping and murdering German citizens in East Prussia. She said, "They slice off the women's breasts and nail them to the barn doors. In this village, they killed everyone, even the children. They want to get rid of us Prussians so the Russians and Polish can have our land."

Another bomb explodes nearby, shaking the house, causing Marike's ears to ring, and reminding her of their imminent danger. As her youngest, Edel, and his cousin burrow their faces into her blouse, Marike feels wetness: their tears. She uses her sleeve to wipe their faces.

Julianna yells, "Are we going to die? I want my *mutti.*"

"I don't like the dark. It's scary," Elisabet says.

Marike hugs the children. Finally, the sirens stop blaring. It's eerily quiet.

"Dear children. Don't worry. It's dark, because the electricity went off. If only we had a candle. We're safe. We're not going to die. Children, your mother will return." Marike hugs Edel and whispers, "Shhh, I hear voices—they sound like they're coming from the other side of this wall."

"I hear them, too. And I hear a scratching. Look, a brick just fell out." A small shower of dirt and a brick land near Heinz.

Astonished, they watch as a candle, held by two fingers, moves through the new hole. When Marike lights the candle with the stove matches she always carries in her pocket, the children grin. Now, at least they can see. In hushed voices, they thank their unseen benefactor. And Marike says a quick prayer of thanksgiving.

A loud *ka-boom* sounds across the street. "Please, Mutti," three-year-old Helena cries, "I'm scared." Marike, hoping to distract her panicked children, promises to sing to them.

The children hum as Marike's clear soprano voice rises, sheltering them. With renewed vigor, Marike sings Goethe's *Heideröslein.*

Elisabet joins her in her favorite song. *"Sah ein Knab' ein Röslein stehn, Röslein auf der Heiden…"*

As they finish, Marike's niece asks her to explain what the song means. Marike says, "A young boy sees a small rose blooming fresh in the morning. He runs to it and tells the rose he will pick her, but the rose defends itself by pricking him. The boy can't complain about the pain, because he brought the pain on himself by picking the rose. He has to endure…"

As the children listen to their mother's singing, they no longer jump at each loud noise. Instead of staring at the bright flashes in the cellar's small window, they watch Marike.

Marike still hears the *ka-boom, ka-boom* of bombs exploding. Sometimes, she feels the bench moving and hears the house creaking. Looking at the candle's flickering light reflected on the children's trusting faces, she sees hope.

Much of the night, Marike tells the children Grimm's *Fairy Tales* until, exhausted, they fall asleep. Their small bodies lean awkwardly against one another.

While the children rest, Marike gazes around at the dusty walls and recalls yesterday's events. *It doesn't feel like yesterday—more like a yesterday that happened long ago.* How had they come to be in this strange, empty row house on Bischofsberg in Danzig? First, while fleeing the war, they had been staying with relatives in another town. Then, German orders had come. "Evacuate immediately." Russian troops had marched in from the east and Allied forces had cut off any escape from the west. Her sister had said they should go to Danzig and the Neufahrwasser Port. Reluctantly, Marike had agreed.

Marike, her four children, and her sister Agathe, with her two small children, had hurriedly boarded the Red Cross bus. It took them to Danzig, where they were to escape on a ship across the Baltic Sea. But when they arrived in Danzig, they found chaos. Enormous throngs of other refugees, Prussians and Germans, milled about. A rendezvous for refugees had been organized at the theater.

When they entered the theater, they found hundreds of refugees crowded together. Marike had to step over people who sat and lay in the aisles. Every place was taken. Babies cried. People shouted to be heard. The noise pounded their ears.

Fortunately, the Red Cross director noticed them as they stood overwhelmed in the entrance. She apologized for the confusion, saying that over a million refugees were trying to leave Danzig. Commiserating with her dilemma and hoping to enlist her sympathetic assistance, Agathe explained they had just arrived with six young children.

"Six little ones," the tired-looking director repeated in astonishment. "There's no room here, and the ships have been loaded, but you can stay at one of the empty row houses on Bichofsberg. Tomorrow, I'll send the bus for you, and you can board another ship."

"Thank you for helping us," Marike said.

The director motioned to the bus driver, gave him instructions, and Marike, Agathe, and the children followed him to the bus.

As they drove over the cobbled streets, the bus driver directed their attention to the magnificent architecture of the many Lutheran churches whose steep roofs lifted their crosses into the sky. When the driver learned they were Mennonites who had never been to the historic city, he pointed out the Danzig Mennonite church. It was a modest, white-washed, rectangular building with a low hip roof. Marike remembered thinking the building symbolized the Mennonites' virtues of faithful simplicity. If only the German government had allowed their men exemption from the military. For centuries, they had tried to follow Christ's peaceful example: substituting non-combatant work for military service and avoiding swearing the military's oaths. Now, their pacifist ways were no longer accepted.

When they arrived at the vacant row house, the bus driver promised to return the next day and take them to their ship. Because the children complained of hunger, they first searched the house for food. Unable to find any, Agathe told Marike to care for her little ones while she searched the city. Since it has been many hours since Agathe left, Marike prays for her sister's safe return.

After many frightening hours of continued bombing, Marike and the children fall asleep in the damp cellar. Abruptly, Marike awakens to the sound of knocking. At first, she thinks it's a dream, but no, it comes from upstairs. Trying not to awaken the children, she carefully untangles herself from their small bodies and climbs the cellar stairs. The noise comes from the direction of the kitchen door.

"Who is it?" she inquires cautiously.

"Your sister! Hurry and open the door!"

Shoving the door open against the debris that fell during the night, Marike hugs her sister. Now Agathe's children awaken, and they cling to their mother, teary and smiling at the same time. The mothers remind the children to step carefully around the broken glass from the shattered windows.

Then Marike breathes a quick prayer of thanks. After righting the kitchen chairs, children and mothers collapse on them.

"Dear Agathe," Marike begins. "We were so worried about you."

Agathe laughs nervously. "Oh, I'll admit I was plenty scared, but I found shelter in the entrance of a sturdy building. The bombing went on all night. I didn't dare leave."

Marike notices the children's eyes keep darting towards Agathe's coat pockets.

Finally, Agathe's youngest asks, "Mutter, food?"

Shaking her head, Agathe kneels and kisses her son Jakob's sooty face. "No, but soon we will find food. Look at you two, like street urchins. I hope, at least, there is water."

As the children leave for the bathroom to wash and get a drink, Marike and her sister exchange worried glances.

"How bad was it?" Marike asks.

"Oh sister, God was watching over us. Thank heavens we didn't board our ship yesterday. The Neufahrwasser Harbor looked terrible—too many ships sunk. As far as I could see, ships, barges, boats on their sides, bows down, wreckage everywhere. I don't know how anyone survived." Agathe pauses, "I was so worried about the children and you. Just think if we had been on our ship. It was sunk."

Elisabet returns from the bathroom and extends her hands for Marike to examine.

"Mutti, the water ran a little and then stopped. I wet a wash cloth, and everyone used it, but we couldn't get very clean," Elisabet explains.

"Pipes are broken," Marike says.

Agathe exclaims, "Marike, how did you ever manage?"

"We were safe in the basement." Marike smiles. "The children were good."

"*Tante* Agathe," Elisabet says, "at first we were scared, but all night long Mutter told stories and sang to us."

"You're right. God protected us," Marike calmly replies.

"But the children must have been so frightened?"

"They were, but so good. Can you believe today is Palm Sunday? Yesterday, we planned to go to church. Now, there might not even be a church," Marike sighs.

"I know, but now we must leave. I heard the city's older section escaped some of the bombing. I hope people survived." Agathe asks, "By the way, the bus…did it come?"

"No."

The children return. With so many layers of clothing, Edel and his cousin can barely walk. Heinz and Jakob wear short pants with suspenders and knee socks, several sweaters, and their coats. Since each family has only one suitcase, everyone wears most of their other clothes. Helena has on her wool skirt and the sweater her mother knitted, over her old skirt and blouse. Her mother helps her with her sister's outgrown brown coat, which she can barely button. Elisabet struggles, with the help of garters, to keep up her too-big knit stockings and proudly slips on her new blue coat.

As she looks at Elisabet's new coat, Marike thinks, *today they were supposed go to Palm Sunday services, but not now. No birds sing or flowers bloom on this spring day. Instead all is silent.*

The children stare in shock at the nearby crumpled buildings, like fallen tombstones, in the early morning light. The sun is just a tiny pinprick in a dark grey, smoky sky. Black ash coats everything. The children complain that the acrid smoke stings their eyes and tastes bad. First, Heinz peers down into the huge crater near the house. As he hurries ahead, he looks at more enormous holes. Marike can't believe that yesterday this was a neat row of houses, and now so much is rubble.

An apartment building, missing its façade, looks obscenely naked, as two tilted floors display their few remaining contents: a tattered couch, fallen lamp stand, and scattered books. *It looks so crazily normal,* Marike thinks. She almost expects a husband to walk in and his wife to hurry from the kitchen with a warm greeting. Instead it remains an empty stage. The nearly deserted street greets them as they step around the debris. *Where are the people? Are they all dead?* Marike shakes her head and forces herself to think of her children.

"Mutti, can we go home now?" Elisabet asks. "I miss my scooter!"

"I want to go home too." Young Helena and the other children echo her.

Agathe and Marike lock eyes and then sadly look away. Marike struggles for the right words. Words that will help the children understand the danger but not terrify them. Certainly, she can't share the fears that make it hard for her to think clearly.

"I wish we could go home too. But now the Russian army occupies our home, which is why we had to leave."

The children nod.

"It isn't fair. Besides I don't see why they want my scooter," Elisabet whines.

"They don't want your old scooter," Heinz declares. "They hate us. They want Germany."

"But we're Prussian," Elisabet argues.

"Children, quiet," Marike says. "If you promise to keep walking, I'll try to explain."

"How can you explain this?" Agathe gestures angrily. "I can't understand. And you expect little children will?"

"Careful, children. Watch where you walk." Marike grabs Edel's arm as he stumbles. "I know it's complicated, but to help you understand: Thirteen years ago, in 1932, the German *Reich* got rid of Prussia's Prime Minister Otto Braun and our Prussian government. The state said military service was mandatory, even though we Mennonites don't believe in war and oath-taking. We try to follow Christ's example of non-violence, but your *vater* and *onkels* were conscripted into the German army. Anyway, this is too much politics for you to understand."

Agathe looks back at the smoking ruins. "I can't stand the thought of leaving Prussia. You're younger than I. You can adjust. I love Prussia. Besides, what if we can't find our cousins? They might not still be there." Holding her two children's hands, Agathe turns around and begins retracing her steps.

"You're going back?" Marike's voice rises in desperation, "I can't believe it. You know the stories—the awful things Russian soldiers do. Don't make me say something in front of the children."

"You're right. I know we have to go." Agathe says as she walks agitatedly back and forth before continuing. "But my Herman, I think he's still in Prussia, maybe Hamburg. I can't leave him."

Marike walks towards Agathe and grasps her hand. "I know, but I think Herman would want you to be safe. I, too, worry about my Horst. How could the army make him, a good Mennonite who doesn't believe in fighting, into a soldier? It doesn't make sense. Anyway, we have to go to our mutter's cousins' home. They're the closest. We'll hope they're there." Marike repeats softly, *"Am Lebenbleiben, Am Lebenbleiben." We must stay alive.*

They walk slowly away from Danzig. The little ones whine. Marike worries that with six little children, it will take a long time. *And if the Russian soldiers find us, they'll kill us—or we will wish we were dead.*

Then, Heinz excitedly points to a wheel protruding from a distant crater. Without waiting for his mother, he scampers into the hole and screams, "It's an old bicycle, but I think it still works!"

"Heinz, be careful, there could be an unexploded bomb," exclaims Marike. "Still, I think you found our transportation."

"You don't mean that old thing," her sister replies.

Marike barely hears her as she looks for other useful items hidden in the concrete rubble. A small stool and some rope reward her search. Soon Heinz helps her tie the rope to the stool and to the bike's handlebars. Marike carefully checks the bike. Even if the paint is worn off, when she turns the pedals, the wheels work. Carefully, she places young Edel on the stool. Next, she helps Helena sit on the torn bike seat. Then Agathe, giving in, places her squirming youngster on the bike rack. Reminding each child to hang on tight, Agathe slowly pushes the bicycle down the road. Marike firmly grasps Elisabet's and her niece's hands. Heinz leads the way calling, "Come, come."

Soon they join a few people leaving the outskirts of the bombed city. Some carry bags filled with necessities from whatever they can salvage. Dressed in long skirts, midway to their calves, wrapped in overcoats with scarves knotted tightly under their chins, the women move steadily forward. Children, mostly young, grasp their mother's hands. If she carries a suitcase or bag, they clutch a corner of her coat. As Marike glances at the women, she sees pain and fear in their eyes, but their faces reflect grim determination. An old man, leaning on his cane, leads the way. He removes his hat and points it at the smoldering ruins behind them.

"It's a shame. Danzig was such a jewel."

"Our first visit," Marike replies. "I'd always heard what a magnificent city it was."

With his cane, the man pushes a brick out of the way. "Oh, where are you from?"

"Petershagen, Prussia," Marike says.

"Since you're not from here, you probably don't know much about Danzig. She was famous—had more than a million citizens. Now, look at her. This is the worst bombing poor Danzig has ever had." He kicks a chunk of concrete. "I taught history, and Danzig had a noble history until Germany's defeat in 1918 after the First War. The victors made Danzig a 'free city,' but it wasn't real. Even though many of Danzig's citizens were Prussian or German, the Poles controlled Danzig until Hitler liberated us. Now, Russia and Poland want her back."

"Why?" asks Heinz.

"Good question, boy. The Russians and Poles want her port for shipping, and they don't care how much they destroy to get her."

Marike barely hears him as he disappears around a bend in the road.

As they follow him, Heinz says, "Mutter, look, a truck."

"It looks like an army truck. Hurry children, maybe they'll give us a ride." Together, Marike and Agathe push the bicycle forward.

"See, they're waiting for us," cries Heinz. Standing near the troop transport, the elderly gentleman helps lift the children into the back, where they join other refugees.

CAROL STRAZER

"I thought you ladies needed some help, so I hailed this army truck. Fortunately, the driver stopped. Said he'd just delivered more troops to the front. Sorry, you can't take the bike."

As the truck weaves around potholes caused by the bombing, they leave the devastated city behind them. Although the transport can take them only to the next town, Marike is relieved that they won't need to walk.

Chapter 2

For two days, Marike and the others stay with their *oma*'s relatives. They live in a tiny cottage of four small rooms. Marike, her sister, and their children manage to crowd into one room and sleep in their clothes on the floor. Although the authorities recommended that their elderly cousins evacuate, they have chosen to stay. Each day their cousins feed them one meal of thin potato soup. Agathe and Marike appreciate their generous hospitality, but Marike is concerned about depleting their cousins' dwindling food supply, which consists mainly of a forlorn bag of ripening potatoes. Also, Marike worries about the advancing Russian army.

Reports have reached them that Russian troops and Polish dissidents are taking over Danzig. Danzig's defenseless citizens, many of whom recently escaped from East Prussia, experience a terrible retaliation. Even though Marike offers to help her elderly relatives flee, they decline. Reluctantly, Marike and Agathe, each carrying a suitcase, gather their children and trudge down the road toward the next village.

As they walk, the youngest children, Edel and his cousin, beg their mothers to carry them. Marike holds Edel in one arm, and her other hand carries their suitcase. They progress slowly until Marike notices a cast-off baby buggy frame, which lies on its side next to the road. Half-buried in the ditch is a crib mattress. Other refugees have passed this way and discarded unwanted belongings. Marike rights the buggy; Agathe places the crib mattress on it, and with a piece of rope she found, ties it to the frame. They hoist the younger children on the buggy and continue their journey to another relative's home. While Marike pushes the buggy, which bumps across the rough ground, her sister carries their two suitcases.

As they approach the woods, Heinz shoves his hair out of his eyes and stares skyward. Suddenly, he yells, "Enemy planes! Run!"

With all of her energy, Marike urges the children forward, crying, "Run! Run!" Soon they stumble into the woods' undergrowth as they, too, hear the Allied planes' whining engines. "Lie down," Marike and Agathe screech as they grab their youngest and flop down on the ground, covering them with their bodies. Marike scans the blue sky but sees only the Allies' planes. Not a single plane from the *Luftwaffe* challenges them. Behind them, on the open road, Marike hears gunfire and terrified screams as the planes strafe stragglers. Frightened, Marike and Agathe urge the children to run farther into the woods, where the trees' springtime buds provide scant protection.

It's a warm day, and the children perspire from running. Elisabet removes her new blue coat and lays it on the buggy, while her aunt pushes. Agathe's daughter also complains that her feet are too hot and removes her shoes, tossing them into the buggy. As Marike anxiously studies the sky for more planes, she barely notices the girls removing some of their clothing.

Later, Elisabet complains, "My new coat, where is it?"

"Your coat, you had it on," Marike replies.

"No, I was hot. I took it off and put it right here in the buggy." Elisabet points to the buggy.

"Me too," her cousin says. "I put my shoes in the buggy, but now everything is gone."

"Where?" Agathe asks.

"Maybe in the woods," Elisabet mumbles, her head down.

"Elisabet, how could you be so careless—your new coat?" Marike scolds as she stares at her daughter and grits her teeth.

"We could go back to the woods and look," Agathe suggests. "They must be someplace."

"No, it will be night soon," Marike states flatly. Her anger thins as she realizes how fortunate they are not to be victims of a strafing.

At dusk, they arrive at their distant cousin's Margarethe's large but plainly built home in Schönau. A broad-shouldered man in work clothes opens the front door.

"Oh, Abelard, I'm so glad to see you," Marike says. "I was afraid you, too, had to join the army."

"Marike, Agathe, when we heard about the bombings in Danzig, we were so frightened for you and the children. Thank heavens you're safe. No, the army said I was too old, and they needed some men to farm. Mutter and Vater were so worried they'd never see you again." Abelard grins and embraces his sisters.

"Mutter is here? What about Freda and your children?" Agathe asks.

"Here, come and see. The children already have their oma telling stories," Abelard laughs.

Marike, Agathe, and their children follow Abelard into the drawing room, where Oma Ilsa sits surrounded by Abelard and Freda's five children. Some are as tall as their petite grandmother. Before Ilsa turns her head and sees her daughters, she continues her story about her childhood.

Abelard, Ilsa's eldest son, interrupts. "Mutter, guess who just arrived?"

"I don't believe it!" Ilsa stands up, tears running down her cheeks. "Marike, Agathe, children, how I've prayed you'd be safe!"

Soon everyone hugs and talks all at once.

Abelard's eldest daughter complains, "But Oma, what about our story?"

Ilsa waves her hands. "Later, I'll finish it later. I promise. Then your cousins can hear the story too. Go and play. Now, I must see my two daughters and your cousins. I was so afraid. I thought they were lost."

As she hugs her mother, Marike sighs in relief. During their terrible journey, she often feared for her parents' and other family members' safety. To have her oldest brother Abelard present reassures her, reminding her of how much she had missed a man's authority. It feels good to loosen responsibility's tight constraints.

Abelard, his rough face softening, squeezes Marike. His eyes question his younger sister. *He wants to know if we were assaulted or hurt.* As she remembers the terrible bombing, Marike answers with a brave smile, even though tears smudge her vision. The children, their eyes bright with anticipation, surround them. Again, several children plead with their grandmother to finish her story.

Impatient, Abelard's wife scolds, "Children, have you no respect? Give your poor grandmother some peace. Surely she has enough to do, caring for *Opa.*"

Lena, Abelard's thirteen-year-old eldest daughter, rolls her eyes and grumbles something about Freda. *How difficult it must be,* Marike commiserates with her, *to be stepmother to your poor dead sister's four children. If it were me, I wouldn't have much patience either. At least Freda has Abelard's and her own little Bettina to console her.*

Greeting her sister-in-law, Marike quickly kisses Freda's cheek. Freda acknowledges Marike's empathy with a grateful nod. The adults, concerned about the advancing Russian army, resist saying anything more in front of the children. Marike expects there will be time enough tomorrow.

Marike's mother gently beckons her to a quiet corner and confesses, "Marike, I've been so worried about your father. I almost forgot to give you a message."

"But who would leave a message?" Marike asks, bewildered.

"Your friend Gertrude. So sad; she lost her parents—all the family she had—in an air raid. She thought you might be here and came looking for you. You just missed them."

"Mutter, you mean pretty little Gertrude Froese, our neighbor in Petershagen?"

"Yes, how Gertrude idolizes you—called you her big sister. And now, poor thing, she lost her husband who died of influenza fighting on the Eastern Front."

"You said them?"

"Her baby boy! All she has left. She stayed only one night. I tried to talk her into staying longer, but you know Gertrude. Had to be on her way, she said."

"Oh Mutter, with everything else, you took time to help Gertrude. You're wonderful. Where did she go?"

Ilsa tells Marike that Gertrude said she would try to escape by the only route possible: by sea, to German Occupied Denmark. Ilsa makes Marike promise that if she finds Gertrude, she will help, in any way possible, the "strong-willed but good-hearted" young woman.

"I promise. I like Gertrude." Marike hesitates. "But Vater…how is he? Ever since we left, I've worried about Vater and you. Has the doctor been able to help him?"

Ilsa begins to say something when her cousin interrupts. She apologizes that she has no more beds but gives Marike some blankets for a makeshift bed in the parlor's corner. Their cousin's house is crowded not only with family (Abelard and Freda's five children, Agathe's two, Marike's four, and their parents), but also with other refugees.

Some might be upset by the household's noisy confusion, Marike muses, *but I find it oddly comforting. Like my childhood in a large family, it feels safe, even though I know it's an illusion.*

Later, after her children have eaten their dinner of boiled potatoes and cold milk, they are sleepy. But first, Marike leads them in their nightly prayers.

Heinz interrupts his Mutter. "You forgot Vater. You didn't pray for him."

Marike winces and says, "Please watch over the children's vater and keep him safe."

"I miss him. I liked it best when Vater would let me ride in his bakery wagon."

"You'd get so excited when he let you help him make the bread deliveries."

"When it would rain, Vater would let me ride inside the bakery wagon." Heinz says, "I could see through a small opening in the back door. I loved watching the farmers working in their fields and the sweet smells of our bread and their hay. Someday, I want to be a farmer."

"You'll make a good farmer," Marike says absently, as she draws a blanket over a squirmy Edel.

"The best part was when we came home," Heinz continues. "After Vater unhitched Nell, he'd ride her into the pond next door and rinse her off. He said when I got bigger, I could ride her. Will Vater remember his promise?"

"I'm sure he will. Well, Heinz, time to sleep now." Marike pats his tousled hair, her fingers smoothing his unruly cowlick.

"Yes, Mutter. Mutter, I wish Vater was here."

"I know. I do too. Goodnight."

Marike is grateful for the dark, which hides her tears. *How can I explain to my young son the terrible message I received just two months ago? It happened when we fled the war. We stayed with our cousins in Tiegenhof.*

Hoping to hear from her husband, Horst, in the German army, Marike tried to get her mail. The Tiegenhof postal center's clerk refused her request, saying something about only officials receiving mail. Fortunately for Marike, her brother Diether was stationed nearby. As a German army officer, he used his position to obtain her mail. When he returned to the house, an excited Marike thought the letters he carried were from Horst. It had been months since she had heard from her beloved husband. Her joy became a foreboding and then anguish as she recognized her own handwriting and the large black letters stamped *EMPFÄNGER VERMISST* (recipient missing) on the returned envelopes.

Her brother Diether stood by helplessly as she clutched the mail to her chest. Frenzied, she rushed past concerned relatives and ran up the stairs to the attic where they stored the grain. Oblivious to the sounds of mice, she fell, crumpled on the pile of grain. Sobbing, she inhaled bits of it.

Less than an hour later, she heard her sister Agathe calling her. Marike rose awkwardly and brushed away the grain kernels clinging to her skirt and blouse. With her sleeve, Marike swiped gritty snot from her face. She stuffed her grief, with the returned envelopes, in her pocket. *I can't think of death now.* "Missing" *means hope. For the children's sake, I must believe Horst lives—maybe in a Russian prisoner-of-war camp.*

At first, when Marike awakes in her cousin's house, she thinks she is still in that attic in Tiegenhof. She shivers with fear as she recalls their narrow escape from the terrible bombing in Danzig and their frantic search for family. *Instead, poor Agathe is disappointed not to find her husband Herman at our cousin's.* Marike prays for their husbands' safety.

The house's turmoil, crowded with family and other refugees, engulfs her. Everyone talks about the war. Their voices rise as each claims to know what is happening. Bewildered by the noisy confusion, Helena cries. Marike reassures her young daughter as her family discusses the many refugees, possibly two million, who have escaped from the eastern provinces. With the approach of the Russian forces and the Allied troops, they agree they are separated from the rest of Germany.

For the first time, everyone, except for the small children, is quiet.

Abelard says, "I've heard the German Naval Commander wants to help take people by navy ships across the Baltic Sea. Already, German ships transport wounded soldiers."

"Which is why, when I heard about the ships, I told Marike I thought we could get on a ship at Danzig. I never thought the Allies would bomb it and the port—certainly not with all of the wounded and many refugees," Agathe frowns.

While Agathe continues to tell their extended family about their terrifying escape from Danzig, Marike half-listens. *If only I hadn't listened to my sister. We could have been killed like so many others in Danzig. How many times have I moved—trying to protect my four young children? When Horst was recalled to the Eastern Front, we moved from our home in industrialized Elbing to Altfelde. In Altfelde, I took Horst's place managing his widowed mother's bakery.*

Even though the house is noisy, Marike's exhausted children sleep. Marike wonders how they will escape from the war zone. Tired, she gives thanks that they are together and safe—for now. Finally, she sleeps.

In the early morning hours, Marike hears cupboard doors banging. Quickly, she dresses and hurries toward the kitchen and bumps into her brother.

"Abelard, what's all the noise? It will wake the household."

"I'm about to find out."

Abelard and Marike enter the kitchen and watch as a distraught Freda wipes a pan, shoves it into the cupboard, and slams the door.

"Freda, dear, what is the trouble?" Abelard asks while trying to kiss his wife's cheek. Instead, she twists away from him and continues to dash around the kitchen.

"Your daughter Lena is the trouble. First of all, last night I told her to clean up the kitchen, but just look at this mess. This morning, when I corrected her, she marched out and left me to do everything."

"Here Freda, I'll help." Marike scrapes and stacks plates.

"And what does Lena do but go to town with your brother Diether, an officer." Freda bites off each word. "I'd already forbidden her to have anything to do with him or any other German army officers."

Marike looks puzzled. "I don't understand why, Freda? Diether is a good man."

"I will tell you why." Freda inhales. "My old minister preached against fighting and the taking of oaths. Some Mennonites I know even said that Mennonite officers should be shunned. I wouldn't go that far, but still I've always believed in our peaceful traditions."

"You forbid Lena, your stepdaughter! How dare you. That is for her father, me, to decide." Abelard's tone softens, "I believe what our new pastor said, that Jesus taught us to place others' needs ahead of ours. Don't you remember in 1933, when Germany said that public interest came before personal interests? Even some Mennonites agreed our society was too permissive. They had heard from Mennonites in Russia about their terrible trials under Bolshevism. They feared the Bolsheviks—called them atheists. Besides, you know what happened to the pastor who preached against the mandatory military service. He was censored."

"I do remember—poor man," Freda says. "Yet, I admire him for his principles. Still I think your brother is wrong. And it was Hitler who said that about the 'public interest.' Like Jesus, I believe to hate anyone is a worse sin. To be a German army officer, your brother had to take an oath. He could have chosen an alternative duty."

"Freda, my brother Diether was just trying to help his family," Marike implores.

"I suppose you'd want Diether to be like *your* brother?" Abelard asks with a hint of sarcasm. "To serve in the Medical Corps and die on the Front, where they send all the Mennonites who ask for alternative service?"

Marike, who wants peace, steps between her brother and Freda.

Freda, as if struck, clasps her throat. In a strangled voice, she says, "That isn't fair. My brother followed his beliefs."

With her hand on his chest, before her brother can respond, Marike says, "Oh Freda, I admire your brother. I believe violence is wrong. Like you, I believe in our peaceful Mennonite ways. But what choice did our men have—concentration camps? Still, if Diether wasn't an officer, I couldn't have received word about my Horst. And we don't even know what else Diether may have done to keep us safe."

"I don't need to remind you two that we're in a war zone," Abelard says. "Now is not the time to argue who is a better Mennonite. Diether is ambitious, like most young people. Besides, he tries to protect us. I don't want to discuss this again. As far as my daughter Lena is concerned, I will talk to her." Abelard shoves open the kitchen door and leaves.

Freda watches him exit and then says, "My dear dead sister always made the children behave. Now look at them. I'm afraid for them."

"Come Freda, sit and rest. I can clean the kitchen." Marike pulls out a kitchen chair for Freda and takes the dishrag from her hand. "I understand. Being stepmother to four half-grown children must be really hard."

Freda places her arms on the table, buries her head, and sobs while Marike rubs her back.

Chapter 3

Two weeks. Marike can hardly believe it has been more than two weeks since they joined her family. Today, they will celebrate their beloved mother's sixty-sixth birthday.

"If only we could make a cake," says Agathe.

"But there is no flour or sugar left. In fact, all I could find were a few old potatoes growing sprouts. And they told us there are no food coupons or any food for us," replies Marike.

"What can I do?" asks their sister-in-law Freda.

"Well," says Marike, "The least we can do is gather the children and sing. You know Mutter, she is always telling us not to make a fuss, and she loves to sing. She'll understand."

Just then, Abelard enters the kitchen. "I overheard you talking about Mutter's birthday. I'm sorry to give you the bad news, but we've been ordered to leave—there is no more food."

"We know. We were just talking. When do we have to leave?" Marike asks.

"Today. We're supposed to take the bus and meet the boat. It will take us to Hela Peninsula where we'll board a ship. Quick—pack, we have only an hour."

"Who told you?" Freda asks. "It could be a mistake. Many people are confused. Besides, a friend told me the Americans gave the Russians bombers. They're bombing our ships. It's too dangerous."

"Someone from the German navy told me. I don't abide rumors. We're surrounded, cut off. The sea is the only way out," replies Abelard, folding his arms.

"What about Vater? When the doctor removed more fluid this time, he punctured his lung. He can hardly breathe," Marike asks.

"There is no choice. We've all been ordered to leave," Abelard repeats. "Hurry, tell the children."

As Marike leaves, her mother enters, and she and Abelard discuss making arrangements for transporting Marike's father.

Chapter 4

It has been a long, dismal day, and Marike is still shivering. They have waited on the dock for seven hours. Frigid winds off the Baltic Sea's churning waters blast them until Marike's teeth chatter. Her children jump up and down, trying to stay warm. Finally, the boat comes and takes them to Hela, where they will board their ship.

Marike recalls the days before the war, when Hela had been a favorite resort of her friends. In those days, they had been able to take a train or car to Hela. Her friends often described to her the thirty-five kilometer, sandy peninsula protecting the Bay of Danzig. Before Germany reclaimed Hela and invaded Poland in 1939, they were dismayed when the Polish army blew up part of the peninsula. *They should call it Hela Island*, Marike thinks grimly.

She sees some thirty German freighters docked, ready to transport some of the two million German refugees attempting to flee to the west.

Marike wishes they didn't have to leave. Late into the night, her family and she had discussed the options, but what else could they do? When an East Prussian refugee, a former customer in the Altfelde Bakery, told them what had happened to her cousins in Nemmersdorf, East Prussia, Marike knew they had to leave. The woman said the Russian troops raped many women and then clubbed or hacked to death most everyone, including old men and children. *There is no choice. We must leave.*

A loudspeaker announces their ship is boarding. Marike urges her children forward.

"No. I'm not going. You can't make me." Elisabet stands resolutely, tears in her eyes.

The family stares at the gangplank, a long board slanting upward from the dock to the ship's deck, and watches as people slowly ascend it.

"C'mon, Elisabet, it isn't that bad. Just follow me. Remember when we used to climb the playpen at home?" Six-year-old Heinz gives his younger sister a playful push.

"Stop! I remember when you folded the old playpen and made a climbing game, but I didn't climb. I was scared, and Mutter didn't make me. Did you, Mutter? I don't have to climb that board, do I?"

"I'm sorry, Elisabet. I know you're afraid of heights, but it's the only way on the ship."

"But look. It's such a long way up to the ship. What if I fall? Please tell me I don't have to. At least, somebody can help me?"

"I'm afraid not. Heinz is helping Helena, and I have your little brother. Heinz will go first and show you how. Just follow him and I'll be right behind you."

"Elisabet, just hang on and slide your hands along the side. You can do it."

Elisabet bends over and grasps the slanted board. Placing one foot in front of the other, she carefully pulls herself up the board. Following Heinz, she is one-third of her way to the ship, when the strong ocean wind moves the board. Her feet slide.

"Help, help me! I'm falling," screams a panicked Elisabet. She looks down and sees the foamy waves far, far below. She freezes. "I can't move."

"Hey, what's going on up there?" yells a man standing below them. "If you don't hurry, the Russians will get us."

"You can make it," yells Heinz.

"I know it is hard, Elisabet," Marike shouts. "But he's right. There's a whole line of people waiting. Don't look down, just straight ahead. Now, move slowly, one hand first, then your foot. That's it, good girl."

Ever so slowly Elisabet regains her grip. Her small, five-year-old hands cling tightly to the board, her toes digging in.

When Elisabet reaches the top of the gangplank, a young sailor grabs her and sets her down. Those who have been watching Elisabet's struggle clap their hands. Elisabet smiles through her tears. Marike thinks they're not just acknowledging her courage; they're relieved they can board now.

Soon everyone is aboard; the gangplank and guy-ropes are retrieved. The large ship slowly leaves the Bay of Danzig, heading out into the Baltic Sea. Oma Ilsa and Opa Eberhard are directed to the upper deck. Marike, Agathe, and their children and Abelard, Freda, and their children are sent below to the ship's hold.

There, the noise is so loud that little Helena clasps her hands over her ears. Mothers rock and attempt to soothe their screaming infants. Young children try to escape their older siblings' restraining hands. Everyone seems to be talking. Someone switches on the lights, illuminating the dark hold.

"Turn those lights off and be quiet," shouts a man. "You want the subs to find us?"

"No, of course not," Abelard says, "My best friend boarded the *Wilhelm Gustloff* at the end of January. I heard a Soviet submarine hit it with three torpedoes, and it sank in less than seventy minutes. An estimated seven to nine thousand, many of them refugees, died. Maybe, a thousand survived. My friend didn't make it. The paper said the machinery to lower the life rafts was frozen. They never had a chance—not in those frigid waters."

"Abelard, please don't say any more," Marike warns. "You'll frighten the children."

Marike looks nervously at the children, fearing they had heard his comments. Oblivious, Elisabet and Christa, her cousin, sit, knees touching, absorbed in playing a clapping game.

"You're right," Abelard says. "Yet, I'm thankful we're here. Before we left, Diether told me if Admiral Karl Dönitz, the German navy's commander-in-chief, hadn't organized this rescue for so many refugees, we would have been trapped. Who knows, he might have even disobeyed orders." Abelard shifts his body as if trying to find a more comfortable sitting position.

At first, Marike is relieved to see her daughter engaged in a normal, childish game, and then she notices Elisabet's grey face. Immediately, she thinks Elisabet must be affected by the ship's swaying as it makes its way out of the Bay of Danzig to the Baltic Sea.

Suddenly, Elisabet spews vomit on her surprised cousin. Barely has Marike begun to wipe Elisabet, when ten-year-old Christa throws up on Elisabet. Relieved of their queasy stomachs, the girls point at each other, laughing, and despite the smell, Marike smiles.

Marike's smile changes to disbelief when she takes Elisabet and Christa to the ship's facilities. As they enter, they nearly fall on the floor. A watery slime from overflowing toilets covers the floor. The mingled smells of excrement, urine, and vomit make the girls gag. Clamping her mouth shut, Marike quickly steers them back to their family. When they return, Abelard, who sees their distress, shoves their pot in front of them. This time, Marike heaves into the pot.

With a weak smile and nod, Marike thanks him. "The facilities, they're awful—too many people and not enough toilets."

"I saw them," Abelard's mouth twitches in disgust. "My pig sty never smelled as bad. Good thing I brought this pot along. When you need it, we'll make a circle around you. Afterwards, I'll throw the contents in the sea. At least you'll have some privacy."

Grateful as she is for Abelard's foresight, Marike wonders how much they will need the pot when they have so little to eat. In the darkness, she feels the ship's swaying motion but has no idea where they're headed. No one tells them—part of the constant need for secrecy, she supposes, and their fear of Russian planes and subs. Meanwhile, Marike hears muffled moans and bodies moving. Of course, she remembers the many wounded soldiers she saw as they boarded. What agony they must be suffering.

Marike and the children sleep on the floor next to the many other refugees. The fetid air, little space for her to even roll over on the hard boards, and noisy passengers make rest difficult. *If exhaustion and fear didn't numb us,* Marike reflects, *sleep would be impossible.*

The next day, sailors enter the hold and bring empty bags. With experienced hands, they place the bodies of two small children, who died during the night, in one bag. The mothers, numb and tearless, rock back and forth, watching.

One mother grasps the sailor's arm and whispers, "What are you going to do with my child?"

The young sailor tries his best to reassure her. "We have orders to bury the dead at sea."

The mother shrieks. Nearby, two women try, in vain, to calm her.

Agathe whispers in Marike's ear, "I heard so many people died last night, they've run out of bags in which to bury them. They have to put two children to a bag. Remember when we wondered why they had rocks piled on deck? They use them to weigh the bodies down, to keep the sharks from getting them. And some say so the Russian subs won't find us."

"Poor woman, they've travelled so far with little food and shelter. It is too much for the little ones." Marike says.

The woman says, "We must have walked miles and miles with nothing to eat. It was so cold that my baby's diaper froze to her. When I tried to remove it, pieces of her skin peeled off. Then, she got sick like the others. If only I could have helped her." With the backs of her clenched fists, she rubs away her tears.

Like the others, Marike turns away. *At least the woman deserves privacy in her grief. How terrible—not even a grave. So many innocents have died. How many more must die? When will this terrible destruction end? I'm grateful,* Marike thinks guiltily, *it isn't my child. But who knows what tomorrow may bring.*

Chapter 5

As their ship crosses the Baltic Sea, it runs a deadly game of hide and seek with Russian bombers and submarines. To avoid being attacked, the ship's captain steers a zigzag course for two days—sailing at night and anchoring in little known coves during the daylight hours. When, frightened and hungry, they finally arrive in Kopenhagen's harbor, it is mid-April. They are forced to stay on board the ship. Marike watches as first the wounded soldiers, then those who died are carried off to the German military hospital. Someone asks the captain what will become of the refugees.

The captain replies briskly, "Some time ago, the German Occupying Force commanded the Danish to provide for the estimated 250,000 German refugees. Danish schools, factories, barracks, and other facilities have been confiscated. Be patient. It may take three days before you can be moved."

"Mutti, when can we get off the ship? It stinks," Heinz says.

"I'm sorry," Marike says. "We're not allowed to leave."

A woman holding a screaming infant complains, "I hope it's better than this ship. All they've given us is a few biscuits and a little tea."

"I doubt the *Dänins* will do much for us," says another woman. "Ever since we conquered their country, they hate us."

Heinz asks, "If they don't want us, Mutti, why don't we go to another country?"

Abelard, in a strained voice, answers. "No one else will take German refugees."

"At least we're alive," Marike says. "I was so afraid a Russian bomber would find us."

As Marike and her relatives wait to be moved to their new "home," Marike reminisces about her past life in Prussia. *It must be like dying, when you remember all the things you did.* Will she ever again see her beloved homeland? Will her children return to Prussia? Smiling, she sees herself as a child like Elisabet, helping her eleven brothers and sisters on her parents' Petershagen farm. As Marike's empty stomach rumbles, she thinks, *Even though we were poor and worked hard, there was always so much food, especially bread. When young, I loved to help my mutti make bread.*

Marike inhales. The warm, yeasty smell fills her imagination. Every day was baking day when she worked at *Frau* Amalia Wien's Altfelde Bakery. Even though Altfelde was a small Prussian village, Marike, accustomed to farm life's slow pace, enjoyed its excitement. Trains on the railroad's main line from Berlin to Königsberg provided patrons to keep the bakery busy.

She pictures Frau Wien's bakery, which typified German architecture. A large, square, two-story concrete building with a flat roof, its structure stood solidly on a well-frequented corner. Loaves of freshly baked bread rested behind the large window, to tempt the passersby. Often, the shopper paused, mesmerized by the dark breads, white breads, and assorted sweets in the glass display case. Marike delighted in arranging the bakery items just so, to create the lingering attention.

Marike remembers how Frau Wiens, a widow, told her how she had learned to manage the shop while she raised her two sons, Horst and his older brother. When Marike asked about her husband's death, Frau Wiens made the same, brief statement she always did.

She said, "He fell off the train at the end of the Great War. The train ran over his legs. Later, he died of gangrene." Even though

Marike expressed her sympathy, Frau Wiens shrugged her shoulders, ignored Marike's concern, and returned to her work.

Marike quickly learned everything Frau Wiens taught her. She most enjoyed waiting on customers, exchanging local news, and inquiring about their families. In return, the customers enjoyed her friendliness.

All would have been well with Frau Wiens, if not for her son Horst and me, Marike thinks. *But then, I admired his confident ways. Four years older, he always knew how to make me laugh.*

One day, as she returned from shopping, Horst suddenly appeared around the corner. Taking the heavy grocery bags from her, he walked with her along the street. She liked the way he talked, so full of plans, but not too full of himself, like some young men. When he described how he felt making and selling the bread, his strong hands punched invisible dough, and he smiled. He made her smile too.

Horst said, "I like you. You always work so hard and are so responsible."

Words too familiar and sometimes onerous to Marike, but she prized them because her Horst said them.

"In a big family like mine, everyone is expected to work hard," Marike said.

Taking her hand, Horst looked directly into her shy face. "You're the prettiest girl in town."

"I can't be. I'm too tall."

Then, he whispered in her ear, "I like tall girls. And I like how determination almost clings to those high cheekbones of yours."

His breath on her ear was like a kiss as his hand lightly caressed her cheek. Her mind whirled.

One quiet afternoon, Horst's mother, with her lips tightly compressed, bustled into the empty shop. Immediately, she locked the door.

Marike wondered what had she done wrong? Did she make a mistake with the receipts?

Frau Wiens stood directly in front of Marike and blocked any escape.

Without hesitation, she said angrily, "Marike, this is no good— you and my son. You are a decent, strong girl. You need to find someone else."

"What do you mean?" Marike stammered. She had an idea, but she hoped she was wrong.

"I mean," Frau Wiens continued, almost as if she had rehearsed what she was going to say, "There are many nice young men. I'm sure you can find one—but not my son. Anyway, I would expect your parents would want you to marry a farmer. That would be more appropriate."

Marike had heard other customers, mostly city women, criticizing the farm folk for their crude ways. She had hoped the proud Frau Wiens was different.

Later, when Horst heard, he angrily declared his love for Marike and said they would get married anyway. They did, but Marike never forgot and hoped that someday his mother would accept her.

How ironic life is, Marike reflects.

"Marike, Marike, hurry, bring the children. The truck is here," Freda calls interrupting Marike's memories.

Chapter 6

With one hand grasping their suitcase and her other holding Edel's small hand, Marike urges Heinz, Elisabet, and Helena toward the crowded truck. Two German sailors from their ship lift the children onto the truck. Marike draws the children around her, where they squeeze tightly together. A Danish soldier, looking bored, leans against the driver's door.

A short, scruffily dressed man with a high-pitched voice asks one of the sailors, "Is it true…what I heard about the *Goya*?"

The sailor glances around nervously. "I'm probably not supposed to say anything, but the newspapers already have the story. Yesterday, April 16, a Russian submarine sunk it. I know the *Goya*. They say there were some seven thousand aboard—mostly wounded soldiers and refugees."

"My brother was a sailor on that ship. Do you know if any people survived?" The man yells over the truck's idling engine.

Freda, standing next to Marike, asks, "Can you believe the Russians would sink a ship clearly marked for the wounded? What about the Hague Convention? I thought they couldn't sink ships carrying the wounded."

The sailor says, "The ship sank so fast—in four to seven minutes. I think about one hundred and eighty-three managed to survive. I'm sorry about your brother."

The short man mumbles something. With his head bent in defeat, he hastily walks away.

"Your poor brother and all those men, to endure so much war and then to drown—I'm so sorry," Marike says to the man's retreating back.

Freda whispers, "Oh my, do you realize we left from the same harbor. It could have been our ship." Freda shudders.

With shaking hands, Marike covers her stricken face. *For the children I must regain control.* As she lowers her hands, she says softly, "God protected us, thank heavens. We must pray for their souls."

"Yes, Mutti," Heinz and Elisabet say.

Slowly the large truck bumps through Kopenhagen's narrow, cobbled streets. Marike and the truck's occupants—mostly women and children—have no idea where they are going. They're prevented from seeing their surroundings in the entirely enclosed truck. Other trucks filled with refugees follow them. Marike knows they can't be too far from the sea. She can feel the damp sea air, smelling of fish.

Finally, the truck parks near what appears to be an enormous, two-story factory. As they enter the cavernous building, a dilapidated sign suggests this may have been an automobile factory. A Danish guard gestures to a huge pile of straw, indicating that each person is to take an armload. Marike notices those who have arrived earlier are sitting or lying on their straw piles. Suitcases are lined up to provide a makeshift barrier between various groups.

A din of people's voices, coughing and yelling, reverberates in the concrete building. Children, finally free of the ship's confines, run in circles. Nearby, a woman with tired features tries to comfort her fussy infant. Wordlessly, she turns a hopeful face towards them. Marike shakes her head. She understands the woman's unspoken plea. They have no food to share, no food at all.

Abelard finds a space large enough to accommodate all of them. Gently, he arranges the straw on the cold concrete and helps his father lie down. The small pile is barely enough for Eberhard to lay his head and upper body. Abelard adds more straw from his own pile and gently tucks the one blanket they each have been given around his father. Abelard looks worried. His vater wheezes, mouth open, gasping at the fetid air.

Around Abelard, his wife Freda, mother Ilsa, and sisters Agathe and Marike try to make straw beds out of the unwieldy straw, which scatters as soon as it is placed. Like other refugees, they line up their suitcases in a makeshift wall around them.

After their long trip, the restless children want to explore their new surroundings, while the exhausted adults collapse. Oma Ilsa calls the children to her and suggests they sing their favorite songs. Soon their tired eyes brighten as they say, "Yes, yes! Please, Oma, let's sing." Little three-year-old Helena's eyes are wide with terror, her mouth opens and closes wordlessly, and she sits frozen, wrapped in her blanket. She seems completely overwhelmed by the noise and confusion. Marike notices her daughter's distress but is soon distracted by Edel, who wanders away. Elisabet impatiently urges Helena to sing, and she dutifully joins the other children circling their oma.

With their straw and blankets distributed and suitcases placed, the mothers rest. To Marike, the concrete floor feels cold and un-yielding no matter how she arranges the straw. She surveys the enormous room, as more bedraggled refugees enter. She hears there are at least two thousand German refugees in just this one building. *At least we are safe from the bombs and the Russians. Tomorrow will be a better day*, she thinks as she rests.

"Mutter, wake up, they're bringing food." Elisabet is excited.

Marike sits up, and then stands, straining to see over so many people. The children are right. Several guards are approaching with a large pail. When they arrive, they give each person a cup of hot wa-ter. Even hot water feels good after so long. Carefully, she helps each of her children drink. Oma Ilsa comes and asks for a cup of water for Opa Eberhard, who is too ill to walk. When the guards learn of Opa's illness, they say they will return to take him to the hospital.

Two days later the guards come with the family's first hot meal and explain that after the family has finished eating they will take Opa, who is struggling to breathe, to the hospital. Everyone is relieved. Marike carefully pours the milk and distributes the loaf of bread and sausage among her children. When hunger makes Heinz stuff the bread in his mouth, Marike reminds him to remove it and eat only tiny bites.

"Why?" Heinz asks.

"Because we've had so little food, our stomachs have shrunk, making it harder to digest." Marike warns, "If you eat too much, you'll get sick."

Tearing tiny bits into her hand, Marike feeds two-year-old Edel. Helena and Elisabet watch their mother and eat ever so slowly.

"Look, Mutter," clever Elisabet says, "I can chew each piece twenty times."

"I can chew more times than that," Heinz adds a piece to his mouth. As he slowly chews, he silently counts on his fingers.

When they hear their cousin Peter throwing up, Marike silently thanks her children for their game. She knew they were terribly hungry, but she had insisted they should wait.

A truck drives up and the Danish guard helps Opa Eberhard into the back. The guard says he will take Marike's vater and others who are sick to the hospital. When the guard learns Bettina, Freda's three-year-old daughter, is also ill, he offers to take her to the hospital.

Freda clutches her baby and says, "*Nein, nein,*" loudly and furiously. The guard hurries away.

Suddenly, Bettina holds her stomach. Freda rushes her to the bathroom just as a brown line runs down Bettina's thin leg.

When Freda returns, she informs the family many others are in similar straits. Bettina lays limply in her mother's lap, her curly bangs drenched in perspiration and her cheeks reddened. Humming softly, Freda rocks her baby.

After she is asleep, Marike and Freda whisper to each other.

"Poor Bettina, she is so weak and sick. Are you sure it wouldn't be better to take her to the hospital?" Marike asks.

"*Nein*, I've heard about that hospital for babies. One woman told me in the bathroom—'If you love your baby, don't take her there—they don't come back alive. Mine didn't.'"

"You mean…" Marike says.

"I'm afraid so. She said that they are putting all the babies who aren't toilet trained in the nursery. They don't separate the sick from the others. The hygiene and medical care are poor. I'll never let them have my precious baby." Freda kisses Bettina's sweaty head and smoothes her curls.

Finally, the noise lessens as the refugees fall asleep. Marike prays for her father and her little niece and hopes the rest of the family stays well.

Helena snuggles next to her mother. "Please, Mutter, tell me my story."

"What story?"

"My favorite story—when I was born."

"All right, but then you must go to sleep."

"Yes, Mutter."

"Before you were born, your brother, sister, and I lived in a cottage in Elbing. Your vater, working in his mutter's Altfelde Bakery, visited on Sundays. Sometimes we'd have a picnic after attending our Elbing church. I loved our Mennonite church where we had such a caring pastor. You were growing big."

"I was in your tummy, right Mutti?" Helena pats Marike's stomach.

Marike grins. "Yes, kicking and giving your mother no rest. Your thoughtful vater suggested I take you, your brother, and sister to the family's cabin in Kahlberg, Prussia, near the Baltic Coast."

"Did my vater and his mutter come too?"

"They were busy with their bakery. Besides, Oma Wiens didn't feel well. She needed your vater and peace and quiet," Marike says ruefully.

It was good Horst understood why it was hard for her to think of moving to Altfelde. Soon enough, Marike knew the day would come. But with the new baby coming, she wanted this time to enjoy her children. Besides, even though she understood her mother-in-law's feelings about her, it didn't make them any less hurtful. Marike's eyes close.

"Mutter, don't sleep. You haven't told my story," Helena demands.

Marike yawns. "Let's see, one day when the sea made lovely, lapping sounds and frost sparkled in the morning light, you decided it was your time—October 6, 1941. Soon, there you were, all pink and crying. Elisabet thought you were a doll and wanted to put you in her doll bed. Heinz asked why you weren't a boy."

"Mutter, was I pretty?"

"Oh yes, you had the biggest, bluest eyes. Everyone said so."

"Tell me again what Helena means?"

"Bright one, torchlight. I believe someday you will light the way for others." Marike pats Helena's head.

"I like it. It's so pretty."

"Now, go to sleep dear."

"Yes, Mutti."

Gently, Marike tucks the blanket around Helena as her eyes close. Heinz curls up, one arm stretched over his head. *Just like his father,* Marike thinks as she holds little Edel close to share her warmth.

Chapter 7

"Mutter, Mutter, wake up," Elisabet shakes Marike's shoulder. "What is it?" Marike inquires.

"Magic, Mutti. There is magic. I saw hair move...in the basket...by the toilets. Come see."

Marike rolls over and carefully moves young Edel aside as she does so. "What is it? Oh, well, we may as well all go and see. Come, children."

Slowly, the children follow their mother. While they wait to use the toilet, Elisabet points her finger at the wastebasket. "Look, see the hair is alive."

A large clump of blonde hair in the basket does appear to move. Young Edel runs to see the basket. Marike watches the hair move.

"Oh, children that is lice. Edel, don't touch."

Edel withdraws his hand and returns to his mother.

"Children, we must try to be clean," Marike says. *But how, with no facilities for bathing?*

When they return to their informal family compound, the children excitedly tell their cousins about the "magic hair," and soon all must see. Marike smiles sadly, thinking how ironic it is that the children can be entertained by lice-filled hair. Chattering about the hair, they return in time to join those waiting in line for their daily food rations.

Young Helena quietly follows the older children. Marike asks her why she is silent. Helena whispers, "Mutter, too noisy, so many people." Tears cloud her enormous blue eyes. Marike lifts her and hugs her until Edel demands her attention.

Danish guards watch and sometimes straighten the long line of mostly women and children. Receiving their food, the family returns to their ill-fashioned camp.

In disgust, Elisabet pushes her bowl toward her mother. "Look, Mutter, black things floating in my soup. What are they?"

"Now dear, just take your spoon and dip them out."

"Ugh, mouse droppings." Elisabet sets her bowl down.

"Here, I'll take them out for you." Marike reaches for her daughter's bowl.

"This is mostly water," Heinz complains. "They said it was barley soup."

Elisabet makes a face, "I think they just gave us the sweepings from the empty grain bins."

"Children, don't complain. It isn't right," Marike corrects them.

"Yes, Mutter."

Later that afternoon, Marike notices people gathering in another long line. Curious, she and the children join them. As they approach the head of the line, a man reaches his scoop into his bucket and seems to christen the woman ahead of them with a white powder.

"Mutti," asks Helena, "Why are they putting flour on people?"

"They look like Heinz when he fell in the flour barrel," Elisabet says, poking Heinz.

"What is this?" Marike asks the Danish guard who motions people forward. When he answers in Danish, Marike tries to understand. *My teacher always said Danish was a hard language. I can't make sense of anything he says.*

A woman behind Marike taps her on the shoulder. "Delousing powder—to get rid of lice," she says as she scratches her head.

"Keep your eyes and mouth shut," Marike hurriedly tells the children before they too look like they fell headfirst into the flour barrel.

"It stings," Elisabet declares.

"I know," Marike consoles her youngsters, "but it will get rid of the bugs."

Freda joins Marike and Oma Ilsa. "Have you seen my children? I've been looking for them since we had that awful stuff they call soup."

Glancing around, Marike and Oma shake their heads.

Freda frowns. "How can I manage five children in a place like this? It's chaos. Don't they care? The children run wild. I tried to talk to a *danisch* guard, but he ignored me. It feels like a prison. Why aren't our German soldiers helping us?"

Oma responds, "Except for keeping us here, the Danes don't seem to care what happens to us. If only they allowed us some news."

The sounds of gunshots, people cheering, and church bells ringing come from the nearby street.

Heinz and his cousins run to Abelard. They shout excitedly at him.

"Whoa, slow down, I can't understand anyone with all of you shouting at me," Abelard claps his hands.

"Is it true? What they are saying?" Heinz asks.

True to his nature as a farmer, Abelard responds slowly, "What now?"

"Onkel, some refugees who are near the entrance said they heard the Danes celebrating because some English general is here in Dänemark." Heinz answers.

"General Montgomery, Vater," interjects Heinz's cousin, "and Deutschland capitulated to the British."

"When did German armies in Dänemark surrender to General Montgomery? It's probably another Danisch rumor," Abelard coughs.

— 45 —

Heinz pulls his uncle's sleeve. "Now can we go home? I mean, I know we can't go to Prussia, but to Deutschland?"

The other adults sitting nearby look hopefully at Abelard, who shakes his head.

Abelard's son says, "Mr. B.—I forgot his name, but he speaks Danish—heard the guards talking. I thought he said, 4 *Mai* was the surrender here in Dänemark. The guards said that after five long years of occupation, they'll be glad when German soldiers leave, even if it's for prisoner-of-war camps. And Dänemark should dump us refugees across the border. 'Let 'em starve,' they said. 'Why should we feed them?'"

Marike turns to Abelard, "Two days ago, May 4, they surrendered here? Do you think the *Dänins* will move us to Schleswig Holstein, where there are so many people and little food?"

"We'll see—can't blame the Danes. This war has been tough. I remember when Germany invaded Dänemark on April 9, 1940. The 'One Day War' they called it." Abelard continues, "They want their country, their buildings back—the ones our army confiscated for us refugees."

Freda, who joins them, comments, "I'm afraid of the Danish Resistance. They're punishing Danish collaborators—shaving the poor women's heads and parading them through the streets. Call them 'mattress women' and their babies 'little German soldiers.' You're too soft-hearted, Abelard. Who knows what they'll do to us."

"It explains why we haven't seen any of our soldiers," Marike replies. "I guess we're fortunate the Danes even let us stay here."

Oma Ilsa beckons Marike's children to join her. They do so readily, begging her for a story or song, while the adults point and laugh at each other's ghostly appearances. Soon, the children are also giggling.

Helena proudly tells Ilsa, "My name is 'bright.'"

"What?" A puzzled Ilsa enquires of Marike.

"Last night, I told Helena why I named her Helena. I said she had such large, bright blue eyes, I called her Helena which means 'bright one, torchlight.'"

"Mutti, tell me again what Elisabet means."

"You were my first daughter, sent by heaven. I named you Elisabet. It means 'pledged to God.'"

"You made a mistake, Mutter. She's not very heavenly." Heinz laughs.

"I am so, aren't I? Heinz probably stands for 'mean brother.'"

"I was teasing." Heinz smiles mischievously. "Don't be so serious, Elisabet."

"Children, stop. Heinz, you were my first son. Heinz means 'household ruler.'"

Elisabet pouts, "He doesn't rule me. Anyway, you didn't tell us what Edel stands for."

Marike pulls Edel to her lap. "Edel means 'noble.' Now, be good to each other."

Heinz sticks his tongue out at Elisabet, who tosses her head and looks away. Marike gives thanks. *Her children are still children!*

Elisabet takes Marike's hand. Marike bends down, "What is it, Elisabet?"

"Mutter, Helena said you told her about when she was born. Please tell me my story about when I was born."

Marike studies Elisabet's serious face. "After your vater and I married, we lived in Elbing, where he worked for a bakery. First, I had your brother, and then I was pregnant with you. You were due to arrive in August, but then Horst received orders to report immediately to the German army. As you know, all eligible German men had to serve. Anyway, barely had he left, when my pains started."

"Did they hurt?" Elisabet asks.

"Yes, but they were good pains, because it meant you were coming. Immediately, I sent your vater a message. I almost couldn't believe it when Horst actually came home. I was afraid he'd left without permission. Fortunately, his commanding officer had understood and allowed him to return for your birth."

"I'm glad Vater was there."

"I'll never forget his face when you arrived; he was so proud. He said that he had prayed for a daughter. I think that is when we decided to name you Elisabet, pledged to God. It suited you."

"Oh, Mutter, I love my story."

Marike looks in the distance, remembering. "We were so happy, the four of us. But the following day, your vater kissed Heinz and you goodbye and hugged me. I didn't want to let him go. I didn't know then, my gentle Horst would be sent to Poland. You were eight months old when he returned on furlough the next March."

Suddenly, the noise seems to diminish. Those around them stop and stare as a truck drives up and stops. A distraught young woman carries her baby toward the truck. When she sees the truck's contents, she retreats in horror. The driver jumps out, grasps her arm, and wrestles the infant from her. No sound comes from the child. While the mother shrieks, the Danish guard places the baby in the truck's bed with the other children—once beloved, now deceased. The bereft mother stands staring at the truck while it moves away. She extends her arms as if reaching for her babe. Someone, possibly a relative, leads her away.

The other mothers, along with Marike, try to distract their children. It is impossible. Even young Helena knows about the truck for the dead. So many young children are dying from diarrhea, dehydration, and disease. Marike, like her sister-in-law, often reminds the children they are fortunate. They are toilet trained, otherwise they would be sent to the nursery where many children don't survive.

It has been two weeks since the children's opa returned from the hospital. Instead of being better, he is worse. Ilsa often sits with him, stroking his hand and talking softly. "If only we could find a doctor or medicine to help him," the family says. "He is a good man—never hurt anyone."

Marike struggles with her father's suffering. Unconsciously, she breathes at each gasping breath he takes. With the news that the war in Germany will end soon, Marike's thoughts turn to Horst. She wonders if her husband is also suffering in a Russian prisoner-of-war camp or in a hospital.

Marike reminisces about when she received the news that Horst had been wounded.

It doesn't seem possible that it was a year ago.

Chapter 8

It was a busy day at the bakery. As usual, Marike rested her chin on her fingers which were laced together, her elbows braced on the bakery counter. She gazed dreamily out the store window. Since Horst had received orders to return to the German army, she operated her mother-in-law's bakery. It had been a hectic day, with many Lithuanian refugees buying bread.

I'm thankful I have this work, my children, and family to keep me busy. I don't want to think about the war. I'm tired of hearing about it. I just pray my husband and brothers are safe. I feel guilty when I hear about someone else's husband, because I'm glad it isn't mine. I know that isn't right. I worry about my children.

From the back of the store, Frau Wiens entered. Marike admired her mother-in-law's erect posture. And even though the woman had been supervising the shop's clean-up, her dress was meticulous.

"Marike, did you forget to lock the door? It's time, and besides there's no more bread to sell," she said.

"Sorry, Mutter Wiens, I'll do that now," Marike apologized automatically.

Just then, a boy rode his battered bicycle up to the shop's entrance. Staring intently, they watched as he carelessly dropped the bike near their doorway. Marike glanced quickly at her mother-in-law, who didn't move. Marike guessed what her mother-in-law must be thinking: *Not my other son, too.* Just a few months ago, Mutter Wiens had received the terrible news about her older son.

As Marike hurried to the door, she hoped the boy had lost his way and needed directions. She hoped anything. When she opened the door, he asked, "Frau Wiens?" Marike barely nodded her head "yes" as he shoved an envelope into her hand. Paralyzed, she watched as he pedaled furiously down the street. Automatically, she locked the door and joined her mother-in-law. As she attempted to hand the envelope to her mother-in-law, Mutter Wiens shrank back against the display case. She refused to touch the envelope, as if it was a hot tray of rolls.

The envelope was addressed to 'Frau Wiens.' *There are two Frau Wiens,* Marike considered. *Does it really matter which one?* Marike sliced open the envelope with the bread knife. *Who cares if it dulls the knife?* Pulling the sheet out, she unfolded it and tried to read, seeing only the word 'injured.'

"Injured," she announced. "It says 'Private Horst Wiens was injured.' Oh, thank heavens."

"He's alive—not like his brother?" His mother beseeched her.

"Yes, oh yes. It says they've taken him to the Berlin hospital. I must see him. When was this sent? Oh, my love, you're alive. I'm coming." Smiling, Marike clasped the letter to her chest.

In a blur Marike barely can recall, she threw a few personal things into her old suitcase, purchased her ticket, and boarded the train.

With no time to write and let anyone know her plans, her visit would be a surprise. She dared not wait—something might happen. He could die or be sent back to the Front.

Shrieking to a stop, the train shuddered. Smoke billowed through an open window, causing a few passengers to cough. Marike covered her mouth. Carefully, she clutched the strings on the bakery box, her mother-in-law had packed and filled with Horst's favorites

Her poor widowed mother-in-law suffered so, already having lost

one son and now this. What if?...But she must not think such thoughts.
Mother Wiens had decided not to come. Someone had to run the bakery.

Soon, Marike found the hospital: a grey, multi-storied, concrete block building. Inside, a stern, uniformed woman confronted her and then directed a worried Marike to the second floor.

Marike mounted the worn wooden steps, taking a breath with each one. *I must be calm, no matter what,* she told herself. After all, she'd seen lots of things, growing up on a farm, with so many children. How many times had she helped her mutter tend one of her brother's wounds after a farm accident?

When she found the ward, Marike used her shoulder to shove open the swinging door. Immediately, a nurse in a stiffly starched uniform and cap blocked her entrance. After Marike explained who she was and why she had come, the nurse moved aside and gently offered to take Marike's things.

It was not the typical smells of alcohol, antiseptic, or even urine that startled her. It was a smell she had almost forgotten while working and living above the bakery. It was the earthy smell of so many men crowded together. She saw bed after bed of men, some gawking at her. A few looked away. Others were partially hidden by bandages and sheets. So many, she felt overwhelmed. Too many—husbands, sons, brothers—all looked so hurt and young. She barely breathed. "Dear God," she prayed.

She searched for him until his huge grin eclipsed the distance between them. Quickly, she walked past the men's stares until she reached his bedside. When she saw Horst's bandaged leg, she cried. He reached up, grasped her blond hair, and pulled her face to his.

For the next two days, they talked. She gave Horst the children's crude drawings, which he studied intently. Then, they laughed at the funny stick figures. Often, they held hands, hungry for each other's touch but aware of too many eyes.

Horst inquired about everyone: the children, his mother, her parents, even her sister who helped at the bakery. When she showed him a photo of their children, his gentle eyes filled with tears. For several minutes, he couldn't speak. When he did, she had to lean close to hear his hoarse whisper, making her promise to always protect their children.

She knew Horst believed she'd always protect them. He said this to avoid saying what neither of them could say—he might not return. In utter agony, she reassured him. The words seemed false, when in truth; she could not imagine how she could cope without him.

With his arm tightly around her, he escorted her to the hospital's entrance. Their last day together would soon end. Her knees shaking, Marike leaned on him—aware of the irony. After all, she was supposed to be the healthy one. When his mouth pressed hard against hers, marking her forever, she was beyond caring.

Later, as she rode the train home, she reminisced about their time together. It had been a miracle—those moments. Unfortunately, she thought grimly, he had suffered only a minor flesh wound. If only it could have been a wound just serious enough to have kept him safe at home. Even though they never discussed the war, she knew, in her heart, that soon the German army would send him back to the Eastern Front.

Chapter 9

Could it really have been a year ago? What would you think now, dear Horst—am I protecting our family? Our precious children starve in this wretched Danish camp. My poor vater wastes away. What can I do? With her eyes closed, Marike's hands smooth her wrinkled brow and tired eyes.

"Marike, Marike, hurry, come here," her mother calls. With the sounds of many voices reverberating around her, Marike rushes to her mother's side.

"Oh dear, he's worse isn't he? We must help him!" Ilsa clutches Marike's hand.

Marike bends over her frightened mother and gives her a hug. "Why don't you sit with the children for a bit? They're bored. I'll stay with Vater."

"Yes, dear, thank you." Ilsa glances at her husband and sighs.

Marike takes the bowl of watery oatmeal soup from her mother's hand. Carefully, trying to avoid the soup's slimy surface, she dips a spoonful and manages to get some between her father's dry lips. With great tenderness, she wipes the remainder from his whiskery chin.

Poor Vater can barely swallow. If only I could help him. Yet, when the Danes brought him back from their hospital, they acted as if he was hopeless. It seems like his body is just quitting. If only I didn't feel so helpless.

With a damp rag, Marike moistens his lips and wipes perspiration off his brow. Mostly, she holds her father's weak, clammy palm. She remembers how as a child, she marveled at her father's large, work-roughened hands. In his firm grasp, she felt his strength and power. And she felt safe. Now, their roles have changed. It's her job to help her vater.

Marike gently lays her head on his chest and hears wheezing sounds. *How much longer can he force air into his fluid-filled lungs? He's drowning,* she thinks, *and I can't save him. If only I could drain the fluid, like the doctor did at home. Maybe the Red Cross or a German doctor can help. There must be someone.* She looks hopefully at the hungry, defeated faces surrounding her, while they turn away. There is no one. *Anything would be better than this agony—watching my beloved father suffer. Finally, I know what I must do.*

Raising her head, she whispers in his ear. "We'll be okay, Vater. You can go now. We love you."

Kissing his grizzled cheek, Marike's tears fall unheeded. Her mother, sister, and brother join them, surrounding Eberhard with their love. Even the grandchildren sit quietly in their tight circle. Suddenly, Eberhard sits up, opens his eyes, and looks at each of them. It is as if he is saying goodbye. Then, he falls back on the straw and takes a few more breaths. Marike strains to hear him. No sound...he is silent.

"Vater is gone," Marike cries.

Tiny Ilsa approaches her beloved husband, folding Eberhard's hands, straightening his clothes, kissing his forehead. "I wish we could have a funeral, a ceremony," she says hopefully.

"Why not," Abelard says. "We'll have to hurry though, before the truck comes. We'll sing Vater's favorite hymn. Marike, you start it."

"With all this noise, you want me to sing?"

"Yes. Vater would like it. He loved your voice."

"All right, but the rest of you must sing too."

Marike's clear soprano voice begins to sing, "Take my hand…"

Other family members join in, and even Ilsa's off-key singing blends in with her family's song.

Although they sing loudly, they cannot drown out the sounds of the approaching truck. It stops nearby. Two men walk up, but Abelard shoves them aside. Gently, he lifts his father's wasted body, walks over, and tenderly places him in the truck's bed. Small children lay, forever still, around his father. "It's only right," Abelard says. "Vater loved the children, now he is surrounded by little angels."

Brushing aside his tears, Abelard returns to hug his mother.

Nearby, an angry woman complains, "It's shameful. Animals are treated better than we are in this awful place."

An old man, missing an arm—but not his dignity—replies, "The Danish guards tell us they are protecting us, hiding us away from their people. They say many Danes, especially those in the Resistance, are angry and bitter about the occupation."

The woman hisses, "That may be so, but we're mostly harmless women and children. What did these little babies ever do to them? At least the Red Cross should do something."

The man gazes sadly at the truck's deathly cargo. "I hear the German Red Cross has been trying to help, but the Danish Resistance keeps interfering. And the Danish Red Cross would help, but Danish officials gave the job to another agency. It's very confusing. I imagine the International Red Cross is trying to intervene, but what authority do they have? Since the war ended, the Danish made the German Sanitation Unit and some doctors stay in Denmark, but not enough to help us. They're busy caring for wounded soldiers."

"Sanitation Unit?" Marike asks.

"They call it that—to remove the mines we planted," the man whispers.

"It isn't right, I tell you," the woman says to Marike. "Your father would be alive if the Red Cross was here." The angry woman whirls around and marches away while the truck moves on to another group.

Abelard sighs, "She is right. If only they'd let the International Red Cross help us."

The family gathers around Ilsa. Someone suggests they say a prayer, and they bow their heads. Abelard's oldest son complains about the lack of medical care for his opa. Abelard reminds him that good Mennonites do not complain. He tells the family that it has been a long day, and they should go to bed early this night.

Marike regrets that there is no coffin or funeral service for their father and wonders where he will be buried. Will it be in a mass grave? She promises that one day she will find his grave and prays the rest of the family will survive.

The next morning, after most of the family has left for the toilets, Marike finds her mother alone.

"Mutter, where were you last night? I was worried," Marike asks.

"I couldn't sleep. After everyone else was asleep, the strangest thing happened. The guard—the one with the kind eyes—came and motioned for me to follow him," Ilsa whispers.

"I'm confused. The guard did what?" Marike's eyes narrow in concern.

"At first, I was afraid, but I followed him anyway. He unlocked a door, and we went to the basement. I couldn't believe it—rows of dead bodies. My heart hurt to see all the little ones, and I began to weep. They reminded me of the babies I buried, but I stopped when I saw the guard's concerned look. I knew he had brought me for another reason. If I lost control, he'd take me back upstairs." Ilsa sadly regards Marike.

"Mutter, you can't possibly mean he took you to see Vater?"

Ilsa nods. "We found Eberhard. The guard moved some bodies to give me room to sit next to him. The floor was cold concrete. I was glad I brought my blanket."

"You can't mean you stayed there all night?" Marike worries.

"Not all night. I had only a few hours alone with your dear vater. Only two weeks ago, we had our forty-sixth anniversary. I was twenty, and your vater twenty-six, when we married. Most of my life, I spent with him. On Christmas Eve, he would have been seventy-two. Eberhard was such a good man. I can't imagine life without him."

"Oh Mutter, I have to confess, when I sat with Vater the last time, he was suffering so much that I told him he could go. I'm sorry." Tears fill Marike's blue eyes.

"I understand. To ask him to suffer any longer would have been selfish." Ilsa pats Marike's hand. "Last night, I prayed and sang. Your vater never minded I was off-key. He used to say he liked my singing, because it gave me so much pleasure. It was always like him to have the right words to make me feel better. I lay next to him and took his hand. Already, he was so cold. I told him I wished I could join him."

"Mutti, you didn't!"

"Oh, I knew he didn't want that." Ilsa takes a deep breath.

"Mutter, if Vater were here, he'd say, 'We have our faith and our family. We must pray and help each other, and we'll survive.'"

"Dear Marike, you sound just like your vater. Don't worry about me. I'm not going anywhere—as long as I'm needed to help with the children."

Later, the camp guards ask for volunteers to help in the kitchen. Some women agree to help but soon return, saying the kettles are too huge to lift. They're afraid they'll spill the boiling contents on themselves. Others prepare the soup. Meanwhile, each family is given one bucket and told to send a representative to get their daily share.

Obediently, Marike and the other refugees form a long line, which winds around the abysmal room. After a long time, Marike returns to her hungry children. When she pours the soup into her children's bowls, something gleams in the dusty light. Astonished, she reaches in and fishes out a razor blade. *What's a razor blade doing in their soup?* She immediately grabs the children's bowls and, despite their protests, dumps their contents into her bucket.

Freda calls to her, "Did you find something in the soup?"

"Yes, a razor blade."

"Well, I just found ground glass in mine," Freda exclaims. "Are they trying to kill us?"

"You didn't eat any, did you?" Marike examines Freda's soup.

"No, I'm throwing it away."

"Why, would anyone do such a thing?" Marike quizzes.

Freda angrily shakes her fist. Marike knows the answer. How many times has she told the children it is wrong to hate anyone? She doesn't want to think of those who hate them.

Just then, Freda beckons her. Marike asks her what is wrong, and Freda says she is having terrible cramps. Even though she didn't eat today's soup, Freda says she has been sick for days. She tells Marike that her stepchildren are old enough to care for themselves, but she worries about her three-year-old Bettina. Without hesitation, Marike carries Bettina to her straw bed, where she sings to her until the restless child sleeps.

Poor baby, she's weak and can barely lift her head. Even though her diarrhea has stopped, she must be dehydrated. Freda may have caught Bettina's sickness. Although Freda asks her to find some sugar for Bettina, Marike disagrees and hopes Freda understands. Sugary treats aren't good for children. She doesn't give them to her own children.

A frizzy-haired woman watches Marike intently. Finally, she speaks, as if she, too, were part of their conversation. "My baby would be alive today if they gave the babies proper care."

"I'm sorry," Marike says. "Were you talking to me?"

The woman shrugs angrily. "I said the babies need fluids—and sugar, too."

Just then, Freda finds some small, hard pieces of sugar stuck in the corner of her pocket. Marike moistens them with some water and then breaks off tiny pieces, which she places in Bettina's small mouth. Bettina's face colors, slightly surprising Marike.

The woman nods encouragement and returns to her older children, who sit a short distance away.

Helena asks Marike if she can help with Bettina. Marike suggests that Helena sit with Bettina while she goes to the toilet. Helena hums her favorite song, and soon her fragile cousin closes her eyes.

The days slide by as Bettina becomes so thin and weak she can no longer walk. Freda, who has recovered, and Marike must carry Bettina to the toilet. Bettina can barely use it. Some of their neighbors shake their heads at "the poor thing." The family prays for her as she smiles weakly at their caring attention.

Elisabet rocks her little cousin and asks Freda, "Is she going to die like Opa?"

Freda lifts Bettina from Elisabet's arms. "No. Don't say such awful things. She will get well. I'm not giving up."

Freda holds Bettina against her legs and places Bettina's tiny feet on her feet. If Freda didn't have a firm grip on Bettina, she would slide to the floor. Very slowly, Freda moves first one leg, than the other, and Bettina moves with her mother. Bettina is so light; it takes very little effort for her mother to walk so encumbered. Bettina cries. Freda scoops her into her arms and covers her perspiring face with kisses. The family offers encouragement. The exercise must stimulate Bettina's appetite, because for the first time in many days she accepts some of the soup her mother spoons into her mouth.

Marike watches Freda and thinks, *the split pea soup may be mostly water and slimy too, but at least it's liquid and will help the child. Freda's marvelous love may yet help her little one get well.* Curious, Heinz, Elisabet, Helena, and even little Edel, who climbs on to Marike's lap, crowd around her to watch Freda and Bettina.

"Will she really live?" Helena asks Marike.

"Yes, of course," Marike reassures her children. "We'll keep praying for her, won't we?"

"Yes, Mutter," her children answer, and their heads bow as Marike says a short prayer.

"Mutter, I don't understand why our army—our doctors—don't help us?" asks Heinz.

Marike swallows and looks down.

"Why, Mutter?" Heinz shakes Marike's arm.

"I guess it's as Onkel Abelard said," Marike says sadly. "There are too few German doctors left, and they must take care of the wounded soldiers. Hopefully, conditions will improve or maybe they will move us." Marike pauses and stares at her youngsters. "But children, you must be careful not to get sick."

Heinz and Elisabet nod their heads as little Edel and Helena watch their older siblings.

Chapter 10

After six months in the camp in Kopenhagen, on the Danish island of Sjælland, Marike and some of her relatives are told they are being sent to a new camp—where they do not know. The refugees are herded onto trucks. While the trucks lumber along, not far from their camp, Marike glimpses a cemetery of small white crosses. Her chest tightens. *Could this be where the little children are buried?* She prays for them and her vater, hoping he isn't in an unmarked mass grave. *Someday, I promise I'll return and find you.* She strains to see more.

As they travel, they glimpse the ancient Kopenhagen Vor Frelsers Kirke, Church of Our Savior. It is a round building and looks like a fortress with narrow slits for windows. The walls are very thick. One of the refugees who visited Denmark before the war says, "Long ago, during battles, the townspeople sought shelter in churches like these. Places that could be easily defended. This church is famous for its beautiful winding staircase."

"It's similar to northern Germany's round church buildings. How I miss Prussia," Marike says.

Finally, the trucks grind to a halt, unloading their passengers in the deserted Danish countryside. October's strong winds pull at their coats as Marike urges her children to the waiting train's cattle cars.

Freda whispers, "You know why the Danes brought us here instead of the depot? They don't want their people to know about us."

"What are they afraid of?" Marike asks.

"Us. I guess they think that we—a bunch of women and children—might rob them," Freda replies.

"Maybe," Marike suggests hopefully, "the Danish people might help when they see how hungry and sick we are."

She notices gentle, undulating farmland—unspoiled by the ravages of war, and she is lost in the land's fertile richness until her brother touches her elbow.

"Kind of reminds you of our Petershagen farm, doesn't it?" Abelard says with a sad smile.

Marike nods as she gathers her children and suitcase and follows her family aboard the cattle car. Soon, the doors are slammed shut, and they ride through countryside that they can no longer see. After the train stops, they take a short boat ride from the island of Sjælland to the small island of Fyn. Finally, they are transported to the larger peninsula of Jylland.

After six months inside their first camp, without being allowed outside, to be outdoors is incredible. Marike savors the moist, salty air. Speculation swirls around her about where the Danish are moving them and why. Marike believes this new camp must be better. It couldn't be worse.

Soon, they board crowded trucks, where their world is again confined. The children, tired and hungry, beg Marike for information. "When will they stop? Where are we going? Will there be food?" These are questions for which she has no answers, only hope. A tired and hungry Edel falls asleep against an exhausted Marike. Marike senses the increasing cold of the late afternoon and shivers. Helena whimpers. Finally, when Marike feels as if they can go no further, the truck enters the gates of what appears to be one of the German army's former camps, situated in a forest of evergreen trees.

Immediately, armed Danish guards order the refugees down from the trucks. Beyond them, multiple strands of barbed wire encircle the camp. Soon, the guards have the refugees in a line and assign them to their quarters. Oma Ilsa; Abelard, Freda, and their five children; and Marike and her four are all sent to the same barracks. The older children quickly enter the building and race down the narrow hallway. The tired adults, lugging their suitcases, stumble after them. On either side of the hallway are large rooms.

When they locate their assigned room, they discover it contains six triple bunk beds—three on each side. The children quickly jump on the mattresses. They may be lumpy and made of straw, but Marike is relieved they will no longer have to sleep on a cold concrete floor. Soon, another family of five joins them. Eighteen people crowd the room. After each child has found a bed, Freda and Marike hang blankets to give their family some privacy.

Edel and Bettina ask their mothers for the toilet while Abelard's twins offer to find it. Not locating a facility in the barracks, they go outside. Within minutes they return, holding their noses and grimacing. Freda and Marike follow the children. Long before they have reached the toilet, they too can smell the odiferous stew.

Never before have they seen anything like this toilet. A low wall makes a complete circle. Inside the middle are mounds of feces and urine. Little Edel is puzzled by this sight and complains he has to go right now. Since the wall is too high for him, Marike eases his trousers down and lifts him up on the wall, while she holds him around the waist. Surprised, he looks to his mother for direction, but she nods encouragement and helps him to partially drape his tiny buttocks over the pit.

Edel gags, twists, and tries to get down. Marike, fearful he will fall, tightens her grip. Through clenched teeth, choking down her own stomach acid, she urges him to finish. The hideous smell stings her eyes and makes her stomach heave. It reminds her of the ship's overflowing toilets.

In one swift movement, Marike helps Edel down and pulls his trousers up. With her hand pinching her nostrils shut, she leads him back to their barracks. As they leave, a child's scream and his mother's horror-filled moan follow them. Other women run to help them. Marike doesn't look. *I can imagine what has happened—unfortunate child. Surely, they will wash him in the shower. It would be wonderful if this camp has showers where we can finally be clean.*

When they return to their barracks, a Danish guard hands each family two buckets and points to the line forming outside the kitchen. Oma Ilsa, Marike, and Freda grip their buckets and join the long line.

I hope the food will be better; the children are too thin. Once, Marike remembers, *I would have to remind the children to finish their meal, but not now.*

When she reaches the kitchen, a woman ladles a white mixture into Marike's pail. Moving ahead, another woman dips a watery substance with oatmeal flakes in her other pail.

At least there is milk, Marike thinks. When she opens the door to their room, the noise bursts out. Marike pours the oatmeal in her children's bowls and says a short blessing. Heinz whines.

Marike quietly reminds him, "We Mennonites do not complain. At least here we have milk, beds, and our own room. No longer do we have to sleep on the floor with hundreds of people."

Fat tears roll down Helena's thin cheeks. When Marike asks her why she is crying, she has no answer as she sobs. Marike tries to comfort her but to no avail. The other children stare at their sister and then resume eating.

Soon, Elisabet bends her head near Helena's, and in a loud whisper, says, "Helena, we're tired of your crying. We would all like to cry. Think of others."

Helena rubs her red eyes with her small fists and stares at her big sister. Slowly, she picks up her spoon and stirs her oatmeal.

"Mutter, where are Tante Agathe and my cousins?" Elisabet asks asks. "I thought they'd be here."

"I did too, since they left Kopenhagen two days before we did. Ever since we arrived, I've asked everyone, but no one has seen them." Marike sighs. "Before Agathe left, she said that the guards wouldn't tell her anything—gave her half an hour to pack. It was just like when they told us."

"Maybe we could send her a letter—tell her where we are," Heinz suggests.

Abelard, who helps Freda feed their children, says, "Remember the Dane's rule: We can't send or receive any mail."

Marike reflects sadly. *It seems like Agathe and her family have disappeared. Suddenly they're gone, like so many others we've known, who were sent to other camps. No time to say goodbye or find out where they are going. The winds of war scatter us like daisies. We can only pray we land on safe soil.*

After the children quickly finish their oatmeal, they beg to be allowed out of the crowded, stuffy room. Their parents, hoping for some quiet time, agree. Immediately, they leave.

Abelard says, "Before we left Kopenhagen, I heard some news."

"Are they sending us back to Prussia, or maybe Deutschland, like our soldiers?" Freda asks.

"They can't send us to Prussia—it's no more," Marike says. "It's occupied by Poland and Russia. If I know the Russians, they probably sent most everyone who lived there to Siberia or to a worse fate. They want our land for the Polish or Russians."

"What I heard," Abelard continues, "is that except for about one thousand troops kept back to remove land mines they planted, most German soldiers in Denmark were sent to prisoner-of-war camps."

"We assumed as much," Freda says, "when we heard all the army trucks moving through the streets. Hopefully, they weren't sent to Russian camps. What about us?"

Abelard explains that one of the German refugees who understands some Danish overheard two guards arguing. One guard said that he had been in the Danish Resistance, and his superior told him there are more than two hundred thousand refugees from Prussia, Danzig, and Pomerania in about eleven hundred makeshift camps. "He said that, including the German soldiers, there are seven-hundred-and-fifty thousand of us. It is too many for a tiny country like Denmark to feed and house. Some other country should take them. His friend said no other country would take the refugees. He said it would be Christian to care for these poor people, who are mostly women and children. The first guard said that simply because the German military, shortly before Germany's defeat, decided Denmark would provide for the Prussian refugees, didn't obligate Denmark."

While they consider Abelard's news, he pauses as if preparing his words. He says slowly, "We've all heard how even though the war was almost over, the Allies' firebombed many German cities. Even if we could return to Germany, can you imagine how hard it would be to find food and shelter?"

Marike agrees with her brother. Whether or not they return to Germany is not their decision. Who knows, even now her sister Agathe may be with refugees being repatriated across the border to Schleswig Holstein. She must pray for those who will decide their fate.

"We may not know what the Danish will do with us," Abelard says. "But, in the meantime, there are other things we can do."

"What do you mean?" Marike inquires.

"The nights are getting colder, and soon winter will be here." Abelard walks over to the beds. "I think I can take apart this top third bunk and make the bottom bunk big enough for your four children to sleep together. Then, they'll keep each other warm."

"Good idea, Abelard."

"It's not much, but it will help." Abelard removes the straw mattress and takes out the wooden slats.

Chapter 11

A week later, blustery winds pelt the barracks' roof with icy rain. In between the large droplets plastered to their small window, weak sunlight struggles through. Elisabet, Heinz, Helena, and Edel huddle together in their bunk.

"I don't care about the rain. Mutti, please can we go out and play?" Heinz whines.

"*Nein*, you'll get sick," Marike replies.

"I'm bored. There's nothing to do," Heinz complains.

"Me, too," Helena and Edel echo their brother.

"I have an idea," Elisabet offers. "Maybe Oma will tell us a story."

Marike turns to her mother and asks, "Do you mind? Then I can knit." When she holds up her knitting to the light, the gray yarn matches the sky.

Oma squeezes her tiny body among her grandchildren.

"My old sweater? You're using the yarn. Good, Marike, you always know how to make do." Oma hugs her grandchildren. "Today, I'll tell a story you all know. It's about when our family began our journey many months ago—when we left our Petershagen farm."

"I miss the farm," Heinz says. "Someday, I'm going to be a farmer."

Oma Ilsa smiles and says, "Remember how clear and cold it was that January morning, almost a year ago? Your opa hitched up two teams to the wagons. We loaded our belongings, including food, bedding, clothes, and even some dishes. The wind was freezing like today's wind, but it didn't rain. Down our road we drove to the main highway to Steegen. Cold and frustrated, we waited all day for a break in the traffic. German military armament and armies, Lithuanian and Prussian refugees streamed by. It seemed as if everyone was fleeing. Discouraged, we returned home to unpack."

"I was happy, because I didn't want to leave," Heinz says.

"I didn't understand why we had to go," Helena whispers shyly.

"I'm surprised, Helena, you'd even remember. You were just three." Oma continues, "I'll explain. That same evening, a neighbor interrupted our happy homecoming. He told us brusquely we had no choice but to leave. He warned us that the Russian army had advanced to Elbing, a mere twenty-five miles away. In fact, he'd heard a rumor Hitler had ordered the city of Elbing destroyed—part of Hitler's 'scorched earth' policy to burn anything the Allies might use."

"Why didn't the neighbor have to leave, and why would the army burn Elbing?" Elisabet asks.

"I know," Heinz answers. "I'll bet the neighbor was Polish so he could stay. They say the Russian and Polish armies want Prussia. They want the Prussians to leave or else they will do terrible things. Hitler said he would burn everything so the Russians would get nothing."

"I remember," Elisabet says. "It was so early and dark, the rooster hadn't crowed. Mutter dressed me in so many clothes. My new coat barely fit. I was afraid I'd rip it. Our family had to fit everything into one suitcase."

"Good children, you do remember. We left everything, but Abelard brought a large pot, which came in handy. Along the way, we stopped at some relatives' homes and warned them. We said our sad good-byes, not knowing if we'd ever meet again. When we reached Tiegenhof, we barely squeezed on the crowded train. Instead of the usual few hours, the trip took fifteen. Someone told us that, up ahead, they were repairing train tracks that had been bombed. We never knew where we were, because black curtains blocked the windows. Often, the train pulled off on a siding to let another train charge by—probably to resupply German troops. When we reached our destination, we stayed the night at a distant relative's home." Oma studies the children. "Now, do you know why I told you this story about when we left the farm?"

Heinz says, "I know why. It's because you want us to remember."

"If we remember," Elisabet adds thoughtfully, "we can tell our children. I'll always remember about later—when Mutter took us to Danzig."

"I think," Marike comments, "your oma is telling you something more. She wants you to know you can lose your home, but you're always safe with family."

"Then, I guess I shouldn't tell my story, about my red scooter?" a dejected Elisabet asks.

"Why don't we save it until after we get our soup?" Marike suggests.

Chapter 12

This morning, overcast skies and grey light fill the dirty window pane. Raising her sewing to the light, Marike carefully loosens the thread from a worn coat. She cautiously winds the thread around three small twigs. She imagines that when she finishes with the old coat, Heinz and Elisabet will have new, warm winter coats.

Freda asks, "Marike, where did you get the coat?"

"When a soldier left, he gave me his extra uniform. Why do you ask?"

"You're not supposed to use a German military coat. The guards told us. You'll make trouble for us." Freda's concerned glance takes in both Abelard and Marike.

"Freda, we refugees are fortunate our soldiers gave us their extra uniforms, sheets, and utensils before they left for the POW camps. I'm glad they gave me this coat. In this damp cold, the children will be sick if I don't make warm clothes for them. We must use anything we can." Marike begins cutting.

Abelard grunts.

"Did you say something?" Marike asks.

"No. Watching you work—I wish I could do something, any-thing. On the farm, something always needed tending to, but here, nothing. I never thought I'd miss all that work." Abelard walks around the room and bumps into Freda, carrying a pail of water.

"Careful, you'll make me spill this. Can't you find something to do besides your endless pacing?" Freda scolds.

"Sorry, dear, I'm not used to being shut up indoors."

"Well, maybe you should, I don't know, find something, anything." Freda places the bucket in the corner.

"I know what, dear brother. I'll teach you how to sew," Marike grins.

"You'll what?" Freda looks at her husband's large hands and giggles.

Red-faced Abelard stares at his calloused fingers.

Soon, he grins impishly. Pinching his right forefinger and thick thumb together and holding up his hammy left hand, he pretends to thread a needle.

Abelard's caricature of a woman sewing is so funny, Marike laughs—and laughs more as she hears her sister-in-law's high giggles. Abelard's belly laughs bring the children running to find out what is happening. When Marike, still laughing, explains, they shrug their shoulders, bewildered, and Heinz mumbles, "*Lache Dich nicht Tot.*"

"What did you say?" Helena asks.

"I said," Heinz whispers, "don't kill yourself laughing. Anyway, let's go play tag."

After they have left, Abelard, still chuckling, says, "I have an idea."

"What?" Freda asks.

"Well, the children have their games. We adults need a game, something like we used to do—maybe, Parcheesi."

"But Abelard," Freda says, "where would you get one? Surely, no one brought a game."

"Oh Abelard," Marike's enthusiasm colors her pale cheeks, "Do you think we really can? Remember how we used to play as children—long after we were supposed to be asleep."

"You just wait and see. I saved the cardboard from a care package. It's big enough to draw a board, and the children have some crayons."

"I've been saving buttons," Freda interjects. "You could use them for markers—remember, four for each player."

"I have some buttons, too, or we could color pebbles. But what will we use for dice?" Marike asks.

"The other day, I found a rusty knife in the garbage pile. I'll sharpen it and carve dice from some wood chips." Abelard's eyes twinkle as he pats Freda's thigh.

Who would think such a small thing as a children's game could bring so much joy? We could call this Camp Parcheesi! Marike giggles. She understands her brother's frustration. Except for the daily line-up for their meals, there is little for him to do. Women stay busy re-making clothes and caring for the children. The few German books shared by camp refugees have been read many times. There is too much time with nothing to do but think about their losses: family members, homes, and even country. When they aren't grieving, they think about food. Even though the food has improved, it's still too little for so many, and their stomachs complain.

Ilsa enters and says she'll be working in the camp kitchen peeling potatoes. Everyone listens hopefully as Oma Ilsa recites the camp's menu. One potato for each person, tea, powdered milk, soup, bread, and oatmeal are the daily fare. She doesn't know if other foods will be added. There is plenty of powdered milk, which will be good for the growing children. Oma Ilsa, who lost her false teeth in their escape and has trouble chewing, offers her potato to the children. The children quickly devour it, while Ilsa softens her bread in her tea. Several family members grumble that their potatoes have blackened with rot. Without replying, Abelard ducks his head and hungrily scoops up his rotten potato. For her children, Marike strains their watery oatmeal and adds some of the precious sugar they've been given.

Since they arrived at this camp in late fall, the weather has been damp and cold. Marike shivers.

Today, Abelard works on the stove supplied in each room. With the little *Toft* they've been given, he tries to make a fire. Everyone watches him while huddled in their beds, trying to stay warm. The children clap as they see a small flame. From under her bed, Marike retrieves a branch, which she gives to her brother to feed the fire.

Abelard's face registers his surprise, but he silently accepts her offering.

Freda and Marike exchange conspiratorial glances.

"What have you two ladies been up to? Not breaking the rules, I hope?" Abelard asks in a teasing voice.

Freda laughs. "Who us? We just found a few branches. The children gathered the needles from under the trees."

"They look pretty green to me—just don't get caught." Abelard says sternly, but his smile betrays him.

Chapter 13

"Mutti, may we play outdoors?" Elisabet asks.

"I wanna play too, can I?" Edel cries.

"It's too cold. Stay covered up. I don't want you to get sick." Marike tucks Edel's blanket around him.

Heinz groans, "It has been days since we've been out. We're tired of staying in bed."

"Only two days. Maybe it will be better tomorrow." From the other side of their room, Marike hears similar complaints from her nieces and nephews. With so many people living in one room, there is little play space. The building creaks as strong winds seem determined to shake apart the hastily constructed structure. Marike shivers when a cold breeze blows in her face, a reminder of their poor protection from the elements.

If only the barrack's boards didn't have so many gaps, we might fill them in with something. If Vater or Abelard had built this, we wouldn't be suffering. Even the hen house they built was better than this.

"Oma Ilsa, tell us a story," Elisabet begs.

From a far-away corner bed, Elisabet's older cousin, Lena, says knowingly, "Tell the slate story."

"The slate story? I'm not sure…do you mean my little brother's story?" Ilsa asks.

"That's my favorite," Lena replies with a smug smile.

"Please Oma, we love your stories. And Lena, I think you always have the best ideas," Elisabet turns her admiring face towards her cousin. Quickly, the other children chime in. "Please, Oma!"

Ilsa's kind face lights happily as she calls the younger ones to her bunk. Soon her tiny frame is surrounded by children and their blankets. Laughing at their squirming bodies, she quiets them. *As only the mother of so many children can*, thinks Marike.

Like any good storyteller, Oma Ilsa quickly glances around at her rapt audience to ensure she has their attention. Even the older children and the adults stop conversing to listen.

"To begin at the beginning, you remember I told you that when I was seven years old, and my brother Gunther was five, we went to live with Onkel Axel and Tante Adelaide Albrecht on their dairy farm. After my poor vater died, we left our farm. Such a sad story about my vater—I loved him so much. I think he had tuberculosis. He would carve small wooden animals and play his harmonica for us." Ilsa's voice trails off.

"You were like me. I was young, too, when I lost my vater. Instead, my vater left for the war," Elisabet says sadly.

"We want to hear about Gunther," Abelard's oldest daughter interrupts.

"Yes, dear, I'm getting to that part," Ilsa continues. "We were so young we didn't understand what was happening. Mutter told us she had to sell our little farm to pay the debts, but we didn't think we'd lose our vater and the farm…and our mutter, too. I'll never forget that sunny day in late summer when she took us to our onkel's. She kept telling us that the only work she could find was in the city at the factory. She said we must mind our tante and onkel and stay with them. Then, she drove away with our baby *schwester*."

"You told us all that before," Lena whines.

"No, she didn't," says Edel.

"She did so." Elisabet folds her arms and looks for approval from Lena.

"Now children, be patient—it's hard for little ones to remember." Ilsa pats Edel's cowlick until his hair is flattened down. "When my mutter left, I felt like a tree. I couldn't move. Gunther bawled and ran after her wagon. Like my mutter told me, I was the oldest so I had to help him." Ilsa smiles at her older grandchildren. "Just as your parents ask you to help with the little ones."

Lena looks at the ceiling and then casts a meaningful glance at Elisabet. Marike recognizes Lena's annoyed look and guesses that her wise stepmother has also seen it. Still, Marike expects Ilsa will add a moral to her story, like those in Grimm's *Fairy Tales*.

"Since Onkel didn't have any children, and he had a big dairy farm, he expected us to help with the chores. When we first arrived, *Tante* Adelaide asked Onkel Axel if I could help her with the household duties. I hoped I could, since I'd often helped my mutter. She had taught me many things—how to bake, churn butter, and wash the clothes in the big tub. I'll never forget my onkel's words, 'The housework can wait. The farm work has to be done.'"

"Is that why you like to bake? Your torte is my favorite," Heinz asks.

"True, I do love baking, but we had to help with the farm work. Before the sun rose and before school, Gunther and I helped Onkel in the cow barn. First thing after school, we helped too. Always, we worked so hard. Sometimes, I think we were nothing but field hands. One day after class, I found my little brother sobbing. When I asked him what was wrong, he couldn't stop crying; instead he lifted his shirt and showed me his back. Big red welts marked his baby white skin." Oma stops and swallows hard.

"He said his *Lehrer* spanked him. When I asked him why, my brother said the teacher said he couldn't read Gunther's work. Gunther explained that his slate was cracked and hard to print on, but his teacher said that was no excuse. If he didn't get a new slate, the teacher would punish him again. I felt sorry for my brother—hurt and humiliated."

"His teacher was mean. What'd you do?" Elisabet asks.

After a few minutes, Ilsa continues in a raspy voice. "I waited until after supper. While everyone ate Tante's torte, even though I was terrified, I asked if Gunther could have a new slate. I explained he couldn't do his homework on the cracked one. His teacher would beat him if he didn't have a new one."

Lena says, "At my school, I knew some kids who said if their teacher spanked them, when they went home, their fathers whipped them with their belts. One boy even showed me the marks from his vater's belt buckle."

"I'm so sorry, Lena," Ilsa says. "Anyway, as I said, I asked, but Onkel Axel said no. Gunther's slate was good enough. He said we should be grateful for the food and home we had. The Bible said that 'to spare the rod would spoil the child.' My poor brother. I heard him crying all night."

"I don't think I like your uncle," Heinz declares.

"He meant well, I'm sure. He just didn't know much about children. In my day, most people were very strict, especially German parents. They often spanked, as did the teachers." Ilsa glances at Edel curled beside her. "Oh look, little Edel has fallen asleep. Maybe I should wait and finish my story tomorrow."

"No, now—finish it now," the children cry.

"All right." Ilsa beams at the sleepy children's renewed attention. "The next morning, Hanna was emptying the chamber pots. Hanna was the hired girl. I think she felt sorry for us, because she often told us little stories. Once, she even gave us a ball she'd found."

"Hanna must have been very kind. I like her," Elisabet says.

"Hanna was, and she asked why Gunther was sad. When I told her about his teacher, she offered to help, saying she would buy him a slate. I knew she didn't have any money, but she said she'd found an old corset discarded in our attic. She promised to sell it and buy the slate. We were so relieved. Gunther and I hugged her."

"How clever of her," Elisabet says.

"Tell her the next part—what your tante and onkel did to Hanna," Lena dictates.

"You're getting ahead of my story. Be careful, or the children will know the ending." Ilsa's eyes glisten and she glances sadly at the ceiling's cobwebs before she hesitantly continues.

"Two days later, before school, Hanna kept her promise and gave Gunther a shiny, new black slate. Even though it was a cold morning, Gunther tenderly wrapped the slate in his jacket. As we walked to school, now and then, he stopped to check his new slate and wrap it up again. He grinned so much I told him his face would fall off. When we got to school, the *Lehrer* tapped his stick and called my brother to the front of the classroom. As Gunther marched up to the teacher's desk, some boys called him dummy while others giggled."

Heinz says, "At my school, my teacher didn't spank anyone."

Ilsa says, "I'm glad. As I was saying, the teacher demanded to know if Gunther had replaced his broken slate. The teacher told the class they would soon see what happened to those students who didn't obey. Suddenly, the teacher grabbed Gunther's collar and raised his stick. Just in time, Gunther removed his slate from his jacket."

Heinz, Elisabet, Lena, and the other children clap their hands.

Ilsa continues, "All the way home from school, Gunther carefully held his slate away from him. He didn't want to smear the new words he had printed. My brother desperately wanted to show Hanna, Tante, and Onkel. As fast our legs would carry us, we hurried."

Elisabet says, "They must have been proud of him. I wish I had something to write on—even a slate. I miss school."

Oma says, "But when we got there, we searched everywhere, but we couldn't find Hanna. Tante said our onkel fired Hanna. We were stunned."

"Didn't you explain?" Heinz asks.

"I did. I begged her to understand Hanna had only tried to help. Tante said Hanna was bad, and she fired her for stealing. Stealing was wrong. I was wrong to ask her to steal. She blamed me, and she said she would write my mutter so she could discipline me."

"So Oma Ilsa, are you telling your grandchildren that it's all right to steal?" Freda, Lena's stepmother, asks in a mocking tone.

Marike answers her softly, "Freda, maybe Mutter means that how we treat others is more important than rules."

Elisabet, shivering in the cold room, says, "I feel sorry for Hanna. It wasn't right. Were your tante and onkel always so mean?"

Ilsa's eyes crinkle as she laughs. "Oh child, they didn't understand children. We were fortunate they raised us. And when they grew old, we cared for them."

The next morning, Elisabet tells Marike she kept dreaming of slates and of her grandmother's tortes. When she awoke, she imagined she could smell one baking on their stove. The other children, who overhear Elisabet, talk about the last time they had the special treat. Half listening, Marike considers how she could fulfill their wish. Her eyes sparkle as she plans to make a torte from their skimpy provisions. *It may not be the same, but we can pretend. The children are starving.*

"Children, today we're going to make a torte," Marike announces.

"But how can we?" Heinz demands. "You need lots of eggs, sugar, and nuts to make it. And we don't have any."

"We have some sugar, bread, and milk. Watch me." Marike goes to their little cupboard and removes some powdered milk, spoons some into a bowl, adds some water, and a little of their precious sugar. Taking a fork she begins whipping the mixture until it becomes a light froth. She places two slices of their dark bread on top of their wood stove. When they've browned, she turns them over. After she has toasted them, she spoons the whipped mixture between the slices, saving some for the top.

Holding it up, she declares, "See, torte."

"Oh Mutter," Heinz says reaching for the cake. As he does so, it falls to the floor.

"You see. It may not be the same, but we can find a way." Marike says.

Heinz reaches down and carefully tries to dust the bread off without removing the sugar.

"It's dirty," Marike says.

"I don't care. I'm so hungry," Heinz quickly devours his torte.

Soon each child has a piece. Elisabet slowly chews. When Elisabet finishes, she wets her fingers and runs them around her bowl, finding tiny crumbs. Delicately, she licks her fingers. Helena and Edel imitate their big sister and scrub their bowls with their small wet fingers.

"Mutter, that was the best torte I've ever had. Thank you," Elisabet declares. Heinz, Helena, and Edel echo their sister.

Marike blinks away the sudden mist from her eyes before she says, "We make do."

As her children run outside, Marike retrieves her knitting and huddles in the square of sunlight struggling through their dusty window. While she counts her stitches, she thinks. *At least the children still have their imaginations, even if it doesn't fill their stomachs. And they're so dirty. I'm afraid of lice. If only there were showers.*

Later that sunny afternoon, the children, coated with dust, return from their play. Marike takes their tea bucket, dips a rag, and instructs the children to line up. She wipes their faces and hands.

"Why do we have to wash with tea?" Helena asks.

"Because," Marike explains, "We have no soap. You don't want lice, do you?"

"Ugh, no." Helena shakes her head.

"I'm hungry," Heinz complains. "Can we have more torte?"

"Please," her children chant.

Marike replies reluctantly, "I'm sorry. There is no more sugar."

When their faces droop with disappointment, Marike almost regrets raising their hopes with the torte. What can she do? Like them, she constantly thinks of food. She most misses the smells: stew's meaty aroma, bread's yeasty invitation, and bacon's oily smell. Even when she nears the camp's huge soup kettles, Marike fails to find any discernible odor emanating from the watery brew.

"Elisabet," Marike says, "your grandmother isn't well today. I want her to rest and for you to take her place helping me carry our two soup buckets."

"Do I have to? We just started our game," Elisabet pleads.

"You can play a little longer," Marike concedes. "I'll wait in line, and you can meet me at the kitchen." Marike puts down her knitting, grasps the buckets' handles, and leaves.

When Elisabet returns to her playmates, she finds they have contrived a new game.

Her cousin says, "We're playing a guessing game. Who can guess what today's soup is?"

Heinz says, "Potato."

"Split pea," his cousin says. "I hate pea soup. It's only good for this." He bends over. "*Furz*," he blows gas, rolls over and laughs.

The other boys imitate him and argue over who makes the biggest *Furz*.

"Disgusting! Oh no," Elisabet cries, "I'm supposed to help my mutter." She rushes to the camp kitchen. Ahead of her, she sees her mother bent over, carrying the heavy pails, spilling some of the contents.

Full of apologies and excuses, Elisabet runs to her mother and offers to help. Marike ignores Elisabet, who follows her into their room. After setting down the pails, a red-faced Marike grasps Elisabet's arm and spanks her bottom.

"I waited and waited for you," Marike complains. "I was the last in the line."

"Mutter, I'm sorry," Elisabet cries helplessly. "I didn't mean to be late."

"Because of you, I almost didn't get any soup. The cook scraped it off the bottom. Some of it is even burned." Marike continues, "We are lucky there was any left."

"I should have been there." Elisabet looks at the floor.

"I forgive you. Just remember, we need every bit of food. I worry—your little brother's legs are bowed." In despair, Marike throws up her hands.

"Mutter, I feel awful. You should spank me again. The other day I was hungry, and I stole a lick of butter," Elisabet confesses.

Marike, resisting a sob, hugs her oldest daughter. "I saw you, but I knew you were starved for some fat. I know you try to be good. Now, call your brothers and sister to eat."

"Yes, Mutter."

Chapter 14

Cold, damp winds swirl around Marike as she carries her buckets filled with oatmeal toward the barracks. Her bare hands are so numb she can hardly feel the wire handles, and she fears she'll drop the pails. Overhead, tree tops thrash about, spewing pine needles and an occasional pine cone. Seeking protection for her wind-whipped face, Marike tucks her chin into the collar of her coat and forces her way forward. When she glances up, she sees her dear mother holding the barracks' door open for her.

Really it looks more like the door holds my tiny mutter prisoner, Marike reflects as her mother struggles to hang on. Marike hurries inside, and the children surround her as they peer at the pails' contents.

"Oatmeal again," Heinz complains. "I'm so hungry. If only we could have an egg."

"There's hardly enough oatmeal for three of us, much less six," Elisabet whines.

"Now children, don't worry. Since I lost my false teeth, I can't chew so well," Oma Ilsa explains. "I'll strain and drink some of the liquid, and there will be plenty of oatmeal left for the children." Ilsa places a loosely woven rag over her bowl, dips the spoon into the pail, and pours some liquid over it. Then, she scrapes the clumps of oatmeal she has collected back into the pail.

Marike frowns. "Mutter, are you sure that is enough for you?"

"It's plenty. I have my tea. Children eat." Ilsa fills their bowls.

For several moments everyone is quiet, except for the sound of spoons scraping. When they finish, Marike collects their spoons and bowls and washes everything, including their food pails.

There is little food left to wash off, Marike thinks sadly. *The children are so hungry.* When she stacks the bowls, a windy blast of air from one of the many cracks knocks the bowls over. Elisabet helps her retrieve them as she chatters excitedly about the approaching Christmas.

"Mutter, did you hear the camp is having a program for *Weihnachten?*" Elisabet asks.

"Is *der Weihnachtsmann* coming? Will he bring presents?" Helena tugs on Marike's skirt.

Marike gathers her children around her. "Yes, he may. The adults were given permission to organize the children and give a little program. I think they said each child who recites a verse, Santa will give them a piece of candy."

"Candy! I want some!" Edel repeats.

"My favorite is chocolate. The last time I had some," Heinz licks his lips, "was when the two English POWs who helped in the bakery gave us some of their chocolate bars from their Red Cross packages."

"Candy? Is that all you can think about? The best time I remember," Elisabet adds, "was my birthday when I got my red scooter."

Heinz groans, "Oh no, not the scooter story again."

"Mutter, Heinz is being mean," Elisabet complains.

"Heinz, why don't you play with your cousins?" Marike suggests.

"Okay, bye." Heinz leaves the room.

Marike observes how quickly he exits, almost as if his insensitive remark was intended to gain him freedom. She recalls when she was young and complained about her brothers' teasing. Her mother would say, "Boys will be boys."

"I want to hear Elisabet's story," Helena says, her blue eyes shining with enthusiasm.

"Me, too." Edel climbs on the bunk bed next to Elisabet, who surveys her audience, takes a deep breath, and begins.

"My story begins when I was little like Helena. I could hardly wait for my birthday. You probably don't remember, but it was after we moved from Elbing to Altfelde and lived above the bakery."

"I do too remember," Helena declares. "Mutti worked in grandmother's bakery."

"You were too young," Elisabet replies. "You just heard us talking."

Helena pouts. "We were upstairs. Mutti and Vater were downstairs laughing. Vater was visiting. He wore an army uniform."

"Mutter, she remembers," Elisabet exclaims in wonder.

Marike glances up from her knitting, "I hope you always recall happy times and your dear vater."

"I remember the first time I saw my scooter. It was in the shop window. It was all shiny red with a handle and a wide place to stand. It was the most beautiful thing I'd ever seen. I begged Mutter to go in the shop so I could see it better, but she was in a hurry to get back to the bakery." Breathless, Elisabet stops.

Marike says, "I was afraid to raise your hopes. I thought it would be too expensive."

"Every day, I begged Mutter for my scooter."

Marike nods.

"On my birthday, Mutter made my favorite cake, and the family sang 'Happy Birthday.' I was so disappointed. I didn't see my scooter. Instead, Onkel Abelard gave me a rusty scooter from the junkyard. Said he'd fix it up for me. I almost cried." Elisabet looks sadly at her brother and sister.

"Don't stop," Helena cries, "tell us more."

"Everyone started laughing. I was so mad. Onkel said he was teasing. That was when Mutter rolled out my new scooter from where she'd hidden it in the closet under the stairs. I kept touching my scooter, because I couldn't believe it." Elisabet hugs herself.

Marike says, "You were so happy and mad all at the same time."

"It was mean of Onkel to tease me."

"You had to ride your scooter right away. You didn't even eat your cake."

"No one had to teach me. Right away I knew how. I rode my scooter every day, and sometimes, I rode all the way to *Tante*'s on the next street. It wasn't long after that when we had to move to Oma and Opa's little house in Petershagen, and I had to leave my scooter behind. There wasn't any room. I still miss it. It's the only thing I miss. Do you think it's still there, or does someone else have it?" Elisabet looks hopefully from her sister and brother to her mother.

Helena says, "I think it is. It's waiting for you. Will you teach me how to ride it?"

Marike gets up. "I'd better look for Heinz. Elisabet, you're a good storyteller, almost as good as your grandmother. You stay here, and I'll return soon."

"Mutter, you didn't answer my question. When can we get it?"

Almost outside the door, Marike turns. In a cheery voice, she says, "One day we'll buy you a new scooter."

As Marike closes the door, she hears Elisabet mumble, "By then, I'll be too old."

Chapter 15

By the time *Weihnachten* arrives, the children have anticipated it almost as much as they had in Germany. How proud Marike is as her children recite their memorized pieces. Even Onkel Abelard congratulates them, and a compliment from him is special. For days, Elisabet has practiced her piece and recites it with a dramatic flourish. She truly earns a reward, but *der Weihnachtsmann* runs out of candy. Marike can see Elisabet's disappointment, but Elisabet bites her lip and holds her head up. When Helena removes her candy from her mouth and offers it to her big sister, Marike swallows her sudden emotion.

Later on, the children grow excited over the package they receive from American Mennonites. Each item—the toothpaste, toothbrush, bar of soap, comb, and brush—is held to the light, carefully examined, and then solemnly passed to the next child. When they unroll the washcloth and find the small top, they laugh with happiness while Heinz winds the string and makes it spin.

While the children play with the top, Abelard brings out his homemade Parcheesi board and challenges Freda, Marike, and his mother to a game. Meanwhile, Freda and Marike make some of their special treat from bread, sugar, and milk they'd saved. When they drink their tea and eat the cake that was warmed on their little stove, they give thanks.

After eating, the adults play Parcheesi while the children tell stories. Soon, Marike notices the children surround them, curious why they're laughing so hard. First, Abelard, then Freda tries to explain. Still laughing, Marike says, "Your onkel named his markers after some of the Danish guards. You know the fat one? Abelard said he got fat from eating our leftover soup. He said soon we'll be fat like the guard. Isn't that ridiculous?" As she says this, Marike glances at her mother, whose tears run into her toothless grin. Freda hiccups in between laughing, and Abelard guffaws.

"It's not that funny," Elisabet says, looking puzzled.

"Adults," Heinz declares. "You can't understand them."

"I never heard them laugh like that," Elisabet says. "How can they laugh after everything that has happened?"

The children shake their heads and return to their game

Chapter 16

"Marike, a letter came from Agathe! Can you believe it? Finally, we hear." Oma Ilsa waves the soiled envelope as if it's a flag.

"Hurry, open it!" Marike clasps her hands together to prevent herself from grabbing the envelope from her mother's shaking hands. Ever since the Danes lifted their yearlong ban on the mail, Marike has hoped to hear from her sister.

"I can't," her mother says. "What if it's bad news? You read it."

Calmly, Marike takes the envelope from her mother and opens it. For long minutes, Marike holds the single page to the light and studies the smudged writing.

"I can't stand it. What does it say?"

"It must have gotten wet. The ink is smeared." Marike continues, "This much I can read: Jakob, Julianna, and Agathe are all right."

Marike's mother closes her eyes with her hands held prayerfully to her lips. "My dear daughter is alive. Thank you. Thank you. But where are they?"

Marike turns the envelope over. "It's stamped Hamburg."

"Marike, isn't Hamburg in the Russian zone?"

"Yes, but her letter says something about her husband. She must have found Herman in Hamburg."

Marike's mother shakes her head. "I don't understand. How did they get there? And Hamburg, the Russians—it's too dangerous."

"I think they're all right." Marike sighs. "I don't know how Agathe did it, but I can guess. How many times have the Danes announced that any refugee who could locate a relative in Germany could return there? Remember when your cousin in Germany wrote to say we couldn't come. Conditions were terrible. They said they lived in the basement of a bombed-out house and were eating almost anything they could find: a dead horse, garbage, rotten vegetables."

"I remember. Do you think Agathe found her husband?"

"I know when Agathe decides something, nothing can stop her. She missed Prussia. I think she found Herman, and he 'agreed' Agathe and the children could return there. He may even know some Russian—that would help." Marike takes a deep breath.

"But the Russian zone," Ilsa shudders. "And what do you mean 'agreed'? Of course Herman would want his family with him!"

Marike hugs her mother. "Unless a relative 'agrees' to provide for us, the Danes won't let us return to Germany."

The next day, with her hands dug into her coat pockets, Marike waits in line for their soup. Her eyes smart and her nose drips from the cold, damp wind.

It's hard to believe another fall. We've been here a whole year and in Denmark a year and half. Now what? Marike wonders as the Danish guard approaches with one of the volunteer refugee translators.

He points to Marike and in rapid Danish says something. Not understanding, Marike shakes her head. The woman translator shouts, "He said you have one hour to gather your things and be over there with the others." She points towards a group of refugees huddled under a tree.

"My *kinder* and mutter—what about them? Where are you sending us?" Marike cries frantically.

"*Ja, kinder*…Mutter?" He shakes his head.

"Mutter's name is Dieck, D...i...e...c...k, Ilsa. Please, she is elderly," Marike pleads.

The guard checks his list and says, "*ja.*" Marike hurries back to her barracks.

Chapter 17

Crowded into the large army truck, Marike clings to her suit-case and small children while her mutter follows with the older children.

"Where are we going?" asks Heinz.

Marike answers softly, "The Danes didn't tell me."

"Will our cousins be there?" Elisabet asks.

Marike says, "I don't know."

Elisabet sighs.

"Children," Oma says cheerily, "this is an adventure."

"I don't want a 'venture. I wanna go home," Edel cries.

Marike dries Edel's face with her sleeve. "Don't cry. It will be all right. I think this will be a better camp. Oma, did you find Freda or Abelard?"

Oma shakes her head, "I couldn't find anyone. If only we could have said good-bye."

"Maybe they'll be sent to the same camp," Marike says hopefully.

A round-faced woman with soft brown eyes says, "I heard the Danes are closing some of the small camps and sending us Germans to larger facilities."

Marike turns to her, "Do you know where they're taking us?"

"Not exactly, but I've heard talk about a huge camp near Jutland's west coast. That's all I know."

"Thanks. It does seem like we're headed west."

Sometime later, Marike glimpses large gates opening for their truck. As soon as their vehicle stops, armed guards motion them to step down. Marike inhales. *It smells like fish. We must be near the North Sea.* From the German street signs, Marike can tell it was formerly a large German military base. *Once, Germany vanquished Denmark. I remember. It was April 9, 1940. Then, Germany was the proud conqueror, but now we are the conquered.*

Bewildered, Marike and her family huddle together in the enormous camp. A guard yells over the noisy confusion: "*Hauptstr!*" With his rifle, he motions Marike and those standing nearby down the street. Dutifully, they walk slowly forward until they find *Hauptstr* Street. The guard directs some of the refugees to enter Barracks A. Marike looks questioningly at the guard, who indicates they must continue down the street to Barracks B.

Soon Marike discovers she shares a room on the northern side of the barracks with nineteen people, including her brother's family. The mother of the other family who occupies their room informs Marike that everyone must follow her rules. She is in charge. Each morning, she must report a head count. In a dull voice, she explains, "In case anyone dies during the night."

"Do many die?" Marike asks.

The woman tucks a stray hair into her tightly braided bun. "Some do, but it's the rule because there are so many of us—some thirty-five thousand. I have to report. More refugees arrive each day as they close the smaller camps. I'm Verna, Verna Schellenberg. I was chosen to be the barracks' leader. Ask me when you want something."

"I understand. Thank you, Verna."

When Verna exits the barracks, Marike asks Elisabet, "What do you think?"

"It is bigger. And at least I don't walk into barbed wire everywhere I turn, like the last camp," answers Elisabet.

"Yes, but don't forget there is still barbed wire and armed guards around the perimeter," says Onkel Abelard.

"Look what I found—a cupboard," exclaims Elisabet.

"Frau S. said we can store our food and things there. See, they have them at the end of each bunk bed."

"Where do you want the pot?" asks Abelard.

"Maybe we won't need it," says Heinz.

"I think we will. I heard it is hard to find the toilets at night," responds Marike.

Young Edel jumps on a mattress. "Look, bugs!" Insects pop up.

"Bed bugs, not again," says Heinz.

"And straw mattresses, too. And you can see daylight between the cracks in the walls," says Elisabet.

"No more complaining. Be grateful. Some of your relatives in Germany have nothing—not even food," says Marike.

"Vater, can I explore?" asks Peter, Heinz's cousin.

"We all want to explore," says Heinz.

Marike looks to Abelard and Freda for their approval. When they nod, she says, "You older ones take care of the little ones."

"Yes, Mutter," says Heinz, as the children run out the door, leaving it wide open.

As they leave, a bulky woman thrusts herself through the doorway. Marike is surprised by the woman's newer, almost clean skirt and jacket. Self-consciously Marike smoothes her soiled skirt and notices her dirty hands. *How does she stay so clean? Only the Danish people look this good.*

"*Guten Morgen,*" the woman says. Her tone is demanding, expectant.

The family quickly returns her greetings.

"I am Adele Muller. You can address me as Frau Muller. I'm in charge here." She pauses, glances at the adults, and marches up to Abelard.

"But," Marike says, "I thought Schellenberg was in charge."

Frau Muller turns around, "Schellenberg, what does she know?" She grunts. "I'm in charge of this whole section. She is only responsible for this little barracks."

"Oh, we didn't know. Our other camp was so small," Marike explains.

"Here we are organized, more efficient. There are thousands of us. The Danish make us responsible. We are elected. You will see. Follow the rules. Don't make trouble. Someone is in charge of everything, even the distribution of clothing. You must obey."

"Yes, yes, we understand. But we have been traveling and have had nothing to eat," says Abelard.

"Well, there is a *Volkskuche*, people's kitchen, to the right of the barracks. Once a day, they'll give you a hot meal—just about now. Each family sends someone with a pail to get their soup. The cold items you may store for your other meals."

"We eat here in our room?" asks Marike.

"Most families want to—to eat with their families. If you don't have any other questions, I have other families I must see."

"But—" says Marike.

It is too late. Frau Mueller has left.

"Who was that?" asks Marike.

"You have just met one of the four hundred," says Freda.

"Four hundred? Who are they?" Marike looks puzzled.

"They are the ones who get their friends to elect them. Put them in charge. Then, they get more rations, better clothes. They can even take our room and squeeze us in with others." Freda's words sound sharpened with bitterness.

"How do you know?" Marike asks, incredulous.

"On the truck, I met a woman whose sister is here. She wrote and told her about 'the system,' and she told me," Freda says.

"Why don't they get rid of them? We don't need managers," Marike says.

"It's no good. They just get replaced. Then, another has her hand in your pocket." With a disgusted shake of her head, Freda grabs her buckets.

Marike rises and follows her. "I may as well get our buckets, and we can get in line together. Wait for me."

Chapter 18

A month goes by as the family adjusts to the camp routine. Marike is concerned about how thin her children are becoming. With torn strips of cloth, she has fashioned belts for each child, to keep the boys' pants from falling off and the girls' skirts from sliding down. In the past, Marike's boys wore short pants with *Hosentrager*, suspenders, but here it is too cold. Like the older boys, they wear long pants. Each morning, Marike combs the girls' long blonde hair, dividing it into plaits and neatly braiding them. As she does so, she checks for head lice and is grateful when she finds none. She hears other mothers' stories of lice and their children who got typhus and died.

The food is only slightly better than at their last camp. Usually, three times a week it is a watery cream of wheat soup with bits of celery, onions, and other unknown substances. Sometimes, they have a very thin split pea or celery soup. So far, they have yet to see the promised meat. Other foods they receive are soggy dark bread or white bread and a little butter, sugar, and tea. The children like the powdered milk.

Today, as usual, Marike hears clomping sounds in the hall. *At least, since the Swedish gave the children wooden clogs, I know when they are returning.* As they enter, she asks each to remove their clogs and socks. She bends down and examines their feet.

While they sit, lined up on their bunk bed, she rubs their feet. *My poor children—they are too young to have so many painful corns and calluses. If only they didn't have such thin socks.*

Sternly, Marike scolds, "Children, don't run. You're ruining your feet."

Ignoring her comments, her nephew Peter says breathlessly, "Tante Marike, this is my new friend Heller. He can run faster than anybody."

Marike greets him and watches as the boy's brown eyes dart around the room.

"Heller, do you have family?"

His voice cracking, he says, "Yes, Frau Wiens. My mutter has ten children. She got Hitler's mothers' gold cross for so many children. I'm the eldest, at thirteen."

He must be small for his age. I'd have guessed twelve, like Peter. Marike smiles, "Well, I'm glad Peter found a friend."

With his hand on their cupboard door, Heller peers inside, quickly closes it, and skips to the other side of the room.

"I have to go now. Got to do some organizing. See you tomorrow, Peter."

Nervously cracking his knuckles, Peter stands by the door. It reminds Marike of how her son Heinz tries to crack his knuckles. *Children always want to be like their older playmates,* she muses.

"Okay. I'll walk partway to your barracks with you," says Peter.

"Well, Heller, next time I hope Peter's parents are here so you can meet them."

Heller barely acknowledges her comment. Then he disappears out the door, followed by Peter.

When Abelard and Freda return, Marike tells them about Peter's new friend.

"I feel sorry for his poor mother. Imagine ten children. 'Course he is proud of her gold cross."

"Gold cross? Oh, you mean those the German government awarded the mothers—more soldiers for the Third Reich," Freda says.

"Where did you say they are from?" Abelard asks.

"Peter said Königsberg."

"Ten children, and to travel all this way," Freda says sympathetically.

"I think she has only six with her now. Heller likes to tell everyone he is the oldest, but his older three brothers are in the army," Marike corrects her.

"But you said there were ten children, not nine?" Freda frowns.

"True, but Heller told Heinz his little sister got chicken pox when they arrived—never got well and died. Also, Heller told Heinz about his brothers. He seems like a good boy, but there is something about him that just doesn't make sense—like his talk about organizing." Marike's eyes narrow with concern.

"Thanks, Marike. It bears watching." Abelard sits on his bunk, removes his clogs, and rubs his feet.

Ten days later, Heinz interrupts Marike's knitting. "Mutter, you won't believe what my friend did."

Still counting stitches, Marike raises her eyes, "Yes?"

"He jumped on a train all by himself." Heinz's eyes widen with admiration.

"He did? But how?" Marike reminds herself of the many exaggerated camp stories she has heard.

"He fooled a guard and hopped on an unlocked cattle car."

Shaking her head, Marike says, "Now Heinz, you must not believe all the words that come from big boy's mouths."

"But Mutter. It's true. Heller told us. He said he jumped off when he saw the Danish police."

Marike sets her knitting down and studies her son. "I believe you. Here, help me roll this yarn while I finish unraveling it."

Dutifully, Heinz winds the yarn into a clumsy ball as his mother unravels it from her old sweater. As he does so, he glances frequently at their door.

Suddenly, Peter bursts in. "C'mon, Heinz, we're waiting."

"Peter, I'm concerned," Marike begins, only to hear the door bang shut as the two boys leave. She hears other children's muffled voices and pounding feet as Peter and Heinz join them, to run in the hallways.

Getting up, Marike pokes her needles into her knitting and grasps the handle of their pail. *Since there is little else happening, what I most look forward to is standing in line to get our food. If only today they would give us something different, something better.* Soon, she is waiting, like the others, stamping her feet to keep warm. In fact, it is several seconds before Marike realizes the woman in back of her is speaking.

"Excuse me, I don't mean to be forward, but are you Peter's tante?"

Startled, Marike turns. "Why yes, but how did you know?"

"All my Heller talks about is your family." In a hoarse voice, she continues, "He says your big family reminds him of ours when we were in Prussia. He likes your brother, Abelard."

Marike stares at the stranger as the woman nervously attempts to tuck errant strands of hair into her brown bun tightly pinned to the back of her head.

As she talks, the woman's toddler falls and begins crying. It seems she is surrounded by young, squirming bodies. "There, there, Hermann, you're not hurt. You just surprised yourself. Children, be still, your mutter wants to talk to this nice lady."

"You have so many children," Marike smiles.

"They're good, my little ones. It's my Heller that makes me crazy." As she talks, the woman spits on a rag, cleans food off one child's mouth and wipes another's leaky nose.

"Heller," Marike repeats.

"Do you want your soup or not?" A kitchen helper demands as she dips her ladle into the enormous kettle.

"Oh, sorry, yes." After her pail is filled with a pale, green liquid, Marike says to herself, "Split pea again?" She turns to continue her conversation with Heller's mother, but she has moved, like a centipede with her brood, in the direction of her barracks.

I'll have to talk to my brother about this. Soon, Marike sees her children and calls them to their meal.

A week later, she is reminded about Heller when Peter announces that Heller has been arrested.

"What do you mean arrested? Arrested for what?" Peter's father demands.

"Oh, I was afraid something like this would happen," Marike says.

Peter cracks his knuckles and balances on one foot. "It wasn't his fault."

"You don't get arrested for nothing," Abelard says.

Peter hunches over, looking miserable, his voice soft and apologetic. "He was just organizing."

Abelard points his finger at his recalcitrant son, "Peter Dieck, you aren't organizing too—whatever that means?"

"No, Vater."

"If I hear…"

Abelard begins slowly unbuckling his belt.

Peter's eyes are huge as he stares at his father. "I didn't do anything. He asked, but I said no." Peter's body quivers. "Please, no."

"Please, don't, Abelard. The boy tells the truth," Freda pleads, grabbing at her husband's arm, but he shakes her off.

"Maybe so, but this Heller is trouble," Abelard growls.

"Yes, Vater," Peter says meekly.

Abelard sits down, but his eyes stay riveted on his son. "For the last time, tell me what Heller did."

"He just organized some cigarettes. A guard promised them to him for some help he did cleaning the toilets, but then the guard refused to pay him. I guess Heller just took them. Most boys would have smoked them. Instead, Heller traded them for some cheese for his family. He said it was covered in mold, but they ate it anyway."

"*Wie meinst du das?* How do you mean? He wanted you to help him steal cigarettes?" Abelard's voice rises angrily.

Peter nods miserably.

"Well, I'm glad you had some sense for a Dieck. I suppose you had to try smoking too?"

Peter coughs, "Just a little. Then I didn't feel so hungry. Please, Vater, I'm sorry."

"From now on, I don't want you to have anything to do with Heller. Do you understand?" Abelard shakes Peter. "He is trouble. You stay away from him."

Marike says, "Now Abelard, don't be too hard on Heller. I met his mother and the poor woman has her hands full with so many children. Heller doesn't seem a mean sort—just needs a father's firm hand. After all, his father is probably on the Eastern Front. Heller said his mutter came from a Mennonite family, and they're from East Prussia. Maybe you could help him."

"Woman, you don't think we have problems enough without looking in someone else's haystack? After all, he knows the rules, especially *no contact* with the Danish. He'll be lucky if they don't send him to another camp."

"I agree," Marike says sadly, and under her breath, "His poor mother."

"There will be no more talk," Abelard says finally.

"Yes, Abelard," Marike replies meekly.

When Abelard turns to leave the room, Freda winks at Marike.

From then on the family discusses many topics: the new refugees, the food, the bed bugs, the many rules, but everyone carefully avoids the subject of Heller. Marike finds it hard to think of anything else. *What if Heinz is like Heller when he grows older? If only my*

Horst were here to help guide the boys. After a while, she believes she is the only person concerned about Heller, until a few days later, when Abelard mentions him.

"I talked to Heller's mother and the camp chief," Abelard states matter-of-factly.

"You did?" Marike looks up from her knitting.

"Yes. I told him I didn't think Heller was a bad boy. He just needs a man's steady hand. He agreed. He said if I would guarantee him, he wouldn't send him to another camp in northern Jutland."

"Oh Abelard, I'm so proud of you." Marike stands and attempts to hug her brother, who shrugs off her embrace.

"It's nothing to be proud of. Just don't coddle the boy. The chief agreed Heller can work it off. He will be busy cleaning the pits for some days now—and no tobacco for it either."

"And his mutter?" asks Marike.

Abelard scratches his beard, smiles, and says, "She said I was a *gut* man. I lifted a heavy burden for her—made her happy, poor woman."

Freda beams.

Abelard glances at the women. "I'll need your help with the boy."

"We understand," answers Freda, as Marike nods agreement.

Chapter 19

Marike reflects. *It is good Abelard helps Heller. In just one month, he has made some changes, small ones to be sure. But he seems less jumpy, more polite. Of course, Peter's admiration for Heller has cooled— that was to be expected. Peter probably liked the excitement Heller's antics produced.*

Marike couldn't blame Peter. Sometimes, she felt as if she couldn't stand the dull repetition of another day. Yet, when the sun's rays burn off the grey clouds, she knows it is time for a walk out- side—alone. She can't remember when she was last alone, away from the chatter, noise of wooden clogs, and a baby crying. And the smell: Even the smoke from the stoves seems better than the smells of nineteen people piled together. As long as she lives, she knows she never will forget the odd stew of smells—from people's gas caused by too much pea soup, to the smell of wet wool clothes, to smoke not properly vented, to unwashed bodies smelling of urine and worse.

Marike lifts her face to the sun, welcoming the warmth. Ahead, she sees the familiar strands of barbed wire and an armed Danish guard. He doesn't look mean or angry, probably some farmer's son. She smiles at him, but he turns away quickly, almost as if she had slapped him. Marike understands. The guards were warned to have no contact with the Germans. "Not wanted," she mumbles to herself. Staring at the barbed wire, she remembers their cows and horses fenced in on their Petershagen farm. *They think we're dangerous animals. What are a bunch of women and children going to do to them?* Beyond the wire, she gazes longingly at the neatly cultivated farmland, so healthy and green, lying so inviting in front of her.

If only they could go home. But where is home? Certainly it isn't Prussia. Does Prussia even exist since the Russians and Poles crossed their border? She doubted it. Where could they go? Questions without answers; she must think of something else.

If only she had a book. How she loves to read, but only a few worn books pass from hand to hand. She yearns for something beautiful. Marike softly hums. Her mutter loves to sing too. As she remembers how her mutter's singing punishes her ears, Marike smiles.

Still smiling, Marike enters Barracks B and walks to their room. Before she opens the door, she hears her niece's strident voice. *Poor Freda tries so hard to be a good stepmother to her sister's four motherless children, and all Lena can do is argue. What is wrong now?* Before she can enter, Lena throws open the door, nearly hitting her, and rushes by a startled Marike.

"What's happening?" Marike asks.

"I have no idea," Freda says. "I just told Lena that at fourteen, she is too young to be with those women."

"You don't mean…?" asks Marike.

"I'm afraid so," Freda says, shaking her head in disgust. "They say, 'nature calls.'"

"Still, it's hard." Marike says, "Some of these women have been without men for so long."

"Marike, you are a good Mennonite. How can you say such things?" Freda scolds. "Those women are nothing more than *Prostituiertes*."

"Don't say that!"

Freda spits out, "What do you think they bring back in those bags?"

Marike looks at the floor. "I guess food. I'm sorry. I know Lena gives you a hard time."

"Well, I know my sister would never have put up with her nonsense. I don't want to take her mother's place, but still, I have let her have her head too often."

"You're right, Freda. She is just a country girl. She doesn't understand these things. I'll talk to her." Marike hugs her sister-in-law.

Freda blinks back her tears. "Oh, Marike, I miss my sister so much. Sometimes you remind me of her."

"And Lena is just like her mother was—used to her own way."

Freda chuckles. "You're right."

"Sometimes being pretty leads a girl astray. Your sister would be grateful."

"I surely hope so," Freda replies sadly.

"It is hard to keep the peace," Marike says as she begins sewing.

How much longer can we endure the camp's harsh conditions? She recalls Heinz and her recent visit to the hospital.

"Boils," the doctor said.

As the doctor lanced first her boils and then Heinz's, she stared at the yellow pus oozing down their legs.

Heinz's lower lip quivered as the doctor swiftly released the pus in his boils. How brave Heinz was. Unexpectedly, the doctor patted Heinz's head. Marike hoped the solution the doctor swabbed on their wounds was antiseptic. She remembered the wounded soldiers on their ship smelling of awful infections and later, some dying of gangrene.

"Why boils?" she asked in German, pointing at Heinz's leg.

The doctor ignored her question, as if he didn't understand German, but he knew the answer. There are no facilities for bathing or laundering their clothing. She had done her best with the little she has had.

Thinking about wounded soldiers reminds Marike of her dear

Horst. *I wonder, Horst, are you wounded, suffering in a Russian POW camp? I've tried to keep the children safe, but it's so hard.*

Today, she doesn't have water so she washes the children with the extra tea. As she firmly wipes them, she bends her head down so they won't see her tears. Their arms and legs are so thin, her thumb and forefinger meet around their skinny limbs.

On the farm, they had had enough to eat, even when the German army confiscated whatever it needed to feed the troops. Now the children complain constantly of being hungry. Ilsa often gives her meager portions to her grandchildren. How Marike admires her mother. Even though she is in her sixties and has raised eleven of thirteen children, her dear mother still insists on helping.

The afternoon grows cold as Elisabet, Heinz, Helena, and young Edel hurry into their barracks.

"Oma, tell us a story?" Elisabet asks.

Soon the children snuggle next to Ilsa under her scruffy down comforter, which she brought from home. Marike closes her eyes, remembering similar afternoons in her parents' small retirement home near their Petershagen farm.

"Oh children, I don't know if I can. Oma is so tired."

For the first time, Marike notices tiny pain lines etching Ilsa's grey face. *Why hadn't I seen them before now?* And her mother's voice sounds breathless and weak.

"Children, come, let Oma rest."

"No, Marike. It is all right." Her mother waves Marike away.

"But…"

"I'm fine. I'll rest later. Now children, you'll have to be very quiet and still as mice."

"We promise," says Elisabet.

"Snuggle up and get warm," Ilsa tucks the covers around them. "When I was little like you, my dear vater would carve small toys for me and sing to us. Oh, how I loved him, but then he died. Anyway, all summer long our tantes brought cakes and visited us on our little farm. When fall came, I helped my mutter load our wagon. And my little *bruder*, baby *schwester*, and I went with my mutter to my tante's home."

"Were you going to live there?" asks Elisabet.

"We thought we were," Ilsa continues. "Anyway, the morning after we arrived, my tante gave us some cake and said she wasn't used to children. She had never married. She said children made too much noise. She told us we would have to leave. Remember when I told you our mutter said she'd sold the farm. Alone, she said she couldn't manage the farm and sold it to pay the debts. We couldn't go home. Tante said we should ask if we could stay with our relatives who had a large dairy farm. They didn't have any children to help with the chores. That is when our mutter drove our wagon to my Tante Adelaide and Onkel Axel Albrecht's farm. Remember, I told you how our mutter left us and went to work in the city in a factory? Gunther cried. It was like we lost both our parents and our little farm. Since the city was far away, our mutter couldn't visit very often. We had to work very hard. For Christmas, all my tante and onkel gave me was a handkerchief."

"What happened to your baby *schwester?*" asks Elisabet.

"Oh, a couple who couldn't have children took her. They gave her clothes and toys. We could see they loved her very much. Sometimes, they would invite Gunther and me to visit. They'd let us play with her toys and eat cake. We could see how happy our baby sister was. We looked forward to those visits. Those were happy times."

"Your tante and onkel were mean to make you work so hard," says Heinz.

"Sometimes we did feel like slaves, but they gave us a home and schooling. When we finished school, they offered to teach us dairy farming so we could support ourselves. Oh…" Ilsa moans and clutches her stomach.

"Mutter, are you all right?" Marike asks anxiously.

"It's just an upset stomach." Ilsa takes a deep breath and slowly releases it. "See, I'm better already. Now as I was telling the children, when I grew up, I met and married Eberhard. Your opa was a good man. When my tante and onkel got old, and even my mutter, they lived on our farm."

"You took care of them after everything they did. I don't know if I could," says Elisabet.

"They gave us a home," Oma Ilsa states calmly.

"Tell us again Gunther's story about the slate," Heinz says.

"Oh yes, please," the other children beg.

Oma moans.

"I'm sorry, your poor oma has to rest," Marike says. "Now go play."

Ilsa collapses on the bed. The children jump down and hurry out the door while little Helena presses her sleeping grandmother's hand to her cheek. With great tenderness, Marike tucks her mother's comforter around her.

Freda rushes in and looks frantically around the room. "Has anyone seen her?"

"Who?"

"Lena. I've looked everywhere!"

"You don't think…" Marike looks worried.

"I'm afraid. She is too trusting." Freda sighs, sits on her bunk, and removes her clogs. "All she talks about are those women. One showed Lena all the food she had gotten just before she hid her bag. I still don't know how the women get past the guards to make their rendezvous."

"Well, I do. I saw the guard talking to one of them," Marike remarks. "Some make some excuse to leave the camp—visit a sick relative in the hospital or say they have a dental appointment. The camp chief believes them and gives them permits. Others trade favors with the guards."

"Really?"

"Yes." Marike nods.

"I can understand Lena," Freda explains. "She hates the barbed wire fence, all the rules. She's bored. To a young girl like Lena, their life looks exciting."

Abelard swings open the door and stomps into the room. "Are all the children here?"

"Yes, all except Lena, but—" Freda begins.

"Where is that girl?"

"What's wrong?"

Abelard sighs. "The Danish police just arrested two of the guards. The third one killed himself."

"Why?" asks Marike.

"You know, consorting with the enemy. I just hope Lena doesn't get it into her head…" Abelard continues, spewing saliva as he spits out the words.

Lena saunters in, swaying her small hips, glances around, and asks, "Why is everyone looking so gloomy?"

Marike covers her mouth so her brother won't see her smile.

Abelard shakes his finger at his oldest daughter. "Where have you been?"

Lena shrinks back. "Just at that little theater. They said I could help with the tickets. They're free. Why?" Lena nervously looks around the room.

Everyone is silent.

Peter says, "Vater thought you were involved with those women."

Lena's cheeks redden as she looks at her father. "I would never do that. I was just curious."

"And?" Abelard asks.

"One nice woman gave me an apple. That is all. What did I do?"

Abelard looks sternly at his daughter. "You're to have nothing to do with those women. They're trouble. And I don't like the way you sashay around trying to be like them. Do you understand me, girl?"

Lena hangs her head, tears streaming down her face. "Yes, Vater, but..."

"Stop," interrupts Abelard. "If we were home, not here, you would know I meant it when you felt my shaving strop." Abelard paces around the room.

"Yes, Vater, I'll be good," Lena answers meekly.

"Tell us about the theater," demands Lena's younger sister.

"We want to go too," say the other children.

Lena glances first at the children, then at her father.

In a low voice, he says slowly, "I shouldn't agree, but, oh well, I guess it's harmless enough. But I don't want to hear any more nonsense about you and those shameful women."

Excited, Lena gushes, "The cast is just a group of refugees who like to sing. But you should see! One is a famous actress from Danzig. Wait until you hear her. Her voice is the most incredible, unbelievable voice I've ever heard. The actors blacken their faces. I think they're doing some kind of Negro play. I've never seen a Negro. I wonder what they look like."

"Can we go, please?" the children ask.

"Yes, we'll go. Right, brother?" Marike asks. She turns to ask her mother if she wants to attend and notices Ilsa is still asleep. *How can she sleep with all of this noise? She never rests—always working, sweeping, or helping in the camp's kitchen. I hope she isn't sick. She hardly eats, gives her food to the children. Maybe she has hunger pains. Still, I wish I could get some help for her.*

Chapter 20

The next morning, Marike finds her mother doubled over, moaning softly.

"Mutter, what is the matter?" Marike asks.

"The pain is much worse," Ilsa gasps.

"Will you go to the *Krankenhaus* now?" Marike asks.

"I guess so, but I'm afraid of the hospital after what they did to my Eberhard," Ilsa barely whispers.

"Freda come and help," Marike urges as each takes one of Ilsa's arms. Somehow, they manage to help her walk. When a guard learns Ilsa is ill, he arranges transportation to the camp chief's office. The camp chief gives Ilsa, Marike, and Freda permission to go to the hospital.

When they arrive at the hospital, the nurse takes charge and directs Ilsa into a small room. She motions for Marike and Freda to wait. They find two straight-backed chairs and sit. Finally, the nurse returns to say Ilsa has appendicitis, and the doctor will operate. The nurse stares at Marike, waiting for her decision.

I don't know what to say to her. If I don't agree to the operation, Mutter may die. If only Abelard was here. Still, what could he do? What choice do we have?

"Yes, please, take care of my dear mutter." Barely has Marike spoken when the nurse turns and leaves.

For some time, they wait in anxious silence until a rumpled look-ing doctor, followed by the nurse, emerges from the operating room. Nervously, he runs his hand through his hair and begins talking to the opposite wall. At first, Marike looks behind her to see if some-one else has joined them.

This isn't good. He won't look at us, and he keeps mumbling in Danish. I can't understand anything. He just looks like he wants to get away from us. Thank goodness the nurse knows some German. Maybe she can explain.

When the nurse describes her mother's condition, Marike listens in shocked silence. It's Freda who thinks to ask if they can see Ilsa, but she is told they should visit her later.

Marike and Freda slowly drag their feet as they walk away from the hospital to their barracks.

"I can't believe it." Marike stops, rubs her eyes. "Last night Mutter was telling the children stories. Now this—it has to be a ter-rible mistake. Surely, the nurse misinterpreted the doctor."

"I wish that were true." Freda takes Marike's hand. "You heard her—paralyzed."

"It's my fault. I should never have talked Mutter into going to the hospital. You know how they feel about us Germans." Marike's hangs her head dejectedly and mumbles, "But then, she would have died from appendicitis." Marike nervously rubs her hands.

"Don't blame yourself. How could you know?" Freda asks.

"Ever since Vater died, Mutter hasn't trusted Danish doctors."

The women draw near each other, forming a sad pair.

"What can we tell the children? They love Oma so much," Marike asks as they enter the barracks.

"The truth. They should know the truth," Freda whispers an-grily. "Besides, she isn't dead. Don't give up."

Elisabet runs up and grasps her mother's waist. "Oma?" she asks, as she looks up at Marike's tear-stained face.

The other children echo her concern.

"Come, sit with me," Marike says gently. "Oma has appendicitis." The children squeeze next to her, sitting on the straw mattress.

"Did they operate?" asks Peter.

Marike nods sadly.

"Is she better?" asks Heinz.

"No, she is worse, much more so," Freda states, her pale face reddening.

"Oh, poor Oma," says Elisabet.

Freda continues, "The doctor said she had appendicitis and needed an operation right away. We agreed. But when they gave Oma a shot to make her sleep, the needle hit the wrong place in her spine. At least, that is what the nurse who translated for the Danish doctor told us."

"Oh no!" exclaims Elisabet.

"Now Oma is paralyzed, can't move, can't swallow food," Marike says softly.

"But if Oma can't eat," says Elisabet.

"Can't someone do something?" asks Peter.

"No. The doctor said he was sorry. He said sometimes this happens. Her condition is irreversible. He said in her weakened state, she won't last long." As she talks, Marike strides angrily around the room.

"It isn't right," Freda says between clenched teeth. "Ilsa is such a good woman. For this to happen now, after all she has been through. How could the doctor be so careless? It is just as if he had shot her. I knew they hated us, but this. She never hurt anyone."

Two days after her operation, Ilsa Dieck dies, just as the doctor predicted. Life in the camp is too hard for the family to give up completely to their helpless frustration. They know their dear mutter and precious oma would want them to continue their struggle. Yet, without her loving support, it seems the family has lost its direction. For a while, anger sustains Marike, until it too becomes a burden.

Marike seeks an answer to her family's deepening grief. *We've lost so much—our parents, the Petershagen farm, my mother-in-law's bakery, Prussia, and maybe, Horst. How can I go on? I'm so tired. If only I could give up—but the children. I promised Horst. At least, we can take comfort that my mutter is buried nearby—not like my vater in some unknown mass grave.*

Everyday tasks such as: knitting, remaking, and mending their clothes; caring for her children; even waiting in line for their daily food help Marike to continue. And like other women in the camp, she finds consolation in other refugees' sad stories.

When I hear how much they've suffered, I don't feel so alone. And when I listen and really hear them, sometimes it helps them. It makes all of us feel better.

As usual, today Marike waits in line for her family's food. Despite the noise surrounding her, Marike hears someone behind her crying.

"I'm sorry," the young woman says, wiping her eyes with her frayed sleeve. "Ever since I got here I have these crying fits."

"I understand. I feel the same since Mutter died," Marike says, her eyes filling with tears.

"How sad for you. Did it happen recently?"

"Yes." Marike wipes her face with her sleeve.

The woman nods her head in sympathy. "I'm Bertha."

"Marike." She has learned not to ask what happened. It is better to listen with one's heart, even when one's heart hurts so much. How often did her sweet mother remind her to care for others?

When Bertha notices Marike patiently waiting, she clasps her hands to her chest and says, "My poor baby died on the ship. Even though it happened some time ago, I keep thinking about him."

"I'm so sorry," Marike says, wishing there was more she could say to comfort her. To lose a child, how does a mother recover? "I remember how my mutter grieved when my little *bruder* died."

Bertha continues, "My poor baby, he cried and cried. I couldn't comfort him no matter how much I rocked him. One woman on our ship said, 'Your suckling needs milk. I've milk. I'll nurse him.' You see my milk still hadn't come in. He was starving. I kept thinking if only I hadn't left home. My baby was due soon. But German soldiers said I had to leave our farm, because the Russian army was invading East Prussia. Our soldiers had orders not to transport refugees, but they gave rides partway to me and some others. When my pains started, I found an abandoned house and even a midwife. He was so small. I was afraid. Afterward, I found a priest to baptize little Hermann."

"How brave of you," Marike responds.

"That night on the ship, I thought how quiet he is, so peaceful. I'm glad he is sleeping, because little Hermann kept the others awake with his crying. We were so crowded together, barely one meter of space, in the ship's locker room. I couldn't see him in the darkness. We had no light because of the Russian bombers, so I didn't know until morning. When I saw how still he was, it was too much. I couldn't stop thinking it was my fault that he died. I wanted him to stop crying. And he died."

"How awful that must have been," Marike sighs.

"They had to pry him out of my arms." Bertha rocks back and forth, "Other mothers were crying too. They sounded so far away. I knew they must have had children die. I didn't care. I just wanted my little Hermann back. If I had been a better mother, he would be alive. It's my fault."

Marike gently touches the woman's shoulder. As she does so, she feels the woman's grief soften. "You did everything you could. It isn't your fault. Many children died."

"Later, the ship's captain told me they buried Hermann at sea with others who died. I guess he thought it would help if I knew my baby was buried. But I felt hollow. And you want to know something funny?"

"What?"

"That morning, that morning after my little Hermann died, my milk came in. Isn't that funny?" She laughs in high, gasping sounds and then sobs.

"I wish I could help more." Marike leans towards Bertha.

Bertha wipes her face on her sleeve and tries to smile. "You did. You listened. Everyone has their own troubles. Not many want to hear about others. I have to go now. They are sending me to another camp. Goodbye."

"May God comfort you," Marike calls.

"Marike," Freda calls. "Wait, I'll walk back to the barracks with you."

Marike stops. "I didn't see you."

"I know. You were talking to that woman. All she does is whine about her dead baby. You'd think she was the only one who lost someone. She should just get over it like the rest of us." Freda closes her mouth in a tight line.

"Isn't she the one who had a nervous breakdown? I feel sorry for her," Marike says.

"You aren't the only one. Why, the camp director gave her some shoes and took her to town to cheer her up." Freda pauses. "I wish somebody would do that for me."

Marike smiles to herself. *I'm glad I met her—for a few moments I almost forgot about my mutter. And that cold, metallic taste in my mouth almost went away. I wanted so much to hold on to my dear mutter, like Bertha with her dead baby.*

As she enters the barracks, Marike hears her family discussing her mother. Each day they keep reviewing the details of Ilsa's illness and treatment, as if something had been forgotten—something that, if found, could help them accept their loss.

It is Elisabet's childish wisdom that moves them. "Remember how Oma loved to sing?"

"Oh no," someone groans.

"And she would start singing from the German songbook they gave us," says Elisabet.

"We had to sing extra loud just to drown her out," Freda smiles.

"Do you think she knew how bad she sounded?" Abelard asks.

They look questioningly at each other and suddenly start grinning. First, someone chuckles, then Freda giggles, and others erupt into loud, raucous laughter. Soon Marike joins in, pulled by an emotional wave she could not have predicted. Her relatives' faces redden with the effort; their open mouths glisten with spittle. Unable to control their laughter, their arms clutch their stomachs. It is beyond anything Marike has experienced and something she has seldom seen in her reserved relatives. Never before has she seen them laugh like this after someone died—or ever. It doesn't remove death's ugly taste, but somehow, it makes it taste palatable.

The next day, Marike still puzzles over the strange laughter but accepts it as she has learned to do with so much else. This morning there is a Barracks B meeting. A new barracks leader is to be elected, since the previous one had been dismissed due to the many refugee complaints.

"Another of the four hundred," Freda complains.

"With her hand in your pocket," agrees Abelard.

"All the candidates have ties to someone important, you can be sure," Freda says, angrily folding her arms.

"Isn't there a chance someone who is fair will be elected?" Marike asks hopefully. "After all, they are Prussians, just like us."

"It isn't right. They get all of the privileges, extra rations, and clothes," Freda folds her arms. "It doesn't matter how many elections. Soon all they think about is their own needs."

"Someone from the barracks asked if I wanted to run," Marike says.

"You said no, of course," Abelard interrupts. "Our Mennonite faith would not permit such a thing—holding office, and you'd have to swear an oath. What would our Anabaptist martyrs think?"

"I was tempted, just to have more food for the children," Marike admits.

Each candidate gives a short speech in German, and then the adults living in the barracks cast their votes. Marike votes for a woman with a kind smile and hopes she will be more generous. Twice she had spoken to the previous woman in charge, requesting more food for her hungry family. Each time, she had been rudely rebuffed. Maybe, this time, an honest, impartial woman would be selected. Instead, another woman with more supporters is chosen.

"You watch what happens now," Freda warns. "Her friends will be getting all the favors."

Disappointed, Marike leaves the meeting. Suddenly, she feels someone's hand tapping her back. As she whirls around, she collides with a small woman.

"What now? Oh my, Gertrude, I don't believe it! You're here, I'm so glad." Marike quickly embraces her former neighbor.

"Ever since I saw your mother in Germany, before the evacuation, I hoped I'd find you." Gertrude's excited voice rises. "Each time they'd send me to a new camp, I'd ask for you. Last night when I arrived, someone told me you were here."

Marike stares at her childhood friend, whose fingers twirl her bright blonde curls. "My Gertrude, look at you. You're all grown up and so beautiful. I'm sorry about your parents. Mutter told me. It must have been so hard for you."

"It was awful. Your mother was so kind. How are your parents?" Gertrude asks.

"Vater died in Kopenhagen. Mutter—well, we just lost her."

"Oh Marike, I loved your parents almost like my own. I'm so sorry."

"Thanks, they liked you, too." Marike pauses, clears her throat. "Mutter said you had a baby?"

Gertrude's enormous blue eyes fill with tears. "Oh Marike, he was the sweetest baby. I tried so hard to care for him. Every time I'd lay him down, he'd cry and make this gurgling sound. At night I'd hold him on my shoulder, so he could breathe better. When he'd nurse, he would take a little milk and spit up. One day, I changed his diaper, and it was bright green and hardly wet. I knew it was diarrhea. He whimpered and then nothing. All I had left to hold onto was gone." Gertrude sighs.

"You've got me now, and my bruder and my schwägerin and our children. There is an empty bunk bed in our room. Why don't you stay with us?" Marike smiles at Gertrude.

The next day, Gertrude moves in with Marike and her family.

Chapter 21

"Marike, you've been so good to me." Gertrude stuffs a small, cloth-wrapped parcel in Marike's pocket. "I saved a treat for you. Don't let the others see. Look at it later."

"Thanks." Marike slides her hand into her pocket, feeling the unknown object. *It feels like an apple. It has been so long since we've had any fruit. I can't imagine where Gertrude could find this.* When Marike turns to question her, Gertrude hisses at her.

"Don't ask," she says, as she glances around furtively.

Later, when Marike walks with her children to the theater, she gives them bites of the apple. First she makes them promise not to tell anyone. While they greedily devour the apple, Marike watches them, feeling sad that she doesn't have more food for them. When they ask where the apple came from, she changes the subject and points at the daisies lining the barbed wire fence. The diversion works. In fact, it works too well. Young Edel, with outstretched hands, runs toward the pretty flowers. Marike hurries after him. At the same time, the Danish guard marches towards them. Marike's eyes fasten on the rifle he holds in his hands. *Surely he wouldn't shoot—not a little boy picking a pretty flower for his mother.* Instinctively, Marike grabs Edel's shirt collar and pulls him, as he plucks the flower, back from the fence.

"Edel, children stay away from the fence!" Marike shrieks, terror shredding her words. Still shaking, Marike places Edel firmly on the ground. Bending down to place her face near his, her voice strained, she says, "Don't ever go near the fence. Do you understand?"

"Yes, Mutter," her children mumble meekly.

"Edel just forgot," says Helena taking her little brother's hand. "He didn't mean to."

"Remember last year, what happened to your cousins?" Marike scolds. "When they first came to their camp, the Danes hadn't finished stringing the barbed wire. When your cousins saw the berries, they ran up the hill to pick them. The guard yelled and fired his gun at them. Even though he shot over their heads, his message was clear. Next time, he wouldn't shoot over them. You must be careful. Remember. Always stay away from the fence."

Marike doesn't like to frighten her children, but this is important. She doesn't know if they are more afraid of the guard or her. It doesn't matter. She must protect them.

Obediently, the children follow Marike to the nearby building called the theater, where Marike hears voices singing. One of the refugees has volunteered his musical talents to organize a singing group. Marike smiles with pleasure.

I remember when I was young, reading in the newspaper about the theater. I wanted to go, but we were too poor to attend any productions. This theater looks like our barracks, hastily built, with daylight showing between the boards. Still, I'm grateful for any diversion from the camp's terrible monotony.

The song leader introduces the soloist, Danzig Theater's famous performer. Even with her remarkable talent, she too is just another refugee. Although Marike has heard she's allowed special privileges sometimes—passes to visit Danish friends. Yet, she isn't allowed to perform outside of the camp.

Cold, damp air blows through the cracks. Marike reminds her younger children to keep their coats on. The noisy crowd, with only a few muffled coughs, quiets at the orchestra leader's introductions. As the soloist's mezzo-soprano voice soars, Marike feels as if she floats far away to someplace safe. For once, her restless children sit quietly; their rapt expressions mirror hers. Marike's body tingles. Each exquisite note defines a rapture she thought existed only in church. The music so completely fills her, her chest aches, and forgotten tears sting her eyes. She vows to never forget this wonderful moment.

Afterward, as they walk back to their barracks, the children are more subdued than usual. *They've had to endure such ugliness; I hope they always remember this moment of beauty.* Later, after lights are out, while Heinz and Elisabet smash bed bugs against the wall, Marike imagines she can still hear the beautiful notes.

I want to mash bed bugs too," complains Helena.

"You can't. You're too little," says Heinz.

"Please," Helena pleads.

"Here, I'll show you," offers Elisabet. "Watch me."

"I can't see."

"All right, then listen. Take your thumb and big finger and catch it. Then, smash it against the wall. Tomorrow, we'll see who has the most blood spots."

"I can't catch them."

"Be still. When you feel one crawling on you, just pinch it," instructs her big sister.

"I got one," says a triumphant Helena.

"Good, now smash it on the wall," says Elisabet.

"Mutter, Mutter."

"What is it, Helena?"

"I mashed one!"

"Good, now go to sleep. You are keeping everyone awake," Marike mumbles sleepily.

"I mashed a bed bug. I mashed a bed bug," sings Helena.

"Go to sleep."

"Yes, Mutter," answer the children.

In the distance, beyond someone sleep-talking, Abelard's snores, and the children's whispering, Marike hears that same incredible voice soaring above their misery. Her eyes close.

The next day, sullen clouds hang over the camp, dripping a cold mist on the shivering refugees as they wait for their daily soup ration.

When Marike reaches their room, she sets her soup bucket on the table. The children eat their pea soup in silence, and soon they crawl into their beds, hoping to warm up from the chilly weather.

"Please Mutter, let me make a fire. It's so cold," begs Heinz.

"No, Heinz. We have no *Torf*. And the last bit we had was so icy, when it thawed it just smoked from the water."

"They said we could burn the dead wood and needles we find on the ground," says Elisabet.

"But the ground is bare with not a stick left, and even the low branches are all gone," says Heinz. "I have a plan. I can put Edel on my shoulders." Heinz demonstrates by lifting Edel onto his shoulders, where he sways, while clinging to Heinz's head. "Steady now, Edel."

"I'll fall."

"No, you won't. I'm holding your legs. Let go of my head. I can't see." Heinz pries Edel's hands away from his eyes.

"You sure I won't fall?" asks Edel.

"No. See, I have you."

Amused, Marike watches and finally agrees to her son's plan. "Wait until it's dark and the guard has made his rounds."

"Yes, Mutter. We'll be careful."

"If you get caught…" Marike warns.

"I know. We could be sent to another camp or worse," says Heinz. "If we don't get some wood soon, we'll freeze."

Marike's young friend Gertrude has also been watching Heinz and Edel. "I'll help, Marike."

"How?" Marike asks.

"Don't worry, I'll distract the guard," Gertrude confidently reassures her.

"Are you sure?"

"Yes. I'll be all right. I think I know who the guard is tonight."

The rest of the afternoon, the children, excited about the evening's adventure, huddle in their beds until Marike thinks they will grow tired of this new game. After the signal for "lights out," she watches as her sons and Gertrude creep out the door. She listens for the telltale sound of squeaky boards. When all is quiet, she realizes they know where to step. Any minute now, Marike expects to hear a guard shout, but still it is quiet, except for her brother's noisy snores.

She should be sleeping, but not now. Even Peter volunteers to be the lookout. *Have we all become criminals? No, I must not think about that. It seems like forever. They must have been caught.* Finally, the door creaks open.

"Mutter, come see," whispers Heinz.

In the inky darkness, she feels the bushy boughs and hugs Edel, Heinz, even Peter, in relief. But where is Gertrude?

"Didn't she come with you?" whispers Marike.

"No," says Heinz.

"We don't know where she went," Peter says. "As soon as the guard and she walked around the building, we started tearing down branches."

Tired from the excitement, the children soon fall asleep. Marike lies awake late into the night as she listens for the door to open. In the morning, when she awakes, Gertrude greets her with a yawn.

Gertrude acts like this is just a typical morning. How can she? Where was she? If I say anything to her now, I might arouse suspicion.

Marike worries about Gertrude. Whenever Gertrude and she are together, she feels the men's eyes following Gertrude. Who can blame them? Petite Gertrude, with her dimpled smile and clear skin, reminds Marike of her childhood and the porcelain doll she wanted but never received.

Once, when they were children, she felt jealousy prick her at all the admiration her friend received. Instead, young Gertrude's innocent, generous nature soon appealed to Marike's nurturing instincts. Without her parents to protect Gertrude, Marike fears for her. All morning, Marike waits to talk to Gertrude alone, without anyone overhearing them. Finally, she suggests that they go together to get their daily hot meal. Gertrude reluctantly agrees.

Outside the barracks, Marike says, "Thanks again for distracting the guard."

"It was nothing." Gertrude bends down and adjusts her stocking.

"I waited up for you, but I guess I fell asleep," Marike says.

"What soup do you think they'll serve today?" Gertrude says. Her voice sounds distant. "I wish for potato. Let's hurry." Gertrude walks quickly ahead, shoving her hands into her sleeves and bending her head to the cold wind tangling her curls. In a few long-legged strides, Marike reaches her.

"Which guard, Gertrude?"

"What are you talking about?" Gertrude stops, her face turned up while the taller Marike studies her.

"The guard last night...was it that handsome Dane who is always watching you?"

"You don't know anything." Gertrude looks beyond Marike at the trees. "Did the boys get the branches? They didn't fall, did they?"

"The boys are fine." Marike looks at the tree, which is missing upper limbs. "We hid the branches under the bed until they're dry. But I worry about you."

"Don't worry. I'm fine. I'm a grown woman." Gertrude straightens and throws her shoulders back.

"Still, you don't know how men can be. If your vater were here, he would say..."

"It is not as you think. He is kind. He even speaks German. He learned it from his German grandmother. He gives me the news. Not all the Danes hate us." Gertrude backs away.

"Is it the guard Klaus?" Marike asks as Gertrude hurries into the camp's kitchen barracks, greeting a friend as she does so.

With a resigned look replacing her frown, Marike follows Gertrude. So many "what ifs" on her tongue, but now she swallows them in frustration. *Should I tell my brother my suspicions? Maybe I shouldn't. After all, Gertrude is not a relation. Besides, already Abelard has so many responsibilities.*

Since Gertrude arrived, Marike recalled their many conversations and what Gertrude shared about her marriage to her neighbor Albert, whom she had known from childhood. As soon as the marriage ceremony ended, he had to return to his unit. Although no German man of eligible age was exempt from military service, true to his nonviolent Mennonite beliefs, Albert chose to serve in the medical corps. Like most of the other medical corps members, he was assigned to the front lines. When he returned home on leave, Gertrude became pregnant. Then he was sent to Leningrad on the Russian Front, where German forces had been fighting. When Gertrude heard Albert had been killed, she stayed in bed for days, not eating. *Now, in her loneliness,* Marike wonders, *has Gertrude become involved with someone?*

Marike remembers the first time she noticed the Danish guard Klaus. It happened when her son Heinz begged for her permission to play in Klaus' athletic games. All too aware of her son's boredom, Marike agreed, and then followed him outdoors to watch the games. As Klaus demonstrated how he wanted the boys to run, Marike found herself admiring the Danish guard. It had been so long since she had seen a young man so well formed. Near the war's end, she had seen only wounded soldiers and old men. Even Klaus's sweat-stained shirt stirred a forgotten urge deep inside her. It had been so long since she felt her husband's touch.

CAROL STRAZER

But then, several other mothers joined her, and their admiring comments made her smile. Marike imagined an innocent but romantic encounter with Klaus. Anything, she thought, to relieve the never-ending boredom. Still, she chided herself. That was no reason for a good Mennonite wife to behave like some of the other desperate camp women.

During the previous weeks, Marike observed some of the young women whispering and giggling. During the day, they combed each other's hair, attempted to clean their stained clothing, and straightened their stockings. In the evening, they disappeared. Often they returned toting bags filled with mysterious contents, which they quickly hid. When Marike shared her observations with an acquaintance, the woman remarked that one of the women lived in her barracks. Further, before the young woman could hide it, she had seen food, chocolates, and even salt. Marike told her she would give anything for more seasonings, salt, or anything to improve the bland soup. Her friend asked the woman how she got out of camp so easily, without being discovered by the guards. The young woman boasted how she told the camp chief that she had to visit her sick mother in the hospital, which was outside camp. Once she had a pass, she would quickly visit the hospital—but then meet her boyfriend.

What if Gertrude participates in this sort of deception? How else can she explain the extra food? I must have a talk with her; but to see Gertrude alone is not easy. I don't want to incur her wrath—making her angry solves nothing. Yet, I owe it to my mutter to try.

In the afternoon, Marike asks Gertrude to walk with her. As usual, Gertrude makes excuses, but Marike insists.

"I don't have time," complains Gertrude, hurrying down the path.

"I understand, but we must talk."

"Talk about what?" Gertrude asks while smoothing her blonde curls.

"There is a problem…" Marike begins.

"There is nothing," Gertrude interrupts.

"You and that Danish guard. You know we're forbidden contact."

Gertrude turns back toward their barracks, and Marike grabs her arm.

"Let go. You can't tell me what to do." Gertrude twists away from Marike. "You aren't my mutter."

"Please, Gertrude, listen. I care about you. I don't want you to get into trouble."

"You think just because you're older you know everything. If you don't stop bothering me, I'll ask to be assigned to a different barracks." Gertrude's eyes widen, and her voice is low, threatening.

"Don't. I'm sorry," Marike pleads. "I care, and I worry about you."

"Well, worry about your four children. I can take care of myself."

Gertrude enters their barracks and slams the door. Marike stares at the door, then opens it quietly and enters.

The next day, Marike catches Heinz poking a chocolate in his mouth.

Marike grasps her son's cheeks and forces him to expel the chocolate, catching it in her hand. She holds it, almost as if were a bullet about to explode.

"Mutter, that's mine." Heinz reaches for the chocolate.

"Where did you get it?" Marike asks her son.

"Gertrude gave it to me."

"I should throw it away." Marike raises her hand as if to throw the chocolate in the nearby bush.

"Please, Mutter, I've already sucked on it." Heinz tries to catch his mother's hand while she waves it away from him.

Marike can barely look at her son's hungry eyes. *I should teach him a lesson not to accept Gertrude's ill-gotten gains. But how can I refuse him?*

"All right, but never again." Marike looks sternly at Heinz as she hands him the sticky glob.

"Yes," he mumbles, stuffing the candy in his mouth before she can change her mind.

I must convince Gertrude that this is not right. Yet, my poor children have so little to eat. On their small rations, how else can I feed them? What if Gertrude is caught? I must stop her.

As she argues with herself, Marike is interrupted by rapid knocking. When she opens the door, a smartly dressed woman fills the doorway.

"You need clothes? Adela is here. You ask. I'll help you." Before Marike can respond, the barracks' *Hausmeisterin* has continued on her way and is knocking on another door. Marike enters the hallway, where she joins a long line of other women. *If only Adela, who is in charge of the distribution, would have some shoes.*

"What do they have?" she asks the woman in front of her.

"Who knows? It could be from the Swedish. I hope it's from the British or Americans. Swedish clogs hurt my feet too much." The slightly built woman bends down and removes her clog. "If someone would give us heavy socks, they wouldn't hurt so much."

Marike nods sympathetically as the woman rubs her swollen foot. Beate introduces herself, saying she just arrived. She explains, "My feet didn't get this way from the clogs. It was the Frisches Haff."

"We came across the lagoon, too," Marike says.

"Were the Russians bombing you?"

"No, we went across at another point, in the spring," Marike replies.

Beate moans as she removes her socks.

"Do your feet hurt a great deal?" Marike stares at Beate's misshapen feet.

"Not so bad. But you can see, they look terrible," Beate replaces her socks. "I'll never forget that miserable winter day. There were so many of us, mostly women and children, some wagons piled high and pulled by horses. There were long lines of people waiting to cross the frozen lagoon, most of us walking." Beate slowly slides her foot into her clog.

"I heard it was bad," says Marike.

"You can imagine, with tears in our throats, so sad leaving our homes. At first, when the German soldiers told us we had to flee our small village, they helped. They said since the Red Army reached the coast of the lagoon near Elbing in late January, East Prussians must evacuate. To reach the coast, the Vistula, or Danzig, where there were ships to help us, we had to cross the Frisches Haff. But then, our soldiers were ordered to retreat. They just left us. One family so feared the Russians, they tried to kill themselves in the nearby woods. We found them. A girl survived."

"How terrible," Marike says.

"That was just the beginning of the witches' brew. As we were crossing, the Russian planes bombed us. Soon, huge holes appeared in the ice. Terrified, everyone ran furiously. You can imagine. My child and I ran as fast as we could. The drivers couldn't control their frightened horses. My neighbor, his wife, three children, horses, wagon—all disappeared in an icy void. We could do nothing to help. We couldn't stop or we might fall in." Beate crosses herself.

"But you…?" Marike asks.

"Another neighbor offered to take my boy in their crowded wagon. They didn't have room for me, so I ran after them."

"You poor, brave woman," Marike says, searching for words of comfort.

"With the weight of the wagons and people, water was now on the ice. My feet were so cold and wet. I couldn't feel them. They felt so heavy, but I kept running, following the wagon. I had to keep going—for my child."

"Is he all right?" Marike asked.

"I haven't found little Frederick yet. They are good people. If they're still alive, they'll care for him. It's my turn. I have to go. Thanks for listening." Beate smiles at Marike.

"I hope you find your son soon."

"Thanks, goodbye." Beate enters the room.

When it is Marike's turn, she is disappointed to find only a stack of paper blankets. Marike had heard about the blankets made from paper, but she hoped that this time they would receive better blankets. As the woman hands her a paper blanket, Marike admires her clothing. Dressed in a smart wool skirt and white blouse, she is unblemished by dirt or stains. *Definitely, there are advantages to being one of the four hundred. If only...but that only happens to those who know someone in power, and I'm too poor to know anyone.*

Remembering her manners, Marike thanks the woman in charge, takes her blanket, and turns to leave. She thinks her children will be disappointed, another in a long list of disappointments. Each time they receive some donated clothing, there is too little for her family. As Marike walks past the long refugee line, she hears her name called.

"Marike, over here," calls Katharina.

"Katharina," says Marike.

"I wanted you to know I took my old sweater, unraveled it, and am knitting your little girl, Helena, a sweater. I hope you don't mind," the woman stretches her bent back.

"She'll be thrilled. She'll be five come October.'"

"Good. It should just fit." Katharina coughs.

Marike quickly hugs her, having to bend down to reach the shrunken Katharina. Tears cloud Marike's vision, and an ache chokes her words, "You're too kind. You hardly know us."

Katharina smiles, "It's nothing. The sweater had many

holes—not much yarn for anything. I should finish it next week. You're in Barracks B?"

"Yes. Oh, thank you. Helena will be pleased." *I'm embarrassed. If only I could return to my barracks. How could I lose control like this? Yet, Helena will be thrilled to have a new sweater.*

While they've been talking, the line has moved, leaving a large space between Katharina and the rest of the line.

Someone yells, "If you aren't in line, we'll go around."

"Oh no, I've waited two hours already. I'll hurry," Katharina says as she hobbles forward.

"Bye," Marike says. She remembers when she first met Katharina while waiting in the food line. It had been soon after Marike and her family arrived in camp, and some rough boys had mimicked Katharina's crablike walk. Marike felt sad for Katharina, whose twisted back interfered with her ability to walk. Katharina shook her bucket at them. Then, the leader grabbed the bucket, and the boys started throwing it to each other, laughing and playing catch, taunting her while she pleaded with them.

Marike thought someone would stop them, but the other women just watched, as if helpless.

"Heinrich, halt," Marike ordered when she recognized the leader. "Give the lady her bucket now!"

Heinrich eyed Marike, who stepped in front of him. His grin was replaced by a scowl. He glanced at his friends, who backed away.

Marike didn't move. "You've had your fun, Heinrich."

Heinrich hesitated, looked embarrassed, and then handed the bucket to her. "Aw, Frau Wiens, we were just fooling."

"Your vater would never allow you to do such things."

Heinrich shrugged, kicked the dirt, and walked away.

"Are you all right?" Marike asked.

"Oh thank you, dear, for standing up to those terrible boys." She

smiled and introduced herself as Katharina. Marike handed her the
bucket.

"Those boys aren't bad. They remind me of my older brothers
when our father wasn't around—always fooling around. Not enough
men here to make them behave. My family knew his family back in
Petershagen."

"Please, how can I repay you?"

"It isn't necessary. Well, school should start soon and that will
give the boys something to do instead of bullying people. They were
lucky a guard didn't see them," Marike said.

"Thank you," Katharina answered.

Marike laughed. "I'm happy to help."

Recalling the incident, Marike swallows twice. Why did
Katharina's gift cause her so much pain? The dull blankness she felt
before was better than this. It has been some time since the boys
taunted Katharina. As she predicted, life has been quieter since the
children began attending school.

One afternoon, she notices Elisabet with a stick, drawing letters in the sand. Elisabet explains that the only writing paper they
have is the rough side of the brown paper they use at the toilets. She
says they sit on the floor and use their benches as desks. As Marike
watches, Elisabet draws more letters, telling her mother how much
she likes to write. Marike praises Elisabet on making clean, straight
letters and corrects only one error. At least, she is pleased that her
children receive some education. Since there are few books, most of
what is taught is by rote. Heinz has a good memory and often tells
Marike about the day's lesson.

Since the teacher has no blackboard or other teachers to
help, the older children help the younger ones. Quite often, the
teacher leads the children in song. Since the camp has been given
songbooks, printed with only the German words and not notes,
the children learn many songs. Elisabet especially enjoys singing

and, like her younger sister, easily remembers both the melody and words. Marike appreciates that though they have lost their Prussian home and country, at least they can cling to their beloved German language and music. Frequently, while she sews, Marike and the children sing.

Chapter 22

Today is mail day. As usual, the refugees line-up to wait impatiently until their names are called. Those who receive letters, tear them open, hoping for good news but fearing the worse. Some share their letters.

Many of the women, married to German soldiers, have not heard from their husbands for several years. During the war, the men could not write about their whereabouts. To tell where they were stationed might allow military information to become known to the enemy. The wives do not know if their husbands were wounded, in POW camps, or dead.

From the letters, they learn and share the latest news. During the war's final months, many German cities of little military value were firebombed by the Allies. The incendiaries caused horrific fires, spreading from street to street. The fire crews could not contain them. Many citizens, trapped and unable to flee, died. Although Berlin was bombed repeatedly, its wide streets prevented the fires from spreading.

Gertrude enters their room. "Marike, did Horst write?"

"No," Marike answers quickly, too quickly—as if anticipating her friend's question. Ever since she'd received her returned mail, before their escape from Germany, the words have haunted her. *Missing in action! What did they mean? I hope Horst is a prisoner of war, or maybe in a hospital.*

"I'm sorry," Gertrude says.

Marike studies her pretty friend. "Thanks. I am too. I want us to be like we used to be—best friends."

"Do you think we can?" Gertrude asks hopefully.

"I'll try." Marike smiles encouragingly.

"Oh Marike, I've missed our talks. I've always admired you."

Marike says, "And I've always liked you."

Gertrude pulls a bag from her coat. "Please Marike—for your children."

Marike looks at the bag and then away. Her hungry children—how they would devour the contents, but it would be wrong. Softly, apologetically, Marike says, "I can't."

Gertrude kicks the bag under her bunk bed. "How can you call yourself a mother and let your own children suffer? Look at little Edel. He can hardly walk, because his legs are so bowed. It's probably from rickets. You're stubborn like your vater's bull. And just like him, you think you can push the rest of us around."

"Oh Gertrude, I love you. I don't want anything bad to happen to you," Marike pleads.

"Take the food." Gertrude pulls the bag out and thrusts it forward to Marike.

"For the children then, but if you get caught, I'll never forgive myself." Marike hides the food under her bed.

"That will never happen. Tell the children it is magic food." Gertrude tosses her head. "It just appeared—like the manna for Moses' people in the desert."

"Oh Gertrude, I would never tell anyone about you. Yet, I'm afraid for you. You know the camp chief's orders. No guards can have contact with the enemy. And we're the enemy. They could send you to prison for two months, like those women they caught at that party," Marike says while she grips Gertrude's shoulders.

"Well, Klaus says—" Gertrude claps her hand to her mouth.

"Wait, did you say, 'Klaus?' The guard who helps the children? I thought so!"

"Please don't tell," Gertrude glances anxiously around. "He is good. It's not like those other women who use the men for food. I just want someone to love me. You have your children. Who do I have? I'm not good like you." Gertrude strides angrily out of their room.

"You are. Oh Gertrude. Don't leave." Marike collapses on her bunk bed. What will happen to her innocent friend? From the time Marike was seven years old and Gertrude was a baby, Gertrude's sickly mother often depended on her. Marike had watched her own mother change her brother's diapers, and soon, with safety pins held tightly between her teeth, Marike bathed and changed her little neighbor. Forgotten, Marike's raggedy doll lay on the closet floor. With her new responsibility, Marike liked to think she was grown up. What would their mothers think now? Were they looking down from heaven and crying to see their daughters fighting?

Marike's children enter.

"Mutter, why are you crying?" asks Helena, as she caresses her mother's back.

"I'm fine. Where have you been? I worried about you," says Marike, drying her tears with the back of her hand.

"It's Gertrude, isn't it? She's mean, making you cry. We saw her. She was all red in the face," says Elisabet knowingly.

"I'm all right. It's hard on Gertrude with no young people her age," Marike reassures her children.

"What do you mean? There are many. Oh, men. You mean men," says Elisabet.

"Gertrude told us you had a surprise," says Heinz.

"Tomorrow," Marike says. "But you must promise not to tell anyone. It will be our secret."

"Yes, Mutter," they agree.

Now I must lie to my own children. Marike stands up, picks up the broom, and begins sweeping furiously. *If I tell them the truth, they might say something, and Gertrude would be arrested.*

Marike tries not to think about the food hidden under her bed. *When everyone leaves to line up for their food, I will give my children Gertrude's gift. I won't tell them it's Gertrude's. I'll tell them I found it, but they must promise not to tell anyone.*

"Remember Oma's torte, and she'd pour big glasses of fresh milk—real milk—not like the colored water we have here. It would be thick and creamy." Elisabet licks her lips.

Edel says, "Where's Oma? Is she hiding?"

Marike hugs Edel. "I miss her too, baby. Remember, we told you Oma is with Opa."

"I want her back to tell me a story." Edel pouts.

"I'm sorry, Edel. Oma is in heaven. She can't come," Marike says.

"I want Oma, I want Oma," Edel chants.

"I do too, but Oma is gone. Come, Edel, time for your nap," Marike helps slide him under the covers. Edel's words reverberate, becoming Marike's chant. *Oma, please tell me what to do. I promised you I'd protect Gertrude, but now she is going another way, not our Mennonite way. I'm afraid for her."*

Several days have passed since Marike has seen Gertrude. Each night, Gertrude steals in, long after lights are out, and everyone is asleep. In the morning, she rises early and leaves before the children are awake. Gertrude doesn't return to eat her noon meal with Marike and the family. No one comments on Gertrude's absence, not even Abelard.

Marike wonders if Abelard has noticed Gertrude's strange behavior. Possibly he has corrected her. His silence signals to the rest of the family that Gertrude is a closed topic.

At first, I worried Gertrude would be caught; now, I'm afraid others know. In Prussia, she would be shunned. Instead she avoids us. I'll keep praying. I took the food she gave me. Gertrude was right. My hungry children ate so quickly. I thought they would vomit. I'm guilty like Gertrude. I don't care. The children need food. I don't care how late it is tonight; I'll wait up for Gertrude—even if I have to go against my own brother.

After lights are out, for a long time Marike listens to the sound of straw rustling from her restless children.

"I got one. My third, smashed him good," says Heinz.

"Me too," says Helena.

"Did you mash it on the wall?" asks Elisabet.

"I can't see," whispers Helena.

"Wait, there is the moonlight. I'll hold it in that. Now, do you see?" asks Elisabet. She holds her arm out until she is silhouetted in brightness.

Marike stares at the brilliance streaming through their barracks' window. Quietly, she slides out of bed and peers out. Large, white areas surround their barracks, as if lit by a gigantic searchlight. *Where is Gertrude? How can she risk being out on a night like this? What if the guards catch her?* Quieting the children, Marike listens intently. *Did a board creak? Could it be my friend's stealthy step? No. It is only the boards making noises. If only,* she prays. Their usual game of smashing bed bugs forgotten, the children sleep. Soon, too, despite her best intentions, Marike's eyes close.

Chapter 23

As the morning light struggles through their dusty window, Marike glances furtively at Gertrude's neatly made bunk bed. It's too late. The others have also noticed the empty bed, which stands like a terrible judgment of Gertrude. Abelard's face flushes crimson, and his mouth twists as he thrusts aside his blanket and lurches across the room to Gertrude's bed. His body shakes.

"Where is she?" he thunders.

Everyone cowers under their covers.

"Did you hear me? Where is she?" he repeats.

"I don't know." Marike pleads, "Please, Abelard, she is so young—been through so much. Remember, Mutter told us to help her."

Abelard strides across the room to Marike's bed, blocking her, pinning her with his eyes.

"Marike, if you know something, tell me now," he demands.

"Please brother," Marike cries, searching his face for a line of leniency. Finding none, she confesses her concerns about her little friend.

"If she gets caught, the Danes could send her to jail," Abelard growls. "We could all be sent to other camps. How could Gertrude, from a good Mennonite home, do such a thing?" Shaking his fist at Marike, he erupts on her, his nearest target. "Why didn't you tell me?"

"I thought you knew," Marike mumbles apologetically, aware of how pathetic she must sound.

Her brother turns his back to her and slams out of the barracks, leaving them, even the children, to shudder in silence.

In a daze, Marike rises slowly from her bed, slides her feet into her wooden clogs and straightens the clothes she sleeps in to stay warm. Without thinking, she reaches into the cupboard at the head of her bed and removes some dark bread and a small pat of butter, placing them on the table.

"Mutter, don't you want me to help?" asks Elisabet.

"Oh, yes," Marike murmurs.

Elisabet places five bowls, cups, and spoons on the long, rough table, while her brothers and sister climb on the benches.

Freda says, "Marike, he was too hard…it's just he worries so about his family, and Gertrude is like family." As Freda hugs her, Marike sighs.

"He's right. I should have said something. I kept hoping. I was wrong. It's my fault." Marike sinks into herself as she lays her head on her folded arms.

"Mutter, don't cry," says little Helena, patting her mother's back.

"Here is the powdered milk," says Elisabet.

Her family's concerns arouse Marike. She wipes her eyes and begins to attend to their needs.

All morning the family is busy with their chores. They wait. Marike sees but ignores their questioning eyes. Gertrude does not return. Fearful of attracting more attention to Gertrude's plight, Marike doesn't ask anyone about Gertrude's whereabouts. She reminds the children not to say anything. In their fear of the wrong word being overheard and reported to the Danes, no one speaks, instead communicating in silent gestures.

Later, as the time approaches for them to stand in line for their daily food, Abelard returns and sheepishly offers to get Marike's bucket filled. Startled, Marike notices Freda watching. She might have known. Even though she still hurts, Marike hands her bucket to her brother. As she does so, his rough hand firmly enfolds hers. His humble gesture speaks his simple words. She is overwhelmed, and her eyes are moist.

"Oh Abelard, I'm sorry. Please forgive me," Marike whispers.

"No, I was wrong to place blame on you," Abelard gruffly replies.

"You were right. I should have told you." As she gazes out the window, Marike asks, "Oh Gertrude, where are you?"

"I guess I should tell you," Abelard's rough face droops in sad lines.

"What? You know something?" Hopefully, Marike searches Abelard's face.

"I wanted to wait until the family was together before I said anything, but it is better that I tell you now."

"Please, what is it?" Marike clutches her brother's arm.

"I went to the camp chief's office."

"You did what?" In disbelief, Marike stares at Abelard. "I can't believe you would do that."

"Hush. When Gertrude didn't return, I looked everywhere, all over camp. I thought if she was my child, I would want to find her. I knew then what I had to do." Abelard rubs his knuckles.

Marike finds this familiar gesture of Abelard's comforting.

Abelard continues speaking slowly, methodically. "I knew the camp chief was a fair man, from when I helped him with the boy, Heller. As soon as he saw me, he said *he was just coming to talk to me.*"

"Tell me. I can't stand this," Marike demands.

"I'm telling you—" Abelard says, as he is interrupted by the children, who crowd in, asking about their meal.

"You children behave and sit down," Abelard orders. "I'm talking to Marike about Gertrude."

"Did she get arrested?" asks his son.

Abelard glances at the questioning faces. "I guess everyone knows anyway. Last night the guards caught Gertrude sneaking back into camp. She wouldn't give them the name of the Danish man she was meeting. The camp chief said the police planned to send her to prison with some other German women they caught with Danish men. However, he said he knew we cared for her and were a good Christian family."

"She is still here?" asks Freda.

"No, they were transferring some refugees to another camp farther north. Gertrude went with them," Abelard explains.

"But," Marike cries, "she didn't even get her things or have a chance to say goodbye—my poor baby."

"A baby she's not. I guess she showed us." Abelard pauses, speaking slowly. "I wish no harm for her. But you children take heed. No more complaining about too many rules." Abelard gazes sternly at the children until they look down, and he is answered with a chorus of meek responses.

Marike walks quickly from the barracks. *If only I'd found a way to make her listen. Now this. I wish I'd never taken her food—even if the children needed it. What will happen to her?* Marike hurries along and turns her face away when a friend greets her. *I can't bear the thought of anyone's conversation. Not now, not after this.* To avoid contact, Marike walks along the camp's perimeter until confronted by the many strands of tightly strung barbed wire that encircle the camp.

She moves nearer the fence. *Did the sharp spikes tear my friend's flesh? Is that blood on the barbs?* Instead, it's a bright red flower growing near the post. Marike reaches out her hand to pluck the flower, but the Danish guard removes his gun from his shoulder and waves it at her. Frightened, Marike steps back.

Beyond, she can see the emerald green farmland gently undulating to the horizon. A tidy farmhouse snuggles in a small fold. The peaceful pastoral scene makes her heart ache. *No large bomb craters or faceless buildings mar the landscape. It's as if the war never happened.* Marike is struck again by the pleasant appearance of the camp's entrance, bordered by flowers, freely embracing the sea air. *Any unsuspecting Dane, looking at the camp from the outside, would never guess at the misery within these walls. It is no wonder I, like many other refugees, avoid this section.*

"*Standsning, halt.*" A Danish guard yells in German as he approaches Marike.

She looks around to see if he is talking to someone else, but they are alone. She recognizes him as the kind guard who teaches the boys' athletic games. Klaus.

He motions for her to come closer. Hesitantly, she obeys. She is surprised when he speaks to her in halting German. Worry creases his handsome features.

"You're Gertrude's friend?" he whispers.

"Yes, but—" Marike answers.

"She asked me to ease your mind. She's all right. She'll write as soon as it's permitted." He glances over his shoulder. "I know what it's like for some guards. They use the women. But not me!" He turns his intense gaze on Marike and continues, "I love Gertrude. Please—tell no one."

A group of refugees approach, while talking and laughing.

Suddenly, Klaus' demeanor changes, and he stares menacingly at Marike. He shoulders his gun and marches away.

Marike's acquaintance yells at her, "What did the guard want?"

Marike answers quickly, "Oh, he just warned me to stay away from the barbed wire."

Satisfied, the woman rejoins her friends.

Marike sighs with relief. She knows if Klaus had been caught talking to a refugee, he would have been punished. Her friend talks too much, and Marike doesn't trust her. She saw her receive extra rations under questionable circumstances. At the time, she told Marike she did extra work, but Marike didn't believe her. She knows some refugees exchange information for food.

It's wrong that some take advantage, but, in my present circumstances, I can't judge others. Without the extra food Gertrude gave me, my poor children might not survive. Yet, I don't want to make trouble for anyone. Should I tell Abelard about the guard? Abelard might tell the camp chief. Sometimes, Abelard can be so contrary, though his heart is big.

Chapter 24

"Marike."

"Yes, Freda?"

"You were gone so long. We worried something had happened to you," Freda says as she approaches.

"I'm fine. I just needed a walk," Marike says, trying to sound normal.

"You look worn out. Let me help you." Freda grasps her sister-in-law's arm and leads her towards their barracks. "I'm sorry about Abelard. You know your brother loves you."

"I know. It's just so hard with all of us living on top of each other."

Freda gives Marike's arm a gentle squeeze. "Soon we'll leave like some of the others."

"But where can we go?" Marike asks. "The Russians and Poles occupy our homes in Prussia. Some refugees have relatives in Germany they can go to, but you read that letter from our cousin. They don't have enough food to feed us. There's no one else to ask."

"Don't think about it. Abelard said to bring you to a meeting," Freda says, her face flushed with excitement.

"What meeting?"

"There are some Mennonite missionaries who say they can help us. I doubt it, but Abelard believes them, because they're Mennonites. I promised him that I'd bring you."

Freda motions towards the barracks used for meetings.

"I don't see how I can go. I'm so tired," Marike yawns.

"Come Marike, it will be good for you."

Marike walks through the doorway while her sister-in-law holds the door open for her.

As they enter the meeting room, which also serves as the building for performances, Marike is amazed to see her mother-in-law, Amalia Wiens. As Freda joins Abelard, Marike sits in the empty chair next to Amalia, who looks small as a mouse, her few chin hairs now white. As Marike hugs her, she is touched at Amalia's grateful response. Could this be the same former employer now mother-in-law whom she once feared?

"Amalia, when did you get here?"

"Yesterday. They closed our small camp."

"I'm glad. I've been worried about you. It's been a long time since Germany. Someone told me they saw you in the camp at Kopenhagen. But when I looked for you, the Danes had sent you to another camp. Each time we moved to a new camp, I hoped we'd find you. Are you all right?"

"Just the usual old aches and pains. I was sent to a refugee camp, kind of a converted resort in the forest. I hated being there, but it wasn't too bad. The Danish administrator was kind. I asked everyone if they'd seen you and your family. When they started shutting down the smaller camps and sending everyone to several enormous camps, I thought I might find you here. Heinz, the children, your parents, are they in good health?" Amalia's voice is imperious, reminding Marike of when she worked for her in the bakery.

"I'm sorry to say my vater died when we first came to Kopenhagen, and recently...we lost my dear mutter."

The speaker clears his throat and taps the microphone.

Amalia whispers. "We'll talk later. I'm glad you're all right."

With typical Mennonite modesty, the speaker introduces himself. He says that some twenty-five years ago, he decided to leave Germany. At the time, his father and two older brothers, serving in the German army's medical corps, had been killed during the Great War. The destructive war had left him homeless. He feared there would be another war, and he would be forced to serve. He believed war was wrong. Jesus had taught him "to turn the other cheek." Neither did he want to swear an oath of loyalty to Germany. He and his new bride wanted to live their faith as missionaries. He had been investigating various foreign missions when he read about Paraguay.

Enthusiastically, he continues that Paraguay seemed to provide the perfect answer to their prayers. Since Paraguay lost many of its male citizens in the War of the Triple Alliance, the country had been seeking immigrants—especially industrious Mennonite farmers. In fact, the government wanted the Mennonites badly enough to allow them to educate their children in German, administer their own institutions, and practice their pacifist beliefs.

A man, missing one arm, stands up.

"Yes?" the speaker asks.

"You said we could practice our pacifist beliefs. Does that mean our sons would not have to serve in their military?"

"Right, the Mennonite men are exempt from service in the Paraguay military. I thought I said so."

Various people in the audience stir and whisper to each other.

A woman raises her hand. When the speaker calls on her, she asks, "Are you talking about the mission Filadelphia? Our church sent care packages to them. I heard there isn't enough water, and the land is hard to farm."

The speaker pauses, seemingly to collect himself. "When Filadelphia was first founded in 1932, it was tough farming the arid land. However, the hard-working early settlers were successful in locating water. Their peanut, sesame, and sorghum crops support the community. Also, their crops have attracted many birds, hunters, and even photographers."

Marike glances anxiously at Amalia, who seems mesmerized by this missionary's fervent portrayal of Paraguay. He continues and says that since the early twentieth century, German immigrants have settled there. Also, Canadian and Ukrainian Mennonites have immigrated to Paraguay. He promises that fellow missionaries will offer assistance to any Prussian Mennonite refugees who want to settle there.

As the speaker continues to extol Paraguay's climate, people, and opportunities, Marike reaches for another dream. *What if Horst is alive—in a POW camp or hospital—just waiting to hear from his wife and children? Wouldn't it be wonderful if we all could go to Paraguay? We could open a bakery. The children could go to school, a Mennonite school. And we could live and worship in peace in a community where we are wanted. We would be free to come and go and do as we please. No more armed guards, barbed wire, and endless rules. There would always be plenty for us to eat.*

The speaker asks those who are interested to show their hands. Amalia raises her hand and looks expectantly at Marike. Dutifully, Marike slowly puts her hand up. *Is it really possible we will go to Paraguay? But if we do, how will Horst find us?*

After Amalia and Marike complete some forms, Marike accompanies Amalia to her barracks. With the ocean breezes blowing her dreams in many directions, Marike's impatience cannot be mastered, and she asks, "Have you heard from Horst?"

"No, have you?"

"Nothing, but if we go somewhere else, how will he find us? I wish we could just go home," Marike says wistfully.

"To Prussia? Surely not. Haven't you heard? There is no more Prussia. The Poles and Russians have it," Amalia says.

"Yes, but I keep hoping."

"Foolish child. If we had stayed in Prussia, we would be in Siberia or worse by now. The stories they tell…awful."

Marike nods. "I know. You're right, Paraguay is better. But some Mennonites are going to America."

"I've been thinking about America. I have a cousin on my mother's side there who married a farmer." Amalia stops, frowns. "But, it takes a long time to get a letter to America."

"You decide. I'll follow you," Marike says dutifully. As they walk, Marike stays slightly behind her mother-in-law, partly in deference to her but also to assist her if she should stumble.

"I hear it is hard to get permission. And those Americans, they may be rich, but not so smart. Remember their President Roosevelt, before he died, so friendly with Stalin and the communists. What was Roosevelt thinking?" Amalia stamps her foot in frustration.

"Then, you want to go to Paraguay?" Marike takes a breath.

"I don't know about Paraguay. It sounds like life is hard. Here are my barracks. Tomorrow, bring the children. Goodbye dear."

"Bye, Amalia."

Confused, Marike returns to her barracks. *What can I do? I've always been told to respect my elders. It's only right that my mother-in-law should make the decision, but she doesn't seem to know what she wants. I feel like the Biblical Ruth who followed her mother-in-law. But Ruth's mother-in-law knew where she wanted to go. There is so little time. The missionary said we had to make a decision soon.*

————)(()(————

It has been two days since the Mennonite missionary from Paraguay spoke at their camp. The opportunity for complete religious freedom and to return to their agricultural roots has enticed numerous Prussian refugees to join others going to Paraguay.

Even though Marike has tried to elicit her mother-in-law's decision, Amalia wavers. Marike concludes it must be all the losses Amalia has suffered—her husband, her sons, and the bakery, everything Amalia held dear. Never before could Marike remember her mother-in-law indecisive, except after her oldest son was killed.

Needing guidance, Marike seeks the wise, spiritual counsel of her Mennonite pastor. Ahead of her, she notices he is leaving his barracks. "Wait, please," Marike calls.

Thin as the Bible he carries, Pastor Behrends turns his stooped shoulders toward her. His kind smile reassures her, even as she notices he has recently lost several teeth. Even in these terrible conditions, he cares for others. He, too, must miss his Prussian farm, his small Mennonite church, and most of all, his two sons who died on the Eastern Front.

"Dear Pastor Behrends, I don't like to trouble you. Oh my, what happened to your teeth?" Marike asks.

"My teeth, oh yes, just rotten, I guess you could say less to brush," he chuckles.

"I'm sorry. I hope they don't give you too much pain?"

"Not now," he says as his hand covers his mouth. "The dentist gave me something for the pain—kind man. Enough about me. How may I help you, Marike?"

"I don't like to trouble you, but I don't know where to turn. You heard the talk about Paraguay? It sounds good, but then we thought we might immigrate to America. My poor mother-in-law, you know, Amalia Wiens? She keeps changing her decision. What should we do?" Suddenly, Marike presses her hands to her chest and bends over. "Oh no," she pants.

He places his arm around her, steadying her. "Child, what is it?" She hears the concern in his voice.

Marike shakes her head. *If I don't move, maybe the terrible pain in my chest will go away.* She sucks in her breath to ease the pain.

"Is it your heart? You're too young for a heart attack. We should go to the *Krankenhaus*. Come, I'll help you." His hand is under her elbow, guiding her.

Marike pulls away. "No, it's nothing." She coughs. "Don't worry, just a cold that won't leave. Please help me with my mother-in-law."

"All right. Still, maybe you should go to the hospital. Since you asked me, I think you should make the decision about where you will go to live. If you want, I'll speak to your mother-in-law."

"No. I'll talk to her tomorrow. You've been a big help. Thank you." As Marike hurries away, she coughs: dry, seal-like sounds.

When Marike looks back, she sees her pastor watching her. Then, he turns and walks away.

Marike enters their room in Barracks B and is relieved to find it deserted. She decides everyone must be waiting in line for soup or at school. She stuffs her cold body into her bunk bed. At the same time, she retrieves the German army jacket she dismembered. With care, she winds the threads on her sewing ball. If the cuts she plans are correct, she should be able to fashion a jacket for Heinz and hopefully something for little Edel. Talking to Pastor Behrends helped. As soon as he said it, she knew what her decision would be. Now, how to tell Amalia? She must find a way that will not wound Amalia's pride. With an experienced hand, Marike cuts into the heavy fabric as she follows the lines she has drawn.

She is grateful for her sewing. It distracts her from the constant pain. Pastor Behrends surely thinks she is an obstinate creature, but there are many reasons why she doesn't want to go to the hospital. Her children, for one: Who would care for them? Besides, she doesn't trust the medical care. Remembering her mother's and father's hospital experiences, Marike resolves to rest more and get over her cold. She closes her eyes and sleeps.

I hear voices, but I don't recognize them. They sound strange, as if my ears are water-logged. My body aches. I feel like I've been swimming underwater for a long time. I can't breathe. I have to get to the surface. "Help, please someone help me."

Frantically flinging her arms against the current, Marike awakes. The jacket she has been sewing falls to the floor. When she retrieves her sewing, Marike counts only fifteen neat stitches, while the needle dangles on its long thread—a silent accusation. Children's voices come from the hallway.

Her coughing begins again, lasting longer this time. When it finally stops, she licks perspiration from her lips. Suddenly, the pain in her chest sears its way into her belly. It reminds her of when her sisters and she played dress-up with their grandmother's corset. It is like when her sister Agathe planted her foot on Marike's back and pulled mightily on the corset strings until Marike saw black spots and collapsed. With tears streaming, Agathe untied the strings. She begged Marike not to tell their parents, saying repeatedly, "I'm sorry." And Marike never told.

Now her sister-in-law Freda's face appears bent over her, and Freda's cool hand brushes wet hair back from Marike's forehead.

"She's burning with fever," Freda announces.

"Could be pneumonia," says a distant voice.

"Or flu," says Abelard.

Elisabet gently lays a wet cloth on the top of her mother's head. Marike smiles weakly, reaches up, and slides it down on her forehead. Helena strokes her mother's hand, and Edel tries to crawl into bed with her while Heinz questions her.

"My poor children, if I die, what will happen to you?" gasps Marike.

Chapter 25

Usually ebullient, Elisabet quietly enters the hospital ward. Her tante Freda speaks softly to the ward nurse, who directs them to her mother's bed at the far end of the long, narrow room. Other patients stop talking to stare at them. When Elisabet reaches Marike's bed, Marike is on her side, her back to them. The sheet lays flat on her still form.

"She isn't dying, is she?" whispers Elisabet. "I've been so afraid she would die. With our vater gone, who would care for us?"

"I think she is only resting. Marike, we've come for a visit." Freda gently shakes Marike's shoulder.

Marike wakes, sits up smiling, her arms outstretched. "Elisabet, you came. I'm so glad. I've missed you so much."

Elisabet hesitates, looks at her aunt, who nods, and then hugs her mother.

"Don't worry, Elisabet, I'm not dying. You can hug me. Happy birthday."

"Oh Mutter, you are the best birthday present. I couldn't believe it. I thought everyone forgot. When I woke this morning, the first thing I saw were the paper dolls. They're wonderful." An excited Elisabet spins around until she bumps into the bed.

As Marike laughs, she begins coughing and gasps for air. Covering her mouth, she motions with her hand for Elisabet to come closer.

In a hoarse whisper, Marike says, "I saved this for you," and puts a small object wrapped in a napkin in Elisabet's hands. "Careful."

Elisabet cautiously opens the rag and peeks inside. Astonished, she exclaims, "An egg! A real egg, just like I used to collect in Oma's hen house."

Freda takes the egg from Elisabet and examines it. "Are you sure, Marike? The nurse must want you to have this."

Marike takes the egg and returns it to Elisabet. "I have enough. This is for Elisabet."

Elisabet says, "Remember how scared I was when I had to collect eggs? How Oma's old hen would try to peck me? Oma said if I acted brave, the chicken wouldn't know I was frightened and wouldn't peck me. Oma was right—that mean hen left me alone and—"

Freda interrupts, "What does the doctor say?"

"Pleurisy," Marike whispers. "But I want to hear about your birthday, Elisabet." Marike turns away and covers her mouth as she begins coughing.

Elisabet pats her mother's back until Marike stops coughing and turns over. "There, there, Mutter, that's better. I couldn't believe you remembered my birthday. Where did you ever get paper dolls?"

Marike chuckles, "Some time ago they came in a missionary package. I hid them to surprise you. I asked your tante to give them to you on your birthday. Do you like them?"

"Oh yes, they're wonderful, with all the beautiful clothes." Elisabet dances around on her toes. Then, she pauses. Tiny frown lines crease her small brow. "What's pleurisy, Mutter?"

"They tell me it's an infection of the lining of the lungs," Marike says. "I'll be fine, don't worry. Tell your brothers and sister I love them and think of them every day."

Freda bends over the bed, smoothing the covers and kisses Marike's forehead. "How long did the doctor say?"

"He said maybe six months. I'm so sorry." Marike's sad eyes stare at her hands.

"Don't say another word. My baby—I would have lost her when we were sick if you hadn't helped," Freda declares.

"Your five and my four children are not too many?" Marike, exhausted, collapses, unable to sit up any longer.

"We've tired you out. Come Elisabet. Let your poor mother rest. We'll come and visit again when you're stronger. Goodbye."

"Thank you: bye." Marike rolls over, burrowing her face into her pillow. *How can I bear this? It is as if my chest pain is four separate pains. They need me so much. How can I lie here doing nothing? Tomorrow, when the doctor visits, I'll tell him I'm better.* Overcome with weariness, Marike embraces the descending darkness, kissing each of her absent children's faces.

Chapter 26

With her eyes still closed, Marike wonders if she imagines someone is calling her. There it is again: "Marike. Marike."

"Amalia, I'm sorry. How long have you been standing there?" Marike struggles to sit up.

"Don't trouble yourself." Amalia slides a chair next to Marike's hospital bed and sits. "I've just a few minutes to visit. You need your rest. I wanted to come earlier, but my arthritis is acting up. Before that, I took the children swimming in the North Sea."

Fully awake now, Marike protests, "But they don't know how to swim."

Marike watches as her mother-in-law lifts her proud head. In superior tones, Amalia describes her adventures with her grandchildren. "I can't believe you never taught your children to swim."

Marike groans, "I know, I should have. When the guards said we could swim in the North Sea, I thought I'd take them so often. But, as you know, the rule is that we must swim before seven in the morning, before the Danes come to the beach. Between the cold mornings and my sick body, I rarely made it."

"No matter," Amalia says briskly. "I told them how important it is to be able to swim. I wanted to teach them, as my parents taught me. I'd swim and tell them to watch. Then, I'd hold each one and move their arms. But they're impossible." Amalia shakes her head.

"You have to understand. They're young, and all of these changes—it's hard for them."

"Nonsense, after I went to all of that trouble." Amalia stands. "Edel dug holes in the sand. Helena kept crying, 'It's too cold.' Elisabet paddled around, not really swimming. Heinz, dear boy, tried but couldn't even float. If your children would listen and mind me, I could teach them to swim."

"I'm sorry," Marike says.

"Your children, they are frightened for you. Helena asked me if you were dying like her oma and opa. She said if you die, they will be all alone. I could hardly make out the words, she was crying that hard. I tried my best to tell her it would take a long time—six months—for your healing. I said I would help, but then she cried harder. Your children, I don't understand."

Marike sighs, "They are young and have suffered much. I'm certain it must be very hard for them. You've tried your best, but they need their mother."

"Here comes the nurse." Amalia stands and carefully replaces her chair in its original location. "I have to leave now. Be sure to rest."

"Wait, Amalia, we need to talk. Have you heard from your cousin in America? Are you still okay with my decision? I think we should…" Helplessly, Marike watches as her mother-in-law, without turning her head, strides out of the ward.

Chapter 27

Each week, Freda faithfully visits Marike. As the weeks become months, Marike's health slowly improves. Today, Heinz visits.

"You've grown four inches in just months. I can't believe it. Are you all right?"

"Yes, Mutter. I'm fine. Look at my back." Heinz turns his back on Marike and lifts his shirt, revealing his thin back and four red lines.

"Those marks across your back—what are they?" Marike asks, concerned.

"Growth marks," Heinz proudly replies.

"I've never seen such a thing. Are you sure?" Marike traces the marks with her finger.

"Yes. I'm fine," he grins.

"Oh Heinz, you're growing up, and I'm not there to help. How can you grow on so little food? Here, take this. I saved it just for you." Marike grasps Heinz's hand.

"Mutter, I don't think you should be giving us your eggs. You need them." Heinz thrusts the egg at his mother.

Marike pushes his hand away. "Nonsense, you need it to grow. Hurry now, your Aunt Freda is waiting. Be good and help her."

"Yes, Mutter." Heinz awkwardly hugs Marike, his averted cheek barely touching her face.

"Goodbye Heinz. Tell your sisters and brother to mind their tante and onkel." *He is growing up too fast and embarrassed to give his own mother a kiss. Horst—if only you were here, you would know what to do. Where are you, Horst? Your family changes. They can't wait for you. If only you could send us a letter, then I could write to you. I don't know if I made the right decision. If you return, will you be able to find us in America?*

"*Stoppen*," the Danish nurse blocks Heinz's exit from the ward. Grabbing his arm, she pries open his fist and takes the egg.

Terrified Heinz tries to explain, but the nurse puts her finger to her mouth. Then, she grabs his shoulders, shaking him, and scolds him in Danish. Even though Heinz shivers with fright, Marike admires him for not crying. *I must explain and tell the nurse I gave him my egg. It isn't fair.* Marike struggles with the bed clothes, which have become tangled around her legs. Finally, she is free, but it's too late, the nurse has shoved Heinz through the door. *If only I wasn't so weak, I could have helped him. But how can I explain when this nurse doesn't speak any German, and I know only a few Danish words. It isn't fair that the Danes will allow us to learn other languages, but we're not allowed to learn Danish. I suppose they think if we learned their language, we might escape and steal from them. Maybe, they're afraid Denmark's ordinary citizens would find out about us.*

Marike walks unsteadily to the door and is just about to open it when the nurse barges through it.

"Please understand—he didn't do anything. It was my fault." Marike forces the words out between frantic gasps for air. Wordlessly, the nurse takes her firmly by the elbow and steers her to her bed. Too weak to resist, Marike allows herself to be put to bed.

She treats me like a child. When she glances out the window, she sees Heinz walking dejectedly in the direction of his aunt. *Heinz may try to be a man, but he is still my boy—my first-born child. All the plans Horst and I had for our inquisitive Heinz. Now what? What can*

I do? So much has happened: the war, conscription, Horst's disappearance, the bombings, our flight, and now this camp.

They may call us refugees, but we're criminals to them. The Danes hide us away. They don't want to see us. We're a problem—too many to feed and house. Probably lots of Danish people don't even know we exist or that there are these German refugee camps.

Marike reminisces about her childhood, and the first time she was invited to visit a schoolmate who lived on a neighboring Petershagen farm. Even though Marike's family was poor, her mother helped her dress, taking longer to brush Marike's hair and adding a bright blue ribbon. Excited, young Marike hopped first on one foot and then another until her mother threatened to swat her bottom. Finally, she was ready and was warned to mind her manners and not to overstay her welcome.

That is the problem. We've worn out our welcome. They didn't even invite us. Before the end of the German occupation, the German army told the Danish government they had to take us. Where else could we go? No country would take German refugees. It wasn't our fault. Where can we go now? It's awful being where you aren't wanted. Marike closes her eyes, pulling a curtain on thoughts that are too painful.

Today, Freda arrives alone.

"Marike, I've brought you mail." Freda hands Marike a thin, wrinkled envelope.

"Who could it be from?" Marike tears open the envelope and takes out a single, thin sheet. She squints at it and sees Gertrude's signature. Quickly, she replaces it in the envelope.

"Horst?" Freda asks.

"No, it's not from Horst, but thank you for bringing it." Marike stares at the envelope.

"I have to leave." Freda buttons her coat. "I just wanted to bring your mail. I'll be back tomorrow."

"Goodbye. Thank you again. Please tell my children I love them," Marike says to Freda's retreating back.

After Freda leaves, Marike struggles to find enough fading sunlight to illuminate the letter's cramped handwriting.

My dearest friend Marike,
How worried you must be. I'm sorry I didn't get
to say good-bye, but by now, you know why. You must
be so ashamed of me. What I did was wrong. I admit,
at first, I thought it was an easy way to get extra rations,
and I was so bored.

Stretching her head back, Marike studies the ceiling, where a spider busily gyrates along its web towards a struggling fly. "Oh Gertrude, you're like that fly," Marike whispers and continues to read.

I didn't expect to find love again. Not after all that
has happened. When they arrested me, I thought our love
wouldn't last. Still, I didn't give them his name.
Each day was agony. Oh, the Danish guards
treat me okay. Instead of prison, an army truck took me
and other Prussian women, accused of fraternizing
with the Danes, to this small refugee camp in
Northern Jutland. As we went through town,
some Danes hurled epithets at us, like they did at their
mattress women. We were grateful we weren't guarded
by the Danish Resistance men. If they were our guards,
maybe they would have shaved our heads as they shaved
their Danish women's heads.

The nurse arrives. Marike quickly stuffs Gertrude's letter under the mattress. Silently, the nurse hands Marike an egg and motions for Marike to eat it so she can write in Marike's chart that Marike has complied. Marike makes a wry face but peels and eats the egg. After the nurse has left, Marike continues to read Gertrude's letter.

> *Instead, we're restricted to our barracks. Yesterday,*
> *one woman broke the rules. We have many rules—even more*
> *than you do. The police came and took the woman to prison.*
> *At first, I didn't care what happened to me. I felt awful.*
> *Then, I received his letter. He loves me, and after all of*
> *this is over, he wants to marry me. He said he talked to you.*
> *Please understand. I love him. Don't tell your family, but do*
> *tell them I'm fine. I miss you. Please write.*
> *Your friend, Gertrude*

Marike rereads Gertrude's letter, memorizes her address, and tears up the letter.

Oh Gertrude, I wish I could write to you, but I don't have paper, pencil, or even a stamp. Instead, I'll send my prayers that you will be safe, and that Klaus and you will be happily married. He is a good man.

The letter puts Marike's mind at ease, yet she wonders how Gertrude paid the postage. Did she have to sell her mother's ring?

Chapter 28

Marike lies quietly listening, trying to remember where she is. The clogs clomping in the corridor certainly don't sound like the hospital. Yesterday, after six long months, she returned to Barracks B. The children had organized a welcoming celebration, with everyone singing her favorite songs. Before Marike left the hospital, she felt strong, but this morning her strength feels used up. She knew it would take time, but her children need her now.

And Marike senses something else is happening. What is it? Oh yes, last night when she thanked Freda and the others for caring for her children, Freda spoke too quickly and kept glancing at Marike's brother Abelard, as if they had a secret. *What a good sister-in-law she is, more like a sister. How had she ever managed nine children?*

Marike observes her children aren't as clean or polite as before her sickness. In fact, they seem to run in the hallways like caged animals. She can't blame Freda or the children—they're bored.

Today, Marike insists that she is strong enough to stand in line. When she returns with her pail of soup, she hears laughter, which grows louder as she enters the barracks. Setting the pail down, she gazes in astonishment at her relatives, whose faces are distorted with laughter.

Before she can ask, Abelard thrusts in her hand a torn brown sheet, which she recognizes as their toilet paper. A German poem is penciled on it.

"Let me see. It says, 'Ode to Our Wonderful Home.'" Marike reads,

"There are those who know not
How fortunate it is to be
In a shelter where there are
Open spaces for you and me
To feel the ocean breezes
And if you don't like sea air
Because it makes you freeze
Yet, it's good for your hair
Join us by our fire
Mostly just smoke
We're not the liars
Because toft makes you choke
It's our wonderful home
From which we'll never roam."

Marike begins chuckling.

Helena asks, "What is so funny?"

"The poem makes fun of our barracks, the cracks between the boards, our wet fuel, the damp, cold sea air, and the fact we can't leave," Marike explains.

"I don't get it," Helena whines.

"The poem tells us that all of this is good for us. Sometimes, we have to laugh through our tears," Marike chuckles.

"Grown-ups, I'll never understand," Heinz says. "Come on, let's play hide-and-seek." As the children leave, Marike and the other adults laugh.

"One thing you can say, the Danes didn't make a rule against laughter," Abelard says.

"Ha ha, they can't ration laughter, either," Freda says.

Chapter 29

The next evening, Abelard says, "Marike, we need to talk about Paraguay."

Even though he speaks abruptly and sounds his usual grumpy self, Marike knows he cares for her and her children. "Yes, of course. I, too, want to talk."

"There is a problem. I promised our mutter I'd look after you and the children."

"Why? I don't understand." Marike's eyes widen as she stares at her elder brother.

"Because we received permission...we leave tomorrow."

"For Paraguay?" Marike asks.

Abelard shakes his head, "For Enkenbach, Rheinland-Pfalz. We won't be going with you, your family, and our cousins to Paraguay."

"Oh Abelard, I should have told you. We aren't going to Paraguay," Marike says.

"I thought—didn't your mother-in-law want to go to Paraguay?" Abelard paces, digging his hands into his pockets.

"She did. But she kept changing her mind—first Paraguay, then America, then Paraguay. I decided America would be best, where we have a sponsor—Amalia's cousin. But you, how did you manage to return to Germany?" Marike asks.

Abelard ducks his head and looks out the window. He mumbles,

"Freda's brother in Enkenbach offered to sponsor us. Our Prussia is no more. Now, it's part of Poland. We, Prussians have been forced from our homes. Stalin will never let us return."

Marike's shoulders sag. As other family members rejoin them, Abelard and Freda instruct their five children to prepare for their journey. Marike's pain is too great to be shared, and she leaves quickly.

For Marike, each day seems identical to the previous day, until Marike demands that something, anything, should be different. The dull sameness is so boring and pointless. Why did she wish to find a new home? To lose Abelard and his family, especially Freda whom she loves and trusts. Poor Heinz and Elisabet will miss their older cousins. The dull pain grows and twists, like branches to her other losses, almost strangling her. Marike walks around outside the barracks, hoping the sea air and walking will untangle her thoughts.

When she returns to their room, Abelard and Freda stop packing, while the children excitedly chatter.

"Hush," Abelard commands and the children obey.

Marike hugs Freda. "I'm sorry. I'm being selfish. It will be better than the camp, a new start for you." Marike swallows, rubs her eyes with her sleeve.

"Dear Marike, we'll miss you and the children so much. I wish there was some way you could come," Freda says wistfully.

"I will miss you. Sometimes, I wonder if I made the right decision," Marike begins.

Freda stops packing, "It may take you a long time to get visas. In the meantime, the Danish are trying to empty the camps."

"If we had relatives left who could take us in, we might have returned to Germany like you," Marike reflects.

"Don't give up," Freda says. "Maybe, Horst or one of your family will find you."

"I don't see how anyone could find us here," Marike's lips turn down in discouragement.

"Remember the forms we filled out when we arrived. I met a woman, a refugee like us, who came from another camp. She volunteered in an office with a hundred German refugee women. All day they filed those forms. On the wall were postage stamp-sized photos of children, separated from their mothers during their flight to Denmark, and others, searching for their missing relatives. Row upon row of boxes, containing information about some of the over two hundred thousand German refugees, filled the shelves. When a letter came, asking about a refugee, they matched it with their information. Once, we were a slip in a box waiting for someone to find us. When my brother in Germany wrote, hoping we'd escaped to Denmark, they located us."

"Oh Freda, what will I do without you? I can't bear the thought. Your sister would be proud of what you've done with her children."

"I don't know. Lena still resents me," Freda says.

"That's because she's young. She'll get over it," Marike reassures her.

"Marike, you always make me feel so much better. I'll miss you and the children. They're like my own. Your Heinz is becoming something of an athlete. You should see him play in some of the games."

"What games?" Marike asks.

"You remember Klaus, the guard who organizes athletic games for the boys. The camp director encourages Heinz, and it keeps him and the other boys out of trouble. Heinz says Klaus' German is terrible, but the boys regard him with awe, follow him everywhere. Heinz said Klaus competed in the Olympics."

"Really, did you say Klaus?" Marike repeats.

"It may not be true, but watch Heinz and the others this afternoon."

"I will. But when do you go to Ehrenbach?" Marike asks.

"First, they said we have to go to a transition camp. The Danes want to make certain we don't have any bugs or diseases before they let us go. If we do, it's their fault," Freda says.

When Heinz returns to their barracks, Marike questions him closely about the guard and his games. She worries Klaus' influence will cause more problems for her family. Heinz reassures her and makes her promise to come and watch him play. Marike hesitates, struggling with her fears. She refuses to say, "I forbid you." Instead, she agrees to come.

Soon she finds herself seated on the grass, with other mothers watching the games. First, Klaus has the boys go through a few calisthenics. Then they form a circle, and he tosses a large ball to them. Heinz glances quickly at Marike, to make sure she is watching, and then tosses the ball back to Klaus. Marike is surprised as she watches the ball's smooth arc.

The woman seated next to her says, "Your son—he is so talented."

"Yes, but he is really too young for this."

"He may be, but he is very good. See how Klaus corrects him. He doesn't do that with everyone."

Marike watches as Klaus adjusts Heinz's grip on the ball, while he quickly glances at Marike. Something about Klaus' gaze makes Marike feel uncomfortable, as if he is trying to communicate something. As the other boys leave, Klaus continues talking to Heinz until Marike approaches. Soon, they are standing alone with Klaus's hand on Heinz's shoulder.

Klaus says softly, "Heinz good."

Marike smiles proudly.

Klaus says, "I help."

"I know you've been good to Heinz."

Klaus shakes his head, "I help you…Heinz leave."

Marike can't believe what she is hearing. Maybe he has some German words confused. "Are you sure?"

"I help," Klaus says again. Two guards, laughing and talking, approach them.

When Marike turns to answer him, he has disappeared.

Chapter 30

Ever since Klaus spoke to her, Marike has questioned whether she correctly understood him. If he is really planning their escape, can she trust him? She has heard about other refugees who have tried to escape, but were caught and punished. She hopes he understands that she can't leave the camp without her four children and her mother-in-law. Surely, it is impossible to even think of such a thing with the barbed wire and guards. And where could she go? Certainly, she couldn't escape to the Danish countryside? Unable to speak Danish and with her dirty, torn clothes, she would be spotted instantly. If only she could talk to someone, but she doesn't dare say anything.

If only Freda was still here, but they've left for the transition camp where they will be checked for communicable diseases like tuberculosis, typhus, and even measles. From the rumors she has heard, the camp authorities also make certain no one has lice or scabies. Unconsciously, Marike touches her greasy hair, trying to remember the last time she really bathed. Except for last summer's few ocean swims, all she can do here is use a bowl of thin tea and a bit of soap and rag to wash. How her little ones squirmed while she scrubbed. Sometimes, Heinz and Elisabet tried to distract them by tickling them, making a game of her attempts at cleanliness.

She remembers some of the things her dear mutter taught her

as a child. How important it was to keep clean. How she would help her mother with the heavy basket of work clothes, standing next to her and handing her more clothes. Sometimes, she would press her face into a flapping sheet, inhaling the fresh, clean scent. Her brother would tease her about her love of clean clothes, saying she was "too German." When his teasing bothered her, she'd hide in the corn crib until she couldn't bear the cobs poking her.

If Abelard, Freda, and the children pass their tests, soon they will leave the transition camp for Ehrenbach. *Will I ever see them again?*

"Castor oil, castor oil," outside, the Danish nurse yells at the children.

Heinz and Elisabet rush in and grab their spoons from the storage shelf.

"Don't forget your little sister and brother," Marike reminds them.

Without answering, they hold up two spoons each.

Marike chuckles to herself. At home, they complained when she gave them their weekly castor oil, but here, they're so hungry, they welcome it. As she follows them out the door, someone grabs her elbow.

"What—" she starts to ask, but is shushed and hurried to the deserted area behind the barracks.

"Tomorrow night, be ready," a masculine voice says.

"Klaus?" she whispers, but when she turns around, no one is there.

If only she could have asked him all the questions swimming, like the North Sea's frightened fish, in her head. *Where are they going? How? Who is taking them? What if they are caught?* Maybe she can take the risk, but can she risk her dear children? And what about her mother-in-law? It would be safer to stay here. Wait until—until what? Until she hears from her husband, but how long will that be? Other husbands wrote to their wives when they returned to Germany from POW camps. She had hoped, but not received anything—not a word since the day her letter was returned marked MISSING.

One of her friends, whose husband managed to escape from a Russian POW camp near Leningrad, told her how he, with the other captured German officers, was shot by Russian soldiers. Although wounded, he lay very still and pretended to be dead. For several days, he hid in the woods until discovered by partisans who helped him return to Germany. Too often, she hears women crying as they receive news of their husbands' deaths.

It has been hours since my conversation with Klaus. Maybe I just imagined it. Why would he risk everything for my family? If only I would hear about our American visas. Why are they taking so long?

Marike walks toward her mother-in-law's barracks when a young woman stops her.

"Marike Wiens?"

"Yes." Marike stares at her. "Do I know you?"

"You won't remember me. We met some time ago. I'm a friend of Gertrude's." To Marike, the tightly knotted scarf around the girl's dark hair and her threadbare coat fail to disguise her youthful beauty.

"You know something about Gertrude?" Marike asks—her interest piqued.

"They moved her to another camp," the girl answers.

"Which one?"

"It doesn't matter."

"What do you mean, it doesn't matter?" Marike is irritated.

"Shush, someone will hear."

"Tell me."

"Klaus told you. Tomorrow there will be a transport to Germany," she says into Marike's ear.

"Who are you? How can we?" Marike whispers frantically.

The girl looks around and places her finger to her lips. "Can I trust you?"

"Yes, of course," Marike answers. "Tell me, I must know." *How hard I've worked to convince my mother-in-law to apply for American visas and now, to change our plans and return to Germany. What if I'm wrong? If we stay and the visas never come, what will we do then?*

"All right, but you must not tell anyone. Our lives depend on it. Of course, you heard our German troops planted over a million land mines in Denmark during the occupation?"

"I don't see what that has to do with us," Marike says impatiently.

"Listen. A German officer was put in charge of removing them. I remember him from my brother's letters. He said the same officer helped him when they were surrounded by the Russians at Stalingrad. I guess the Danes respect him, because at the end of the war in Denmark, he stopped his own German troops from blowing up an important Danish bridge." The girl pauses.

"What does this have to do with us escaping?" Marike asks.

"When he finished removing the mines, he began helping Prussian refugees to return to Germany. And some Danish officers assisted him. I guess they help him, because it's their chance to get rid of us and send us back to Germany." She winks at Marike.

"But how can they do that?" Marike asks, her face a question mark.

The girl pauses and glances around. Marike follows her gaze. When the girl is certain no one can hear them, Marike asks again, "How?"

"Klaus said they've obtained Danish army trucks and phony documents for the British border guards. And some Danish guards, who want to help, ask Prussian families they can trust if they want to leave. I wish I knew more."

"Oh, thank you for telling me." Marike clasps the girl's hands.

"I did it for Gertrude." She stares sadly in the distance, almost as if she could see Gertrude. "Together, Gertrude and I would meet our boyfriends. She saved me. If Gertrude had given the guards my name or Klaus', I wouldn't still be here. Klaus was afraid you and your family wouldn't go."

Before Marike can reply, the girl joins another woman walking in the direction of Barracks C.

I don't even know her name. I guess it is better I don't, in case we're caught. I'll have to prepare the children. If I tell them the truth, they might accidentally say something. I'll tell them we're playing a game. They'll mind me. They're such good children.

The next day, Marike helps Amalia move her things to Marike's room. Carefully, Marike folds and packs her mother's soiled down comforter and their few belongings. She instructs each child to wear every bit of their clothing, even though they've outgrown many things. Since a cold, damp wind blows, no one notices their extra clothes. As Marike watches, other mothers make similar preparations.

"Come children, we will go to the kitchen," Marike says.

"We can't! It is past curfew," says Heinz.

"Don't worry. It's just part of our game. Hurry up now and be very quiet," Marike whispers.

"Yes, Mutti," says Elisabet.

Silently, the children follow her from their barracks into the darkness. As they reach the other refugees climbing into the two army trucks, Heinz whispers frantically, "Mutti, is Helena with you?"

"No, I thought your grandmother had her."

"I haven't seen her," Amalia replies. "Fifty people got on, but not Helena."

Marike hugs her children to her, "Where's your little sister?"

"Mutti, they say we have to get on the truck now," Heinz says. "They're leaving."

"Maybe I didn't see her get on a truck," Amalia says hopefully.

"No, she'd never do that, not alone." Marike looks around frantically.

"They say we should look for her later. They won't wait for us,"

Marike's mother-in-law replies. "Do you want the children and me to get on the truck while you look?"

Agitated, Marike drops her bags, sits on them, and rubs her face. When she looks up, her eyes meet those of Gertrude's friend. With a puzzled look, the girl leans out toward her from the truck's bed, but it's too far away to talk. Desperate, Marike shakes her head while the girl nods sadly.

Marike says, "We've been through so much. We won't be separated now. Amalia, if you want to go with them, I'd understand."

"Come children, let's help your mother find your sister," Amalia says.

In the quiet darkness, Marike hears the trucks' engines idling. *I know they can't wait or they'll be caught. Helena, where are you?*

As the family returns to their barracks, they find three rough-looking boys leaning against the door. Inside, they can hear the muffled cries of someone pounding on the door.

"Helena, is that you?" Marike yells as she runs toward the barracks.

"Mutti, Mutti, let me out," Helena cries.

Before Marike reaches them, the boys dart away. Heinz runs after them, shaking his fists.

"Heinz, forget them, come here." Marike bends down just in time to catch Helena bursting through the open door.

"Those mean boys—they grabbed me and threw me in here. I begged them to let me go, but they wouldn't let me loose. I'm sorry. Did we lose the game?" Helena sobs into her mother's arms.

"It's okay, dear. You're safe now," Marike reassures her.

"I recognized those boys," Heinz says. "They're the same ones who were nasty to your friend."

"Who are you talking about?" Marike asks.

"You know, the boys who stole the old lady's bucket, and you made them stop," Heinz says.

"Now, I remember, Heinrich's friends," Marike says.

"It isn't fair. Because of those mean bullies, we have to stay here, and the others get to leave." Elisabet points to the empty space where the trucks once stood.

Chapter 31

Three weeks later, Marike waits for the children to return from their play when the door bangs open. Elisabet and Heinz burst in, followed by Helena, holding Edel's hand. Their wooden shoes clatter on the floor boards. Usually, Marike would remind them to be quiet to avoid disturbing late sleepers, but so few refugees remain that she doesn't say anything. The children excitedly cluster around her. Behind them, a swarm of fleas regroup in their doorway.

"Mutti, we got a package all the way from America," Elisabet announces.

"Open it," Helena and Edel demand.

"Slow down. I'm coming," Marike takes the large package. "It's heavy."

"Maybe it's our shoes," Heinz says, kicking his clog up in the air.

"I think you may be right," Marike says, as she rescues the address from her children's hands while they rip open the box. "This is the same address of the American Mennonites who asked for your shoe sizes."

"I remember," Helena cries. "You tickled my feet, when you drew around them. I kept giggling. And you said my shoes would be funny looking, because the lines were wiggly."

"It was so long ago. I thought they forgot about us," Heinz says as he grasps the largest pair of brown shoes from the box. Kicking off his other clog Heinz tries to jam his feet into the new shoes.

Laughing, Marike says, "Children, they're not like clogs. You have to untie them first." She watches them as they put on their new shoes and then strut around the room.

"Mutti, is it true?" asks Elisabet.

"Is what true?"

"Oh, Mutti, don't tease us," says Elisabet, dancing around her mother.

"Elisabet wants to know if we're being sent to another camp. The transition camp, where you go before you can leave," says Heinz.

Suppressing a smile, Marike savors this happy moment and her surprising secret.

How her children have grown in these three years. Even though she works hard to remake them, their ill-fitting clothes hang loosely on their scrawny bodies. Even their faces bear dirt smudges from their recent play.

"Mutti, say something, please tell us," pleads Helena, hugging her mother.

"It's true. We're being moved to the transition camp." Marike beams happily at her family. "I wanted to make certain that Grandmother Wiens would be joining us before I told you."

More than three years we've waited in the camps. We're among the few refugees who remain. Our relatives, except for Amalia, have traveled far away. Yet, I feared it might not be true. I couldn't bear to see their disappointed faces. Now the children will have shoes for their journey. We've endured so much, but surely this final camp will be the gateway to a better life.

Marike marvels how quickly her mother-in-law and children ready themselves for their trip. Once they're aboard with the other refugees, the trucks start moving on Denmark's main east and west route. The trip from their camp near the North Sea to their new camp not far from the Baltic Sea does not take long.

"Look, that must be our new camp," says Heinz.

Their truck pulls through the camp gates and parks. Soon, they and their few belongings are unloaded.

Helena says, "I don't smell anything different."

"What do you mean?" Marike asks.

"Heinz said the Baltic would smell different than the North Sea."

"He was just teasing you," Marike says.

"That's mean," says a pouting Helena.

"Come, children." Marike urges them forward. "We have to get processed."

Once processed, they unpack their meager belongings in their new barracks. Marike unfolds and places her mother's quilt on her bed. In the cupboard, Elisabet stores her paper dolls, which have curled up in odd positions. Meanwhile, Edel and Heinz hum pretend engine noises and roll their tiny toy car back and forth to each other. On the shelf, Marike places their toothbrushes, a sliver of soap, a towel, and five bowls and spoons. The family has very little clothing, because they wear what they can. In the bag Marike had knit, she carries her knitting needles, a sewing needle, and some leftover thread. A friend had given her a worn sweater, and Marike had unraveled it and hoped to make a sweater for Heinz. The children admire their new shoes as they sit on the bunk beds and swing their legs back and forth.

Marike's hope grows when camp life seems better here than at their previous camp. Waiting with her children to be examined by the camp nurse, Marike studies the other refugees. Since they're accustomed to long lines, they wait patiently. When the child in front of Marike begins scratching his head, she sees tiny movements in his greasy hair. Carefully, she backs away, hoping her children won't be infected with his lice. His mother, with a hawkish nose and beady eyes, stares resentfully at Marike and roughly pushes her son in front of her. Another boy, so pale and thin she wonders how he can stand, coughs into his sleeve. When he finally stops coughing, she notices his sleeve speckled with tiny, bright red dots. Instinctively, Marike covers her mouth, and with her other arm, presses her children to her.

Heinz struggles against her until he breaks free. "I'm not a baby. Let me go."

Helena's blue eyes look questioningly at her mother.

Talking to a new acquaintance, Elisabet barely notices her mother's protective arm encircling them.

Young Edel stumbles and almost falls, but Marike quickly catches him.

What beautiful children, Marike thinks, *with their blue eyes and blond curls, although now their unwashed hair with its dusty coating looks a mousy brown.* Despite their bulky clothing, their stick-thin limbs make them look like marionettes. *If only they were puppets,* Marike thinks, *then I could control their wild behavior.* She hopes the next move will make them more civilized. After more than three years living in Danish refugee camps, she offers herself a reprieve. It was enough just to keep her children alive.

"Next," orders the nurse.

Marike follows the children into a bare room, where a stout, ruddy-faced man motions for them to sit. She had hoped he'd be one of the few German doctors still left in Denmark, but he is obviously Danish.

First, the nurse begins roughly examining her children's hair. Before Marike can stop her, Elisabet shouts, "We don't have any lice."

The nurse pauses, looks at Edel's head, feels it again, and then shakes her head at the doctor.

Now, the Danish doctor probes Edel's head and studies him. He motions for Edel to walk back and forth.

Edel scrambles off the table and does so. While he feels Edel's spine and rests his hands on Edel's small hips, the doctor has Edel touch his toes. Then, the doctor gently taps Edel's arms and legs.

"Ouch, that hurts," Edel protests.

In Danish, the doctor asks Marike for Edel's age. In German, the nurse repeats the doctor's question. Little Edel proudly thrusts his five fingers in the air.

In a low voice, the doctor dictates to the nurse.

Marike looks to the nurse to translate, who asks for the doctor's permission. When he nods, she repeats, in German, his diagnosis. "He says, 'His skull is asymmetrical, bone tenderness in arms and legs, no evidence of scoliosis, possibly impaired growth."

"But what does that mean?" Marike's voice quivers.

Again, the nurse translates the doctor's orders. "Now, Mother, don't you worry—just rickets. We'll give him plenty of vitamins and minerals with calcium and phosphorus. Just like a boy not to eat his raw vegetables or drink his milk. This time of year, near the Baltic, we don't get much sun either."

"What raw vegetables? We didn't get any," Elisabet interjects.

"Hush, Elisabet. Thank you, doctor. I've been worried about Edel." Marike smiles apologetically.

"The doctor says I'm to give you pills and instructions when you leave." The doctor and nurse exit while Marike helps Edel dress.

"Mutti, it isn't right," Elisabet says loudly. "He made it sound like it was Edel's fault."

Sighing, Marike answers, "What good will it do now, Elisabet? He knows there wasn't enough of the right food, but he can't say anything. Besides, it's too late. They're closing most of the camps. Blame is for the powerful." As they leave, Marike silently accepts the nurse's hurried instructions and the envelope of pills.

They have barely closed the door when a young girl hollers at Elisabet. She quickly joins her.

"We've been here only a day and already Elisabet has a friend," Heinz says under his breath.

"It's good she found someone her own age. Look at them with their arms on each other's shoulders—so happy."

Marike, Helena, Edel, and Heinz stand quietly listening.

Amalia joins them. "What are they singing?"

"*Heut noch sind wir zu Haus,' Morgen geht's zum Tor hinaus, und wir müssen wandern, wandern, keiner weiß vom andern.*"

With a distant look in her blue eyes, Marike says, "It's kind of a German farewell song. Today we're together, but tomorrow we'll leave. We'll wander or travel and not know what has happened to each other."

"Are we going back home to Prussia?" Helena asks innocently.

"Not Prussia, it is no more."

"America?" Heinz asks.

"*Nein*, it takes time," Marike says.

"But it is 1948. You applied so long ago. Surely by now," Heinz looks hopefully at his mother.

"In time, son. There are many people who want to go to America."

"Marike," her mother-in-law says in a low voice, "I haven't heard from my distant cousin in a long time. You don't suppose she changed her mind, do you? In her last letter, she wrote she was ill, but surely she is better."

Lines deepen in Marike's forehead as she replies, "I hope so. Still, Kansas is a long way from Denmark. Don't worry. I'm sure everything will work out."

Amalia grumbles, "Three years and four camps, and we're still here. Most everyone has been sent somewhere."

With a confidence she doesn't feel, Marike reassures her mother-in-law that surely everything will be all right.

I didn't want to upset the children. Yet, I too, wonder why we haven't heard from Amalia's cousin. I hope she hasn't changed her mind. If we can't go to America, then will they send us back to Germany like so many other refugees?

Chapter 32

After several weeks in the Danish transition camp, Amalia, Marike, and her four children travel by train to the French Zone of Occupation in Germany. Three and one-half years earlier, six weeks before the end of the war, they had barely escaped advancing Russian troops. Marike hopes life in Germany will be better now.

As they travel through the French Sector, they are occasionally stopped and asked for their documents. Each time they reach another checkpoint, the children grumble, kick their feet, and argue with one another.

"Children, stop arguing, behave," Marike admonishes them. *I understand they're afraid of the soldiers, but I don't want any trouble— not now.*

While French soldiers question other travelers, Heinz asks, "Mutti, why are those soldiers being so mean to us?"

A nearby elderly man with a ragged goatee hears Heinz's question. He replies, "Some of the French don't like us Germans, and some Germans don't like the French. You have to excuse these French soldiers—poor upbringing, probably no fathers to teach them."

As their train continues through war-ravaged Germany, Marike relaxes when they reach the countryside's rolling hills with their beech and evergreen forests. Her favorite beech trees, for which her country could claim many varieties, exist only here. With red and white trunks, they display their magnificent fall colors. Like old friends, they welcome her home.

"Mutti. I remember those trees—red beech—but why are there so few?" Heinz points.

With a sad sigh, Marike responds, "During the war, some forests were cleared for factories. After the war, I suppose the people used many trees for fuel, because there was so little coal and wood."

"Like Denmark, when we'd burn branches, pine needles, anything," replies Heinz.

"Desperate people need to survive," Marike continues.

"I hope someone plants more. They're beautiful, like princesses displaying their finery," Elisabet adds.

When they reach Koblenz, Marike and her children ride in the trolley car. They peer through a broken window that has been taped together. Boards block other broken trolley windows. Pointing at burned-out and rusting tanks, trucks, and jeeps, the children try to identify whether they are German, French, or American army material. Rubble lies everywhere. Surrounded by three partial walls, an elevator shaft stands in naked relief. Instead of transporting the occupant to another floor, it opens to the sky. A few badly damaged buildings remain precariously upright. Grey-faced, shabbily dressed Germans move lethargically through the streets.

They seem to be in a dream. Then, Marike corrects her observation: not a dream, but a nightmare. The people's mouths are set in grim determination as they push wheelbarrows or pull wagons. A few have bicycles. Most activity appears reduced to that which can be accomplished by hand.

When they pass a cemetery, it reminds Marike of All Saints' Eve. The white crosses, many capped with helmets, stand newly draped with evergreen wreaths. The fact that her beleaguered countrymen still remember those who have died comforts her.

As the trolley pauses for passengers to board and exit, the children study signs placed in a shop window. Neatly hand-lettered in German, the cards advertise various items for trade: ladies' shoes for some wood, a healthy goat for an overcoat, a bag of potatoes for a motor.

"With money so devalued," Marike explains to her children, "many Germans barter their few belongings for basic necessities, such as food and fuel." Marike grimaces. Since the war in Europe ended over three years ago, she had hoped Germany's recovery would have progressed further. Everywhere she looks, she sees the war's awful consequences—rubble, hungry children. When she sees the Rhine, the canal contains sunken barges and boats. She looks away. Thinly clad women, clutching their children's hands, disappear into war-damaged buildings.

Those desperate mothers, how hard it must be for them to find any shelter. I would never want my children in one of those buildings. I would be terrified that it might collapse.

When her children see a narrow-gauge railroad, it is so small they think it intended for very young riders on a Sunday outing. Instead, they find the small cars loaded with rubble.

A fellow passenger tells Marike that Elisabet reminds her of the daughter she lost in a bombing raid. Immediately, the children ask the stranger so many questions about the city that the woman frowns in frustration.

"Children, mind your manners. Please excuse them," Marike apologizes.

"It's all right. I love children." She smiles tenderly at them.

"I can't believe this is Koblenz. It looks so different from what I'd heard," Marike says, staring sadly at the ruins.

"It is. Notice the French signs. They spell it 'Coblence.' Before they could get the trains running again, they installed that narrow-gauge railroad to clear the rubble from the streets. We're lucky to have this trolley."

"Look! Who are those women?" Heinz asks.

"*Traummerfrauen,* rubble women, they pick up bricks and clean them off so they can be used again. For many, it is the only job the government can give them. They're rebuilding our city brick by brick."

Marike notices the edge of pride in the woman's voice. "When we traveled along the Mosel River, the valley with its terraced vineyards and mountains looked so peaceful. Even the villages were tidy. I almost forgot there was a war. But this is much worse than I thought."

"The bombing destroyed much of the city."

"How hard it must have been for you." Marike shakes her head sympathetically.

"We were lucky. My apartment building on Roonstrasse didn't suffer too much, although one corner is gone. Fortunately, the damage was severe enough that the French didn't confiscate it. Did you notice those villas and public buildings which were unscathed? Now they house the occupying French soldiers, their families, and other Allies."

How frustrating for the German homeowner to save his home, business, or apartment building only to be told he has to move. Marike's sad eyes regard her new acquaintance.

"I'm sorry about all the bombings. From what I've seen, I wonder how anyone could survive. It reminds me of when we were bombed in Danzig." Marike shivers at the memory. "Now you have the occupation."

"Oh, we're used to the soldiers," the young woman says without rancor. "Now, if it had been the Russians… I was in East Berlin during the fall of Berlin and managed to escape the Russian soldiers by hanging onto the rods under a railway car. I was terrified. I heard stories about what they would do to a German woman. The soldiers checked all the trains with their dogs. Fortunately, there was an air raid, otherwise I might have been found. I almost didn't make it."

"I know. We barely escaped the Russians, too." Marike relates their Danzig and Denmark experiences. "After the war, it must have been hard in Koblenz."

"Since the Russian troops occupied our most fertile farmlands, we had little food. If it hadn't been for the American Quakers and the Swiss, I'm afraid we might have starved. And many did." The woman looks away.

"I heard some American Mennonites sent care packages, too," Marike says.

"Are you Mennonites?"

"Yes, we are," Heinz interjects for his mother.

Elisabet pipes up, "We're going to America."

The woman looks confused.

Marike explains they've applied for visas. "For now, we've been assigned to a farm family near Zweibrücken, in the village of Heidelbingerhof."

"A farm, that is good. Plenty of food and fresh air for grow-ing children," she nods her approval. "Good luck: this is my stop." As the trolley stops, she clutches her bag and steps down to the pavement.

Later, after they have transferred to the train, Marike enjoys traveling through the Saarland. The Saarland reminds her it was once part of Prussia and how they enjoyed the Rhineland's forests.

"Children," Marike says, "World War I's Versailles Treaty de-militarized the Rhineland. In 1936, when Hitler remilitarized it, France did not attack. For Hitler, it was his career's turning point. After World War II, Germany lost land again. At Yalta, Stalin de-manded that Poland's western border be extended to include part of Prussia and Germany. Before and after Potsdam, twelve million Germans were forced from their homes. We were lucky we escaped to Denmark."

Amalia wakes from her nap and glances out the window. "I dreamed we were in the refugee camp. I wonder why the Danes didn't tell us where in Germany they were sending us."

"I don't know. Maybe, they didn't know," Marike replies.

"Or care. Just glad to get rid of us," Amalia says, gritting her teeth.

"Oh, Amalia, it must have been hard for the Danish to feed so many," Marike says.

"They didn't do a very good job, if you ask me." Amalia folds her arms.

"No one asked them if they wanted to take us. What choice did they have?" Marike says.

"I don't know how you can defend them. After all you've been through."

It's time to look forward, thinks Marike. She remembers that when they arrived in Germany, a social worker told her that she and her children were assigned to a farm family and Amalia to a nearby farm. As grateful as Marike is to be living in the French Zone and not the Russian Zone, she wonders what the new family's reaction will be. Like the Danish, they hadn't been asked if they'd like guests. They had been told.

Since no one meets Marike after they arrive in Heidelbingerhof, she asks directions. Fortunately for Amalia, the farmer she has been assigned to arrives to take her to his home, where she will help his wife. Marike and her children gather their few belongings and begin walking.

Even the cool November wind can't dampen the excitement she and the children feel. The distant sun brightens and gleams off village roofs. Marike inhales the fresh air until she smells rotting garbage as they walk by the village's huge refuse pile. She reflects how the garbage signifies more food, but not adequate means for disposal. Meanwhile, the children dash up the empty road and back again, as if to make certain she is following. Since Marike enjoys her children's energy, she doesn't restrain them.

Suddenly, Elisabet spins in circles until she is dizzy, then sits down. The children stare at her, and then they too begin running in circles. Soon, everyone laughs, until they fall together in a heap. Marike catches up with them and gathers her children around her.

"Look, Mutti, no more barbed wire," cries Elisabet.

"No guards," Heinz joins her.

"No more rules," says Helena.

"No lines to stand in," Edel points to the empty road.

"We're free," Elisabet waves her arms.

"Free, we're free," the children repeat.

Marike doesn't want to end their celebration, but the sun slides below the hills. She feels an urgency to find the farm before dark.

Are we really free? What will their hosts expect of them at their new home? There may be no more barbed wire or guards, but will these people want them in their home?

The excited children run ahead of Marike, pointing at various farmhouses while Marike shakes her head. Finally, farm buildings appear that seem to match the social worker's description—a small, two-story farmhouse with a cow barn and outbuildings on each side enclose what looks like a courtyard. It could be. Certainly, they have walked three miles from the schoolhouse, and the farm is on the left side, as she'd been told. Calling the children to wait for her, she joins them.

As they cautiously approach the farmhouse, Marike notices the buildings don't look as grand as she first thought, but appear neglected. A growling noise intensifies as they near the door. Frightened, the children retreat. Peering through the fence, a dog's small eyes stare menacingly at them, drool dripping from his jowls. Squarely built on short legs, the dog wheezes from his deeply flared nostrils. His growl deepens.

Heinz picks up a large rock and draws back his arm, ready to throw his missile.

"No, Heinz, it's okay. He's fenced in," Marike reassures the children. Gathering her courage, she knocks firmly and is surprised when the door opens abruptly. A tall, angular woman fills the doorway. Behind the woman, Marike hears a man's voice yelling.

"Good afternoon. I'm Marike Wiens, and these are my children. We're looking for the Boehr farm. Could you help us?"

"This is it. What took you so long? We've been expecting you for hours. Well, don't just stand there. Come in."

As the woman disappears into the house's dark interior, Marike hears her shout, "Vater, they're here." In a low voice, the woman mumbles, "*Eine Frau mit vier Kinder bringen sie mir!*"

Helena asks, "Mutti, what did she say?"

Elisabet rolls her eyes and says, "A woman with four children you are bringing me!"

Heinz makes a face. Young Edel plops down, tears streaming down his dirty face. Helena bends over him, wiping his face with her sleeve, talking softly.

The woman returns, followed by a man looking as tough and old as the garden's stubble.

"Hello, you must be Mr. Boehr, and this must be your daughter, Miss Boehr."

"What'd you say?" He raises an ear trumpet to his ear.

"I said hello—" Marike begins.

Suddenly, a small brown animal propels itself into the room, barking shrilly.

Miss Boehr scoops it up. "Pekie, quiet. Don't mind her. She's just trying to protect her puppies."

"Puppies, real puppies? Where are they?" Helena's eyes sparkle with excitement.

"Yes, I warn you, she won't let anyone touch them."

"We saw a strange dog outside," says Heinz.

"He's an English bulldog—guards the courtyard. We let him out at night." Miss Boehr's gaze narrows, "I caution you not to go out after dark. He has been trained to attack and keep intruders away."

"All right, but please, can we see the puppies?" Elisabet asks smiling.

Miss Boehr leads the children into the kitchen's warmth, where four small puppies try to paw their way out of a cardboard box placed next to the stove. Even Heinz, who often says he is too old for childish things, joins in as they surround the box. Soon, each child hugs a fat, squirmy puppy. Pekie anxiously sniffs each child and the puppy nestling on their chests.

"Well, I'll be. She's never done that before." Miss Boehr watches them for a few moments and then, regaining control, leads Marike and the children through the laundry room to the stairway.

They follow her up the narrow, wooden stairs, and through the door. Marike is mesmerized. There is a stove, sink, refrigerator, a table with chairs, and a bed.

"Look, Mutti, a bed," says Helena.

"We didn't know how many children. All we were told was a family would live with us. I put an extra bed in the kitchen. During the day you can use it for a couch. The bedroom has twin beds. You can shove them together."

"Mutti, I have to go. Now!" Edel demands.

"There is a toilet, no bathtub, downstairs off the laundry room. He can use that. I'll bring you some leftovers from our dinner after you get settled."

"You are too kind."

"Nonsense, no one asked us, besides Vater needs help in the fields. When he isn't busy, you can help me. All the food we have is mostly milk and vegetables. The soldiers took most of our cows. Is it true the government will pay you?"

"Only a tiny amount, but you'll find I'm a hard worker."

"You look pretty scrawny to me, but maybe the children can help?"

"They're going to school. They need to catch up," Marike says with a determined look.

Glancing at the children's feet, Miss Boehr says, "Last winter they closed the school in January until it warmed up. Not enough fuel and many children didn't have shoes. Some charity, Quaker, I think, gave one pair of shoes per family. Your children are lucky to have shoes."

"But we…" Elisabet begins.

Marike steps beside her. "All the children had for shoes were wooden clogs. They hurt their feet. While we were in the Danish refugee camp, I traced on paper the children's feet and sent the patterns to a Mennonite family in Moundridge, Kansas. They sent these shoes."

"They'll need them. It's a three-mile walk to the school. I have work. Goodnight." Miss Boehr leaves, shutting the door before Marike can reply.

Helena says, "I'm scared."

"He's mean, and I don't like her," says Heinz.

"Now Elisabet, Helena, this is the best we can do for now."

"Why do they hate us so?" pleads Elisabet. "What did we do to them?"

"Why? The government makes them take us," says Heinz.

"Heinz is right. You saw all the terrible destruction. We're lucky to have a safe place. He's old, and she's worn out. We have to be quiet, work hard, and obey their rules."

Curious, the children walk around the two rooms, opening drawers, turning on the water, even inspecting under the bed. How wonderful to have two rooms just for their family.

Elisabet draws back the bedcovers and runs her hand over the clean sheets. Next, she turns off the light and again feels the sheets. "No more bedbugs," she announces.

Soon, they wash their hands, eat the milk and boiled eggs Miss Boehr gave them, and prepare for bed. Marike tells Elisabet she can have her own bed in the main room while Marike will sleep with Heinz, Edel, and Helena on the twin beds. Heinz complains that Marike treats Elisabet "like a princess." Marike replies that his sister is growing up and needs her privacy.

How old was I when I noticed the bright red spots on my nightgown? Ten years old, and my mother was barely nine when she started. Women in my family develop early. Elisabet will be no exception. Soon, I'll have a talk with Elisabet, but not yet. Let her be a child a little longer.

Later, Marike slides quietly out of bed, not wanting to wake her exhausted children. Leaning on the window sill, she stares at the moon-whitened courtyard below as if it holds answers. Catching movement, she recognizes the bulldog pacing slowly beneath her window. The quiet countryside reminds her of her parents' farm and how much she missed the quiet in the noisy barracks. She'd never grown used to the constant clamor. It has been over three years since she has had her children to herself. During that time in the refugee camps, the children seemed to disappear, always playing with their cousins. How can she help them become a family again? Whispering a quick prayer, she snuggles next to her sleeping children.

In the morning, Marike awakes to the sound of pounding, which seems to come from under their beds.

"Help, I'm sinking," cries Helena, who slides to the floor. In his sleep, Heinz has rolled over onto Helena, pushing her between the twin beds.

Marike lifts her up and listens to more pounding on their floor. It sounds as if someone is using a broom handle on the downstairs ceiling. Through the window, a thin grey streak appears on the horizon.

"Hurry children, time to get ready for school." Despite their protests, Marike pulls back the covers and helps Edel dress.

"Elisabet, take your sister downstairs to the bathroom and get dressed."

"Yes, Mutti, but it's not fair Heinz gets to sleep," complains Elisabet.

Marike touches the mound of bedding.

"Heinz, you'll be late for your first day of school." Marike gives the mound a gentle shove.

"Oh Mutti, let me sleep. Then I'll help you with the chores, just like Mr. Boehr said."

"No you don't, Heinz. You're going to school. No more nonsense. If your father heard you say that, you'd be in for a good spanking."

"But he isn't here. I'm the man now."

"Heinz, no more foolish talk. Get dressed." As Marike leaves the room, she hears Heinz slowly extricating himself from the warm bed. She ignores his complaints as she quickly lights the stove.

"Are you coming with us, Mutti?" Elisabet asks while setting the table.

"I'd like to, but I have to help the Boehrs. They'll expect it. Tell your teacher I'll meet her after school and register everyone. Wait for me and be good."

"You don't have to tell *me*. You should tell Heinz," Elisabet says.

After the children leave, Marike clears the table and stacks the dirty dishes, still smeared with egg, in the sink. *They'll have to wait until after my chores*, she thinks as she submerges them in water. After wiping her hands, she pulls on her coat without buttoning it and goes downstairs. Finding no one in the kitchen, she hurries to the barn. She pushes twice before the barn's heavy door slides open on its rusty hinges.

Manure's pungent smell causes her to hesitate. Marike compares this barn to her father's clean one. Still, she decides, he had strong sons to help him. In the early morning light, she hears the barn cats mewing, begging for milk. Raising her hand to her face, she brushes away a cobweb.

"So, you finally decided to come!" Mr. Boehr, grasping a pitchfork like a cane, leans his wrinkled face near her.

"I didn't see you, sorry," Marike gasps.

"Can you milk?"

"I think so. When my brothers were needed in the fields, I'd help, but that was long ago."

"Well, Bessie doesn't like to be kept waiting. If you pull too hard, she kicks."

Mr. Boehr thrusts the pail into her hand. Marike carefully approaches Bessie's ample haunches.

Running her hand along Bessie's side, Marike croons, "There girl, everything's fine. Steady now."

Bessie's head twists around the stanchion while her enormous black eye stares at Marike. As she softly talks to Bessie, Marike sits on the stool. She places the bucket underneath Bessie and gently pulls at a teat. Nothing comes.

"You'll have to pull harder than that," Mr. Boehr says.

Marike grits her teeth. This time, when she pulls, a thin stream pings the bucket. Soon milk fills the bucket while the cats, with their tails waving, loudly meow.

"She used to be my best milk cow. We had a whole herd of seventy-five once. Now just Bessie."

"What happened?"

"Oh, you know, seems the French needed them more than we did. Kind of like when our German army confiscated my horses—probably made a fine dinner for some officers. What can you do?"

"I'm sorry. I can see this was once a beautiful farm. My vater had a small farm in Prussia."

Mr. Boehr coughs. "Before the war, my boys and I produced

enough milk for half the village. Enough talk. Time is wasting. When you finish, toss some hay to Bessie. Shovel the manure. You can shovel, can't you? I got other work to see to." He limps away.

Watching him limp, Marike whispers into Bessie's heaving flank, "He probably got stepped on by a horse. Vater always said he didn't know a farmer who didn't limp, because some animal stepped on him. I wish Vater was here now to tell me what to do. It's been so long since I worked on the farm. If only Miss Boehr lets me bake. I know how to do that." As if in reply, Bessie flips her tail at the circling flies.

Marike works steadily through the cold November day, until afternoon, when she forces her tired legs to walk the three miles to the children's school. Soon, the children happily compete to tell her about their first day at school. Miss Ebert, their teacher, appears coldly distant, but Marike attributes her demeanor to a long class day. On the walk back to the farm, Marike explains a new game to her children.

"Each of you will have a turn to tell about your day. After you finish, we'll see who can remember the most."

"Is there a prize?" asks Elisabet.

"Not this time, but I have a treat."

Edel pulls on her hand. "I wanna play. Can I, Mutti?" Edel's earnest face looks up at her.

"Of course, you can go first."

After Edel finishes, Elisabet says, "The teacher said I had fine penmanship."

"Mutti, tell us about your day," says Helena.

"How thoughtful you are," Marike exclaims. "Miss Boehr sent me to the store, and when the owner heard I had four children, he gave me four pieces of hard candy. Heinz, you can have one too." *I was surprised by his generosity but then, he said that working for the Boehrs he expected we wouldn't get much. He didn't seem to like them.*

"I don't want any old candy," Heinz says peering over her shoulder at her hand.

Elisabet, Helena, and Edel dance excitedly around Marike as she places the candy in their palms.

"I'm going to save mine," Elisabet places hers in her coat pocket. "If Heinz doesn't want his, may I have it?"

Without replying, Marike slides the remaining piece into Heinz's palm and tightly closes his fingers, giving them an extra squeeze.

"Aw, Mutti."

"You're still a boy," Marike says softly as Heinz's cheeks redden.

Watching the children enjoy their candies, Marike thinks, as her mother would say, "Bit by bit." *Yes, Mutti, we're learning to be a family again.*

The next morning Marike is up early, intentionally making noise while preparing their breakfast. She doesn't ever want to hear the broom handle on their floor again. How wonderful it is to have fresh food. Tomorrow, she will fry the eggs. Yet, she worries whether Edel is getting enough vitamins.

She can hear noises in the kitchen below and interprets it as her cue to find out about the day's chores.

She hurries downstairs and knocks on the door. Miss Boehr washes the dishes while Mr. Boehr rocks slowly in his chair.

"Good morning. What do you have for me to do today?" Marike asks as she begins drying dishes. A cuckoo clock announces the hour. Marike pauses to admire the exquisitely carved clock hanging on the opposite wall. "What a beautiful clock. I guess I never noticed it before. It looks like it's really old. Has it been in your family for many generations?"

Miss Boehr and her father exchange uneasy looks.

Marike suspects she has said something wrong, but she isn't sure what or how to correct her mistake.

"Never mind how we got this…" Miss Boehr says.

"I'm sorry. Did I say something wrong? It reminded me of my mother's clock. It was her favorite possession," Marike says. "She said it came from Triberg in the Black Forest. I even remember the back was stamped 'Weisser.' Marike studies the clock's intricate hand carving of leaves, bird, and rabbit.

Miss Boehr turns her back on Marike and continues washing dishes, mumbling softly, "It is barter."

"What?" Marike asks.

"You weren't here. You don't know. After the war, people had little food. They came to the country to barter."

"But the French gave them ration cards."

"Not much more than one thousand calories, if that. Who could live on that?" She grimaces. "Vater gave them some potatoes, eggs, vegetables. They didn't starve. They gave us some of their possessions that was all. Now you'd think we cheated them. Our own people hate us—almost as much as they dislike the French."

"Daughter, the chores," yells Mr. Boehr.

"I thought he couldn't hear us," Marike says.

"When he wants to, he hears."

As Marike glances around the room, she sees a pair of binoculars on the window sill, a crystal bowl on the buffet, and other expensive objects. Funny, she hadn't noticed them earlier.

Later, the winter light fades as Marike finishes the afternoon's milking. As she carries the steaming milk out of the barn, she glances at the horizon. Four small figures trudge up the road, waving their hands. As soon as they reach her, they want to know when their supper will be ready.

That night, after the children clean the supper dishes and finish their homework, Marike helps Edel get ready for bed.

"It's not fair Elisabet gets her own bed. Last night, after we went to bed, she was reading," Heinz complains.

"Elisabet is becoming a woman and needs privacy."

"I'd like some privacy, too. Besides, she never listens to me." Heinz thrusts his elbow at his sister, who dodges him. "She should obey me." This time, Heinz's quick jab connects with Elisabet's upper arm.

"Mutti, he hit me," Elisabet says as she hunches her shoulders and stares at her older brother with wide, bulging eyes. She shakes her small balled fists at Heinz, who further taunts her by laughing.

Growling in frustration, Elisabet's small mouth is clamped shut, her eyes narrowed, and a hurricane of air explodes through her flared nostrils.

Surprised at his sister's intense response, Heinz swallows his laugh, steps back.

"Enough. I've heard enough. Everyone get in bed," Marike orders.

Later, as she hears the clock's cuckoo downstairs announce the late hour, Marike pulls the covers over her sleeping children.

How sweet they look in their sleep. If only they can learn to be more patient with one another. We need a community, our faith, to help us.

Chapter 33

As Marike and her children leave the church, several Zweibrücken congregation members approach and introduce themselves. The unseasonably warm December day encourages lingering conversation, and Marike's heart warms to her fellow Mennonites' interest. When a farmer and his wife offer Marike and her family a ride in their horse-drawn wagon, Marike gratefully accepts.

On the ride home, Marike enquires about the congregation's membership and history.

The farmer replies, "In 1937, we had about one hundred and fourteen baptized members, but we lost some to the war. The church struggles along, but then, two centuries ago it wasn't easy for my ancestors. They escaped the religious persecution by some state and religious leaders. Long ago, they met in Heidelbingerhof, Ernstweilerhof, and other villages and farms."

"I remember stories," Marike says. "Our pastor told us about the early Anabaptist martyrs in Switzerland. How brave they were, singing and praying, knowing the Swiss might burn them at the stake or even behead or drown them."

"Mutti, couldn't they save themselves?" Elisabet asks.

"If they recanted, and joined the state church, they could," Marike answers.

"But why?" Elisabet persists.

Before the farmer replies, his large hands snap the reins, and he urges the weary horse up the hill. "In those long ago days, the state religions didn't like it that Anabaptists didn't believe in infant baptism. And Switzerland wasn't the only country persecuting them. Our members should remember how their ancestors suffered, instead of complaining they can't use their trucks because of the gas shortage."

"Are we Mennonites Christians? A mean boy at school said we weren't," Helena asks.

"Tell me who, and I'll talk to him," Heinz says.

"Yes, we're Christian," Marike says. "Our faith is based on living our daily lives as Christ did. We are to live simply, in peace, forgiving our enemies, helping others, not taking oaths, or doing violence. Those are some of our beliefs. You know what Pastor Behrends taught you."

"Yes, Mutter, I know."

Turning to the farmer, Marike says to him, "You seem to have an active congregation."

"We do what we can. I suppose you didn't have any Mennonite services when you were refugees?"

"Not at first, but when they sent us to the largest refugee camp, we had a Mennonite minister," Marike says. "He gave us hope after all we lost."

"Mutti," interrupts Elisabet, "they said there would be an Advent Children's Program. Can we go?"

"We'll see. Please excuse my children. I'm afraid they've forgotten their manners after three years in the refugee camps. Now, that we're back in Germany, I hope they'll become more civilized."

With a superior smile, Heinz whispers to Elisabet, "See I told you not to ask. You never listen."

Elisabet turns her back to her brother and sucks on her lower lip, mumbling, "He always has to be right."

Marike pretends she doesn't hear the children, as she reflects on the sermon's theme of pride. A good subject, she decides, since her children help her to stay humble.

"To spare the rod is to spoil the child," the farmer says, clucking at his team to encourage them up the hill.

His wife says gently, "And children need loving patience, too."

As they approach their new home, Marike insists that she and her children can walk the rest of the way.

The farmer's wife says, "We had an automobile, but it was confiscated by the French army. It was just as well. We didn't have any gasoline to run it. They let us keep the horses to work the farm."

After expressing her appreciation, Marike and her children walk home. It had been a good decision to go to church. She needs her faith, and next time, she will arrange for her mother-in-law to join them.

On the following Wednesday, Marike quickly finishes her chores and walks to the schoolhouse to meet her children. From a distance, she sees Helena with a strange boy on the school's playground.

As she draws near, Marike notices Helena's small brow wrinkled with worry.

The chubby boy taunts her, thrusting out his thick lips. He circles around her, chanting, "*Krampus* will get you, *Krampus* will get you. Soon, you'll hear his chains rattling."

"I'll be good. Please don't let the demon get me," Helena pleads.

"Only if you give me your lunch, otherwise he'll lick you with his long tongue and beat you with his switch," the boy grins wickedly.

Before Marike can intervene, Heinz grabs the boy from behind, knocks him flat, sits on him, and shakes his fist in his face. "You leave my little sister alone or you'll be sorry."

"I…I promise. Don't hit me. I thought you Mennonites didn't hurt people." As Heinz rises, the boy rolls over on his hands and knees and gets up. He starts to say something, but notices Marike standing nearby. "I'm going to tell my mutter on you." With his fat legs bumping each other, he zigzags down the road.

Marike bends down and draws Helena to her.

"Are you all right?" Marike asks.

"He told me I have to give my lunch to him," Helena says breathlessly.

"You don't have to," Heinz declares. "He's a fat bully. Anyway, he looks like he already eats too much."

Helena giggles.

"Heinz is right. Thanks, son. From now on I want you children to walk home together."

"Yes, Mutter, but will the *Christkind* find us this *Weihnachten?*" Elisabet asks.

Heinz licks his lips, "And will you make some of your good stollen*?*"

"We'll see," Marike says.

Helena wipes her eyes, returning her mutti's smile.

"Oh Mutti, do you think we could have a tree and sing carols?" asks Helena.

"I liked the *Nussknackers* Opa carved," Heinz says. "Like small soldiers."

"You were so young. You may not remember the many nuts we cracked for all the baking. First, we'd gather them in the fall from the orchard. Then, we'd spread them to dry. Finally, we'd place them on a piece of iron and hammer them and pick out the nut meats."

Marike promises herself she will give her children a special Christmas. After all, they deserve it. They are good children. Just considering her plan and making a mental list of small gifts, Marike tastes tiny bits of happiness. She considers how, after all these years of deprivation, to give her children something special will be wonderful. Every mother should know this pleasure.

Christmas Eve in Heidelbingerhof arrives with the fields serene in their frosty cover. Overhead, the pewter-colored sky promises peace. Marike checks on her sleeping children. She does not want to awaken them—and almost succeeds, when Elisabet's sleepy voice comes from the next room.

"Mutti, is it Christmas Day yet?"

"Shh, you'll wake the others. Yes, it is."

"Can we open presents?"

"Later, after I finish my chores."

"That's so long. It's still dark."

"Go back to sleep, and the time will go by quickly. I have to milk." Marike feels her way to their door.

As Marike makes her way to the barn, she thinks how easily she has slipped back into their Christmas traditions. How much comfort they give her. After they've eaten, she will give each child their gift, a new book. Their stockings will hold a delicious orange. They will snuggle together under the covers, and she will read Elisabet's book to them. The German government paid her so little for her work, she had to be careful, each time putting her few *pfennigs* in a can whose lid she nailed under a loose floor board.

How happy she felt when she told the shopkeeper she didn't want a used book. Not for *her* children did she want one of the dusty books a hungry customer traded for some bread. Her children would get *new* books with shiny covers and unbroken spines. She inhaled the book's inky smell. How very carefully she had studied the titles, wanting to pick just the right one to match each of her children's interests. If reading became as important to them as it was to her, then they would learn and make their way in the world. She could not think of a better gift.

Having milked the cow, fed the hungry barn cats a few milky squirts, shoveled out the cow manure, and replaced it with new straw, Marike crunches across the frozen grass to the house. The remote silvery sunlight gives her little warmth. In her haste, she doesn't notice the stranger standing by the door, watching her.

When Marike learns that the stranger has come to see her, she insists that the woman come upstairs to rest. At first, the woman declines, but Marike persists, saying she should at least have a cup of coffee—even if all she can offer is chicory. The stranger quickly introduces herself as representing the Mennonite Central Committee. North American Mennonites have sent care packages, and she is helping distribute them. Humbly, she apologizes that there are only two for their family. One gift is for the girls and one for the boys. Since the children demand to open them, Marike abandons proper decorum and lets them.

Elisabet tries to untie the bright ribbons on the tightly rolled terrycloth towels.

"Look, Helena."

"Wait for me," Heinz cries as he jerks at the knotted ribbons.

"Let the little ones help," Marike directs. Helena and Edel jump up-and-down with excitement.

Beneath their feet, they hear Mr. Boehr thumping his ceiling with the broom handle.

"Oh, oh, children you're making too much noise," Marike raises her finger to her mouth. "Remember, we promised to be quiet."

"But it is Christmas," Heinz complains.

"Mutti is right. You wouldn't want us to get sent away, would you? Where would we go?" Elisabet asks.

"I feel something, hurry," Helena urges her older sister as she fingers their towel package.

"Toothpaste, a toothbrush, and look—a real harmonica, not a toy!" Elisabet presses it to her lips, breathing into it and making some sounds.

"Edel and I got the same, wash cloths, some socks, and a dumb toy car," says Heinz.

Edel grabs the small car, drops to the floor, and pushes it around the room.

"I guess there is only one harmonica. I'll let you play it too, Helena, but you have to be careful. Wait 'til teacher hears. Maybe she'll teach me some music. You know how I love to sing." Elisabet blows on the harmonica.

Thump, thump, thump.

"Oh, oh, we're too noisy. Why don't you practice your harmonica in the barn? Don't run down the stairs. Be quiet as mice," Marike says.

After the children have left and she has thanked and said good-bye to the Mennonite worker, Marike carefully folds the towels and washcloths. As she does so, a slip of paper, written in German, falls out. "We pray your family and you will find a safe, free home."

Marike reads the words again and then presses the paper to her heart. "If only," she says to herself.

Thump, thump, the floor shakes.

"I'm coming," she says, and hurries downstairs to be greeted by a stern-faced Mr. Boehr.

"Girl, you think I have all day. Just because it is Christmas doesn't mean the chores can wait," Mr. Boehr shouts.

"I'm on my way."

"And another thing, your children sound like a herd of cattle. If you can't keep them from stomping up and down the stairs, you'll have to leave—even if it's Christmas."

"I'll try."

"What'd you say?" He pushes his ear horn against his good ear. "Oh, forget it. Besides, you didn't put the manure where I told you. Don't you know anything?"

"I put it on the pile right where you told me." Marike walks to the door.

"Next to the pile, make a new pile." Mr. Boehr shakes his cane.

"But I thought you said..."

"Don't argue. Now, here is the list for today. See if you can get this right for a change."

As Marike leaves, she hears the old man grumbling, "This woman and her noisy children, why couldn't they send me a young, strong girl?"

Hurrying to the barn, Marike slides her hand into her coat pocket. Yes, the note is still there. The note came from an American. If only someday, they could have a real home—in America. It seems like such a dream. How long ago was it she filled out all of the papers? And yet, still there is no word. She must think about the American gifts she has received—the shoes and now these things. Could they be signs? She will have to work harder.

Marike grabs the pitchfork and begins piling the horse manure in the wheelbarrow. Switching its tail, the horse backs away from her, ears up. Softly she talks to him, reassuring him and promising more feed. Turning to move the wheelbarrow, she is surprised to find Heinz pushing it to the next stall. With the two of them working together, Marike quickly completes her chores. Little Edel follows them, begging to be allowed to help. Instead of telling him he is too small, Marike suggests Edel help carry the milk pail when she finishes milking. Some straw falls on Marike's head. In the barn's dust-filled light, she looks up to the hayloft and hears a harmonica's wheezing notes. Marike calls Elisabet and Helena to join her as she returns to the house. Marike reminds the children that today they will make their Christmas treat. Heinz offers to bring wood for the stove and Elisabet and Helena offer to help her stir the batter. Pulling her coat collar up around her chin against the cold December wind, Marike follows her older children.

She recalls her excitement as a child when her dear mutter taught her how to bake their special Christmas treats. Ilsa was famous for her baking, and when the relatives gathered for a wedding or celebration, they always asked her to bring her baked goods. Rubbing her cold, dripping nose with the back of her hand, Marike reminisces about the delicious smell of her mother's pastries and the happiness she shared with her ten siblings. She remembers her warm and patient mother, and how her father could be strict but still kind. How she yearns to give happy family memories to her children, but sometimes, she feels too tired.

Entering her kitchen, she finds Heinz lighting the fire in their stove. Elisabet places the large mixing bowl, wooden spoon, flour, milk, and precious sugar on the table. After hanging her coat and scarf on the peg next to the door, Marike begins scrubbing her hands in the kitchen sink. The steaming hot water revives the feeling in her numb fingers.

"Thanks, Heinz." Marike stretches her hands over the warm stove.

"What about me? See what I did." Elisabet points to the table.

"Smart girl, Elisabet, you got things ready. Now, I'll tell you what to put in the bowl."

"I wanna help too," Helena says, peering into the empty bowl.

"Help your little brother take off his coat and entertain him. That will be a big help."

"Yes, Mutti, but I want to bake too."

"Next time. Why don't you take Edel in on the big bed? Maybe, he'll take a nap."

"Come Edel, I'll tell you a story." Helena leads him into the bedroom.

"Mutti, why didn't your mutter write down her recipes? It would be so much easier," Elisabet says.

"That's the way she learned. Now I'm teaching you." Before Marike can empty her handful of flour into the bowl, Elisabet thrusts a measuring cup under her mother's hand.

"I'm going to measure everything you use and write them down so I can bake too."

"Good idea, Elisabet. When we finish baking, you can make your gifts. I just have time before I have to milk again." Marike returns, carrying bits of cardboard, ribbon, string, and some broken crayons. Taking some flour, she adds a little water, making a thick paste.

"I have an idea. Elisabet, you fold the cardboard, and I'll draw," Heinz says.

"I want to draw too. I'm going to draw a pretty picture of baby Jesus." Elisabet chooses a crayon and begins coloring.

"I think I'll lie down and rest. When you can smell the stollen, carefully open the oven door and check it."

"Do we still have to share it with the Boehrs? They're so mean. They treat us like servants." Elisabet presses her black crayon so hard against the paper, it breaks.

"It's *Weihnachten.* Give me a few minutes and then wake me," Marike removes her apron and enters the bedroom.

"Don't forget, you promised to read my new book to us," Elisabet says without looking up, intent on her drawing.

"Don't worry, I will."

Later that evening, after they've eaten and snuggled under the covers, Marike opens Elisabet's new book and begins to read to them. Even though Heinz, Elisabet, and Helena can read, they enjoy how real the characters sound when their mother reads a story. Marike treasures their reading time, when her family seems the closest. After they finish their jobs and homework, no matter how tired she feels, Marike checks their homework, making certain they correct their mistakes. Each day, she reminds them how reading and studying will make their future.

She wants their future to be better than the misery they've suffered. Fortunately, the Mennonite worker offered a chance for one of Marike's children to live at a Mennonite school. She promised that the school provides better food, additional instruction, and even music classes.

Ever since their conversation, Marike has pondered which child she should select. If only she could send two children, but the woman had emphasized that Marike would be permitted to send only one child.

One of my children deserves this chance. How can I choose? Yet, I don't want to send any of my children away after all we've endured together. I don't want to rip us apart. I must choose. Heinz and Elisabet are older and able to help while Edel is so young. Rarely does Helena, my middle child, receive anything special, and she is so agreeable. She will be fine.

After they have celebrated Christmas and then welcomed the New Year of 1950, Marike decides to tell Helena about her decision. While Marike prepares their dinner, Helena chatters excitedly about her school project.

"Mutti, see what I drew."

Marike wipes her hands carefully on her apron and holds Helena's drawing up to the fading light.

"A dog. It's very nice dear."

Helena points at the drawing. "Not just any old dog, but the dog, Schlamper, in my book. Remember?"

Marike sits down. "I chose that book especially for you."

"Oh Mutti, I cried and cried when the children lost their dog right after they lost their vater. It reminded me of my vater." Helena looks sadly at her picture, then smiles. "When the children finally found their dog, I was happy."

"Are you going to put children in your drawing?" Marike asks.

"No, Schlamper is lost and looking for them. Besides, I'm not very good at drawing people."

Marike peers out the window at the full moon, which looks cold and distant. Giving Helena a hug, she whispers in her ear. Marike tells Helena she chose her for this honor to attend the Mennonite school.

Suddenly, Helena grabs her mother's waist. Marike gasps.

"I don't want to go. Please don't make me," Helena sobs.

Marike lifts her to her lap and rocks her as if she were much younger than her eight years. "Oh Helena, you're so lucky. It's a wonderful opportunity."

"Send Heinz or Elisabet then—but Mutti, not me, why just me?" Helena says, her face pale.

"I'm only allowed to send one child, and it will do you the most good," Marike says.

"But why don't you send Edel or Heinz or Elisabet?"

"Edel is too young, and Heinz and Elisabet too old." Marike sighs. "Helena, I worry about you. You're so thin. You will get better food to make you healthy. When I was your age, I went to a Mennonite school. It was wonderful. This is your chance to learn more, even more about our faith. Also, you will like the singing. With your good singing voice, you'll learn new songs. It's only for three months."

"Mutti, please don't send me away." Helena shakes while tears cascade down her cheeks. "I'll be good, I promise, please. I don't want to go. I don't want to be far away from you."

Marike continues patiently, "Helena, Bad Dürkheim is in the Rhineland-Palatinate. It's not far. I'll visit. You're lucky. Before the war, many Germans wanted to go to the Kurhaus. It was a favorite spa."

Between sobs, Helena asks, "What is a Kurhaus?"

"Like a mineral bath, but you will stay at the Mennonite School. It will be good for you—healthy food, good education." Marike rises, loosening Helena's hands. Turning to the stove, she resumes stirring their soup. While Helena continues pleading, Marike bites her lip.

If only I could tell her the other reason—all of Mr. Boehr's complaints about my noisy children. Even if he is old and sick, he doesn't have to be so demanding. Still, fewer children would mean less noise. I had to make a terrible choice. I'd rather lose an eye than give up one of my children. Yet, Mr. Boehr could demand we leave and ask for another family. Then, we might be moved to a much worse situation. I feel terrible sending her away, but I'll write her letters and visit her. I want her to be healthy, learn more, and make new friends. She will see. This is good for her. I want the very best for my sweet Helena.

Chapter 34

Two weeks later, having journeyed to Bad Dürkheim with Helena, Marike is reassured to discover friendly Mennonites who welcome them. The modest school includes a dormitory for sleeping and a schoolroom. The Mennonites, some of whom come from Canada, promise Helena healthy German food. Even though the teacher gives her a new coloring book and crayons, Helena's tears stain the cover as Marike puts on her coat. Marike hesitates, but the teacher urges her to leave quickly. As she walks down the narrow hallway, she hears Helena sobbing, "Mutti, Mutti, don't leave me. I'll be good, I promise." It is almost more than Marike can bear.

How ironic it is to be leaving one of my children when I've worked so hard to bring them together. How can it be right? It hurts so much. Yet, it must be good for Helena.

As Marike walks blindly down the street, she enters a small restaurant tucked between the larger wine shops. The waiter approaches, and Marike orders a small coffee. Looking at the empty tables, Marike is grateful the hour is early, and there are no other customers to observe her grief. Returning with her coffee, the waiter sets it gently on the small table and licks his straggly white moustache as he studies her intently.

"Did you visit the Kurhaus, or maybe come for the *Weinstrasse?*"

Marike samples her coffee, absorbed in her tortured thoughts. "No."

"Bad Dürkheim used to be a favorite leisure city before the war, but now it is forgotten, like a maiden aunt. The vineyards, their vines are a tangled mess. How we used to boast of having the largest wine festival. Still, nearby is the *Schlossgarten*. Too early for the flowers, but for a pretty lady like you, a walk in the palace gardens may be a comfort."

"I don't know. I don't have much time. Thank you anyway." Reaching in her purse, she pays for her coffee. It is all she has left.

Walking along the neglected paths, Marike imagines what flowers may be sleeping under the frost-covered dirt. If she had her pruning shears with her, she might begin snipping the rose bushes that have grown wild, as her mother did once, she thinks. Marike compares the neglected plants with her mother's once flourishing flower garden. Sometimes, her father would gently chide her mother for tending her flowers and forgetting her enormous kitchen garden. Marike bends down and carefully removes leaves from a green sprout.

"Dear sprout, you and my Helena grow and thrive. Two months from now, when I've saved enough for a ticket, I'll return. Then, she and I will enjoy your flowers," Marike whispers to the silent ground. Rising, she turns and hurries to catch her ride back to Zweibrücken and home to Heidelbingerhof.

Chapter 35

Marike stares helplessly at her bandaged hands. *How could I have been so careless, to spill hot grease on my hands? For years I fried food and never had an accident. Yet, this time, I had been distracted. What was it? Oh yes, Miss Boehr complaining about something. When I returned to the stove, the grease was smoking. Without thinking, I snatched up the hot pan, and hot grease spilled on my hands. Now, all I can do is wait and hope my hands heal soon.*

Marike thinks about Helena. If only Marike could write, then she could explain why she hasn't visited her. At least, she imagines that when Helena's grandmother visited and explained the circumstances to her, Helena understood. Marike hopes Helena has made friends and adjusted to her new surroundings.

Someone knocks. "Come in," Marike calls. Her mother-in-law enters. "Amalia, I'm so glad to see you." Marike clumsily shoves her bedding aside as she attempts to get out of bed.

"Don't get up. I'm fine and can only stay a minute." Amalia sets a chair near the bed and sits down, primly folding her hands in her lap.

"Why don't you take off your coat and rest awhile?"

"I can't. I have to return and prepare dinner. I just wanted to report on Helena. She doesn't look so peaked and has gained a few pounds, although she had several bouts of tonsillitis."

"Oh no, is she all right?"

"She is fine now," Amalia says. "The teacher said since she made a friend of an older girl, she doesn't cry as much. I told Helena about your hands. Clearly, she was disappointed I'd come and not you."

"Oh Amalia, I'm sorry. I hope she wasn't rude."

Amalia sniffs, presses her lips tightly together. "What can you expect from the child? No manners at all! Oh well, I try. As it is, the least I can do is give you a rest and take the children to the circus that is in town."

Using her elbows to raise herself, Marike leans forward. "Oh Amalia, a circus, it has been so long since they had any fun. And they work so hard. Too bad Helena can't go. She loves animals so much."

"Well, the child was disappointed, but I promised we'd save her a special treat."

"You told her?" Marike asks.

"Of course, you baby her too much. Life is hard. Helena needs to stop feeling sorry for herself. I have to go now. Oh yes, I wrote again to my cousin in America. Maybe we'll hear something soon. Goodbye dear."

"Thank you, Amalia, for visiting Helena. I'm certain she appreciated it. Goodbye." Exhausted, Marike collapses on the bed, murmuring, "It isn't the children's fault. It's mine. If only I'd been more careful."

Elisabet enters, straightens a pillow, and tenderly pulls up the covers over her mother before crossing to the bedroom door.

Marike smiles at her. "Elisabet, you're so kind. I have such good children. I'm so lucky."

"Mutter, why don't you rest now? Heinz and I can do the chores. Edel will bring you some water. It's our turn to help you."

Chapter 36

Marike's hands heal, and the three months pass. When she returns to Bad Dürkheim, spring flowers greet her. Helena, her pale cheeks now rosy, vigorously hugs her mother. Marike rejoices in Helena's renewed health.

That afternoon, on their train trip home, Marike recounts to Helena the recent changes on the farm. Old Mr. Boehr has died from pneumonia during the winter. His daughter, who never liked the farm, has leased it to a woman with four children. Then, Miss Boehr moved to the village, where she longed to live.

"Mutti, do we have to move again?" Helena asks.

"No, they said we can stay."

"Oh good. And now I'll have a friend."

"We'll see. The children are older than you. They may not want to play with you."

"Maybe not. I'll share my surprise. The one grandmother promised me. They'll like that." Helena grins.

"What surprise?" Marike asks.

"The one from the circus. Grandmother said she would buy me a special surprise."

Marike searches her memory but can't recall anything her mother-in-law may have saved for Helena. Maybe Heinz or Elisabet will know.

Helena snuggles against Marike, takes Marike's hand, and holds it against her cheek.

"Mutti, I missed you so much and cried every night. I'll be good. Promise you won't send me away again."

Marike bends over Helena, holding her tightly.

"I promise. But Helena, I didn't send you to the school to punish you, but to help you get stronger. Believe me." Marike struggles to soothe the hurt in Helena's teary eyes.

Finally we're together as a family with the children, their grandmother, and me. It isn't like when I was a child, with many brothers, sisters, cousins, aunts, and uncles. Always, someone shared the work, and when we could, we played. What happy times those were, and we didn't even know it. I wish I could give my children a family like I had. I never felt like a burden. I always felt needed and loved. I've tried to be a wall around my children, protecting them, to be both father and mother. I wanted so much to be the best mother, but I lacked my mother's patience.

Walking along the country road from Heidelbingerhof to the farm, Helena runs ahead of Marike to pick wild daisies. Skipping back, she thrusts her sweaty hand, clutching her bouquet, in front of Marike.

"For you, Mutti."

Marike kneels by Helena. "I love you, too." Even though the daisies are a harsh reminder of Denmark's national flower the daisy, Marike accepts them.

Before long, Helena and her mother return home. Immediately, Helena searches for her grandmother's gift. She asks her brothers and sister if they remember Amalia purchasing something for her at the circus.

Heinz, looks puzzled at first, then exclaims, "I know, just a minute." He hurries to the bedroom and returns with something in his fist. "Helena, close your eyes and hold out your hand."

"What is it?"

"Your surprise. Do as I told you," says Heinz.

Helena meekly obeys, covering her eyes with her left hand and extending her small right hand.

"There." Heinz sounds satisfied as he places a small object in her hand.

When Helena opens her eyes and looks at her hand, she sees a blue blob.

"I wanna see it too," says Edel.

"It looks like a balloon."

"She bought a balloon for you," says Heinz.

As she grasps it between her thumb and forefinger, Helena holds it up for everyone to see. "It's all used up. Look, it's shriveled."

"Somebody had to make sure there were no holes. What good would a balloon be with holes?" Heinz escapes into the bedroom and slams the door.

"But, Mutti..."

"Hush, dear. Why don't you show Edel and Elisabet your drawings?" Marike says, filling a glass with water and placing the daisies in it.

Without answering, Helena tosses the shriveled elastic in the wastebasket and follows her brother into the bedroom.

Marike watches and listens through the open door.

Sprawled on the bed, Heinz pretends to read his schoolbook. Helena marches to his side and stands silently, waiting. Heinz turns a page, than flings the book to the floor.

"Okay, I give up," says Heinz. "If I let you use my new pencil, will you promise not to break it?"

Helena sniffs. "You shouldn't have ruined my balloon."

"Balloons don't last. Don't you know anything?"

"It was my prize."

"Here, you can use my pencil, be careful."

"Thanks." Helena takes Heinz's pencil, holding it gingerly between her thumb and forefinger.

CAROL STRAZER

The next morning is Saturday. As soon as Helena is dressed, she joins Heinz and her mother on their way to the barn. While Heinz forks fresh hay to the cow, Marike milks.

Helena counts the kittens mewing around their empty milk bowl. The mother cat weaves in and out of Marike's stool.

Marike aims the cow's teat and showers the cat with milk. Satisfied, the cat pads away, licking her fur. Her kittens surround her; their tiny pink tongues catching milk drops.

Helena reaches down and captures a kitten, which wiggles and claws her arm.

"They're wild, you know, just barn cats," a voice says from the barn's doorway.

Startled, Helena drops the kitten.

"Hi, Agnes. Agnes Goertzer, this is Helena, my youngest daughter." Marike says to the tall girl twirling her pigtail. "Agnes' mother leases the farm."

"Hi, Agnes, would you like to play with my sister and me? Elisabet is very smart. She writes stories, and I draw pictures to go with them. You could help us."

"I can't."

"Why not?" Helena asks.

"My mother says it wouldn't be right. Besides, everyone knows you're going to America. Some Germans you are," Agnes says scornfully to Helena, before hurrying away.

Helena stares at Agnes' retreating back. "Mutti, I don't understand?"

"It's the old way. Those who own property think they're better and don't want to associate with us workers."

"But why did she say those things about America?"

"Envy, probably. Some people think Americans are rich, and Germans who go to America have an easy life."

"Does she hate Americans?" Helena asks.

— 224 —

"Some do. When Roosevelt signed the treaty at Yalta, many blamed him for giving Russia too much German soil. Stalin gobbled up German soil like it was caviar. But I think Roosevelt was very sick. He died soon after the conference."

Helena wrinkles her brow. "Maybe the Americans don't like Germans. What if they don't want us? We should have gone to Paraguay."

"Everything takes time." Marike tries to reassure Helena. *The child asks what I've asked myself many times. Where are the visas? Why are they taking so long? Why hasn't Amalia visited or heard anything? Maybe her cousin doesn't want us to come.*

Later, as the afternoon sun warms her back, Marike kneels and plants tiny seedlings in the kitchen garden. While she works, she plans a visit to her mother-in-law's home after tomorrow's church services.

The next day, Marike and her four children attend the Mennonite church. After the service, the pastor greets her and asks if they have had any news from America. Marike explains that the children and she will visit her mother-in-law this very afternoon, and they hope to hear good news. Hearing this, the children skip down the road, singing one of the songs that Helena learned from the Canadian Mennonites while she was in the Mennonite School. Birds flit across the newly ploughed and planted fields. Even the sunlight seems warmer, and the air is pungent with the smell of freshly ploughed earth. *Frühling* is truly the season of plans and new beginnings. If Marike wasn't so tired, she'd skip with her children. On a beautiful day like this, she hopes good news awaits them.

Marike is pleased that her children are not only well-behaved but loving when they arrive. Heinz opens Grandmother Amalia's door for them, Elisabet carries the basket of homemade bread and jam, and Helena helps her younger brother Edel remove his jacket. Marike dutifully inquires about Amalia's health. When the children become bored with the adult conversation, Elisabet politely asks if they may visit the animals in the barn.

When the children have left, Amalia sighs, reaches into her knitting basket, and withdraws a well-worn envelope with a United States' postmark. Silently, she hands it to Marike.

Marike withdraws a single sheet of paper from the already opened envelope. As she reads the letter, her smile disappears.

"I can't believe it. She died? I didn't think she was that sick."

"I didn't think it was serious," Amalia says.

"Poor Albert! How difficult this must be for him, to lose his dear wife."

"And for us!"

"Oh Amalia, I'm so sorry." Marike quickly embraces her mother-in-law.

"I didn't think you would want the children to know. They've had enough disappointments. No hope now. My first cousin was our only sponsor. My only American relative! We should have gone to Paraguay when we could."

Marike replaces the letter in the envelope and studies the return address: Albert Heinricks, Post Office Box 306, Brainerd, Kansas, United States of America.

"Please, Amalia, may I borrow a pencil and some paper? I know very little English, but I will copy his address. If I have your permission, the least I can do is send him my condolences. Since his German is good, he will be able to read my letter."

"You don't have to. I've already sent a note."

"I want to."

Discouraged, Marike calls the children to her, and they return home. When they ask about the plans for America, Marike crafts deliberately vague responses. Unaware of Marike's somber mood, the children discuss the new tenants. Marike decides to wait before telling them this latest news. Maybe things will change for the better.

For several days, Marike imagines what she will write while she plants the kitchen garden, milks the cow, and does anything else Frau Goertzer asks her to do. Since Frau Goertzer's four daughters help their mother with household tasks, Marike's chores now involve mostly farm work.

Finally, when Marike writes her letter to Albert—a man she has never met—she imagines how grief-stricken he must be. Feelings she'd ignored leak through her pen. She explains that it has been more than five years since she has heard about her husband Horst, who had been assigned to the Eastern Front. She writes that whenever she has an opportunity, she asks returning German soldiers who have been recently released from POW camps if they know anything about her husband. She sympathizes with the bedraggled survivors who bear little resemblance to the proud young men they had once been. So far, none knew about a Horst Wiens. Some told her of less-than-humane conditions in the camps, especially in the Siberian slave camps. As she writes this, her hand shakes. She stops writing.

Focusing on writing the letter helps her control her emotions. She writes, "I sympathize with your pain and terrible loss. I hope your Mennonite faith in Jesus Christ comforts you as it has me." If only she could find better words. Still, as she addresses the envelope, she hopes she touches his heart.

Sometime later, even the children have stopped asking her when they will go to America, but Marike refuses to give up all hope. To protect her children from further disappointment, she says little but thinks, *when—not if—we go to America*. Already, she has had to accept so much. Even though she wanted to protect her children, to preserve their childhood innocence and her close-knit family, the war has already stolen those things. *We, who believed in peace, had to struggle against the violence that threatened to destroy us.*

All that time she'd been hospitalized, the children had learned to fend for themselves, even though her sister-in-law had tried to help.

They'd survived. They had witnessed and experienced things no child should ever bear. It was too late for innocence. To survive, they had become little adults, independent and, to a degree, self-sufficient.

We can't go back and pretend to be the family we were. That is a past dream. And they will never need me in the old way, because to survive they went beyond what I could give, and I had to depend on them.

With these thoughts, Marike walks down the road to meet her children. Soon, they will have a break from school. As they approach, they dance with excitement, reminding her of her school days. She too, enjoys the fresh smell of hay, a meadowlark's song, and the sun warming her.

Without thinking, Marike suggests a walk to their Grandmother Amalia's. When Heinz questions her, she replies that it is a beautiful day for them to play hooky. Their chores can wait. At first, the children stare at their responsible mother, who is suggesting something so unbelievable. Then they laugh.

Suddenly, Elisabet's face becomes serious as she studies her mother. "Our visas—did they come?"

With her hands in her pocket, Marike shakes her head, but she can't stop grinning.

"You're smiling. You're teasing us," Elisabet says. "They came, didn't they?"

"I thought they would never come. Three long years we've waited," Heinz says.

"Never give up," Marike says, holding the envelope and their future to her chest.

"We want to see! Please, Mutti," Helena and Edel beg, tugging at her skirt.

Marike collapses under a tree while the children huddle around her. With a flourish, she lifts official-looking documents from an envelope.

"I can't read it," Helena complains.

"That is because it is in English. Did you think they would send us German papers?" Elisabet chides her younger sister.

"No, but..."

"Look, you can see your name, Helena Wiens," Elisabet points.

Kicking a rock, his shoulders hunched over and hands in his pockets, Heinz walks away down the road.

"Wait for us," Marike calls. "What's the matter?"

"What good are those now, without a sponsor?" Heinz asks. His voice is bitter.

"How did you know? You must have overheard Amalia and me talking, but you didn't tell the others her cousin died." With new respect, Marike regards her son. "However, her cousin's husband Mr. Heinrick is helping us. His sons and friends will be our sponsors. If they hadn't offered, then we never would have received our visas."

Chapter 37

The train's brakes screech as it nears the station. Marike wakes her sleeping children and urges them to gather their belongings.

"Look Mutti, it says Gronau." Elisabet points at the sign. "I know that name. It was on some of the packages we received from the MCC." Elisabet cranes her neck, peering out of the window.

"Some people from the Gronau Mennonite Church are supposed to meet us. Help Edel with his sweater and hurry. I'll get the suitcase."

"It's too hot. I don't want to wear it." Edel tugs at the sweater.

"I know it's hot, even for July, but I don't want you to lose it," Marike says. "Heinz, help your Grandmother Amalia with her suitcase."

"You're a good boy, Heinz, just like your father." Amalia lurches forward, grabbing the seat back and steadying herself.

"Why are we getting off here? We're almost at the border," Heinz asks.

"Your mother wrote the MCC. The Mennonites in Gronau will help us with our travel arrangements," Amalia answers.

"Look everyone, someone is waving at us." Marike leads her family to a white-haired man who introduces himself as Mr. Peter Dirksen from the Mennonite Central Committee—the MCC.

Mr. Dirksen assumes the role of guide as they travel in the direction of the MCC housing. Pointing at the Gronau meetinghouse, he explains it was bombed in an Allied raid, but its replacement is nearly finished. Marike asks him to convey their appreciation for the packages they received from their MCC membership. The children chime in, telling him about their memories of the parcels. Mr. Dirksen assures them he will express their gratitude to the Director of the Mennonite Central Committee.

After they arrive at the MCC camp, they find conversation with Mrs. Dirksen more difficult. Her Dutch accent is hard to understand. Yet, they need no words when she gestures towards the meal she has prepared for them. "Until 1922," Mr. Dirksen explains, "the pastors and membership spoke Dutch, though they were MCC members and part of Germany. Their Dutch ancestors, as pioneer industrialists, helped establish Gronau's large cotton textile mills and their church. Since 1946, the Mennonite Central Committee had helped many refugees from Russia and Danzig emigrate—even to Paraguay. Their location on the Dutch and German border in Westphalia, Germany, and their small membership had aided many. With their understanding of Dutch, they helped those traveling to Rotterdam's ships."

After his long discourse, Mr. Dirksen pauses and clears his throat. "They told me you have visas for America and have booked passage on the Volendam. Even though our membership is small, we'll do what we can to help. The needs are great, and we have little money left."

Marike reassures him that Mr. Heinricks has provided them with both tickets and some funds. Aware of the MCC's limited resources, Marike refrains from mentioning how meager their funds actually are.

Following their meal, Marike and Elisabet remove the tableware and, despite Mrs. Dirksen's protests, wash the dishes. Amalia sits glumly at the table, staring out the window at the nearby barracks.

When Marike returns, wiping her hands on a towel, Amalia rises quickly, upsetting her chair. "Thank you and the Committee for your kindness, but we must leave."

"But you can't—your photos, papers…We must help you," Mr. Dirksen says loudly.

The children stop talking and stare at their grandmother.

Marike hurries to Amalia's side. "What is it?"

Amalia's facial muscles twitch as her mouth moves without any sounds. Whispering, she says in a shaky voice, "The barracks. I can't stay in barracks, never again."

As she reassures her mother-in-law, Marike tells Mr. Dirksen why Amalia is upset.

His bushy eyebrows, raised in puzzlement, soon relax. "Three years? You spent three years in refugee camps? Now, I understand. Come, there is a hotel nearby that is not too damaged. It's managed by a kind widow."

After thanking their hosts, Amalia, Marike, and the family leave. Carrying the family's green wooden chest, Mr. Dirksen leads the way. He says, "Tomorrow will be soon enough to take photos and complete papers."

Two days later, Mr. Dirksen drives Amalia, Marike, and her family to the station, where they board a train for Rotterdam.

As they cross the German border into the Netherlands, Heinz says, "Mutter, I never thought this is how I'd spend my birthday. July 10, 1950, has to be the happiest day of my life."

As the train sways from side to side, Rotterdam appears. Workers thread their way through rubble. Like a phoenix rising from the ashes, some newly constructed buildings stand proudly beside the decimated, bombed rubble.

Heinz says, "Mr. Dirksen said not to be surprised at how terrible Holland looks."

Elisabet interrupts, "You mean the Netherlands."

"All right, the Netherlands. He said years after Hitler bombed it, they're just rebuilding Rotterdam."

"Why did he bomb it?" Helena asks.

"He thought the Dutch would give up easily. When they didn't, he sent in the *Luftwaffe*. The heart of the city was destroyed, and many lost their homes. It was his warning, so they capitulated."

"War is bad," Helena states.

Thoughtfully, the children look out the train window. Marike studies the other passengers, wondering what they're thinking. Seated behind them, a noisy German family stops talking as they, too, look at the devastated city. Except for the sound of the train wheels clacking, everyone is silent. *I wonder what they feel—guilt, regret, or pity—when they see so much destruction.* To distract her children, Marike asks, "Who knows how Rotterdam was named?"

"I do," Heinz says. "Our teacher said Rotterdam was named for a stream called *Rotte* or *Rotta*, which means 'muddy,' and they had to build a dike on it to keep it from flooding."

"The Dutch built a dam, so *Rotta dam*. I see," Elisabet answers.

"I had it first."

"Yes, you did," Amalia smiles proudly at her grandson. "It is one of the largest, busiest ports in all of Europe, and soon we'll board our ship, the *Volendam*."

Elisabet groans, "Oh no."

But Marike barely hears her as Heinz says, "I remember Vater told me how long ago we Mennonites came from the Netherlands."

Soon Marike and Heinz are discussing how the Dutch showed the early Mennonites how to build dikes to drain the marshes. Later, when Russian Queen Catherine invited them to settle Prussian marshland, they applied the same techniques and became successful farmers.

The conductor interrupts their conversation to announce their destination. After leaving the train station, they find local transportation to the harbor.

Chapter 38

"Elisabet, what is wrong?"
"Oh Mutti, I can't do it."
"What?"

"Don't make me go on that ship." Elisabet stops walking, sits down, and hugs her knees.

Other people, following them on the pier, walk around her.

"Children, wait, come here," Marike says.

Breathing heavily, Amalia stops, "Now what? We'll be late. Elisabet, don't make one of your scenes."

Elisabet buries her head in her arms.

"Marike, you must control that child."

"Amalia, watch the other children."

Marike kneels beside Elisabet, her arm around her shoulders to protect her from Amalia's thoughtless comment. Elisabet shudders.

"I don't mean to make trouble."

"So many years ago, and I thought you had forgotten when you had to climb the ship's ladder. Am I right?"

"Please don't make me. I'm scared. I'll fall and drown."

"I promise this time will be different. You'll see."

Hesitantly, Elisabet stands. Marike squeezes her shoulder.

"Marike, hurry, there isn't time," Amalia yells something more, which disappears in the loud blasts from a ship's horn.

When Marike rejoins Amalia, she discovers Amalia talking to two uniformed officials.

The taller man of the two says sternly, "Sorry, we can't let anyone board without first seeing their visas and papers."

Amalia turns to Marike, "Well, show them our papers."

"I put them in my little suitcase for safekeeping. And the suitcase with our chest was loaded with the other luggage. How was I to know we'd have to show our papers before they would let us board?"

Elisabet asks shrilly, "Does that mean we can't go to America?"

"Hush, I'm sure there must be a way." Marike looks imploringly at the kind-faced official. He hails a sailor, explaining their dilemma. The boyish-looking sailor urges Marike to follow him onto the ship and down into the hold where their luggage is stowed. At first, Marike has difficulty identifying her suitcase among so many, but then she finds it, hidden behind their green chest. This time, she makes certain she has everything as she withdraws their visas, photos, and other papers before closing the suitcase.

Returning to the officials, she shows them their documents.

"Who are your sponsors?" he asks.

"My cousin's husband, Albert Heinricks," Amalia says.

"I don't see his name listed. Each person has to have a sponsor, a place to live, and some means of support," the tall official recites in a bored voice.

"Amalia, remember Cousin Heinricks is too old, so his two sons and their families are our sponsors?"

"Housing?"

"Yes, Mr. Heinricks has a house for us."

"Job?"

"I'm to live with and care for Mr. Heinricks," Amalia replies proudly.

"Are these your four children?" he asks Amalia, sounding

perplexed. "They're listed on your papers. And who are you?" he asks Marike.

"I beg your pardon?" Marike asks, peering over Amalia's shoulder at the paper and seeing Heinz, Elisabet, Helena and Edel's names printed under Amalia Wiens' name.

"What now?" Amalia asks.

Marike points at the paper. "There must be some mistake," she pleads. Behind her, weary travelers complain about their long wait. "These children are mine."

"I'm hungry, Mutti." Edel clings to Marike.

"Max, forget it, let the poor women go." The younger official smiles at them. "Someone always makes a mistake." Although weary, Marike returns his smile.

Sighing, Max waves them aboard the ship.

Chapter 39

Several days later, Marike and the children sit in deck chairs, watching the ship's bow as it rises and falls below the distant horizon. Black storm clouds appear in the distance. Each time the *Volendam* drops into another huge trough, sea water streams across the deck.

Heinz yells, "Look Edel, lift your feet," as Heinz raises his own feet above the water.

The children laugh and lift their feet as the water slides in their direction. When the viscous mass retreats, they place their feet on the deck and wait for the next wave. It becomes a game of who can wait the longest before removing their feet while the sea water curls around them.

"Where's grandmother?" Helena asks.

"Inside...eating...can you imagine? I never want to eat again. I'm so sick," Elisabet clamps her mouth shut.

"None of us can, except for your grandmother," Marike says.

"I want to go home now. My tummy hurts." Edel slides off his deck chair as the ship slams into a huge wave. Marike quickly grabs Edel's arm and pulls him into the safety of her chair.

"There, there, hang onto my chair. Soon we'll be in our new home."

"America?"

"Yes."

"Today?"

"No, not for almost a week." Marike gently rubs Edel's shoulders.

"I heard the captain tell someone we're headed through the Straits of Dover. Soon, we're going to stop in Le Havre, France, for more passengers. Then, we'll go through the English Channel, across the Atlantic, and some people will disembark in Halifax, Nova Scotia," Heinz exclaims.

"I want to go home. I'm afraid my kittens will die," Helena's mouth quivers.

"The Goertzers will feed them. We'll get some more kittens in America. You'll see," Heinz says.

"I wish I could as easily replace my friends from school—Lena and Anna," Elisabet says. "It's not fair. As soon as I make friends, we have to leave. Oh no, I think I'm going to ..." She runs to the railing, where she vomits.

"I thought if we stayed on deck, the fresh air might help. Look, it's starting to rain. Come inside. A cool washcloth will help you, Elisabet. Watch your step. The deck is slippery." Marike helps them step over the portal.

Heinz and Edel turn to their right while Marike, Elisabet, and Helena step to their left. As they leave, Marike hears Edel's cries.

"I want my mutti. Let me go, Heinz."

"Come on, Edel. We have to stay with the men. Only babies get to stay with their mutters. Don't you want to be a big boy?"

"I guess so."

"Besides, Mutter and Elisabet are seasick. They need to rest. You know men aren't allowed in the women's dorm. You can stay in my bunk, where we can look out the porthole."

Chapter 40

"Mutti, Mutti, you must come and see." Elisabet grabs her mother's hand, pulling her forward towards the ship's bow.

"What? Wait, I have to help Edel with his shoe."

"Look, the Statue of Liberty, just like they told us." Heinz points excitedly at the enormous statue.

Helena holds a pretend torch over her head and spins around. "I'm going to be just like her."

Heinz catches her. "Silly, you're going to fall down."

"Are we there yet?" asks Edel.

Tying Edel's shoelaces, Marike says, "We're here. New York Harbor."

"When do we get off the ship?" Edel asks.

"We'll go down below and pack, but it will take time for a big ship like ours to dock and unload."

"Mutti, are we going to that island—Ellis Island?" asks Elisabet.

"Didn't you hear the captain announce we're going to Hoboken, New Jersey?" asks Heinz.

"Is it near Kansas? I have to pee," Edel jumps up and down. Marike takes his hand and leads him inside. Hesitantly, Heinz, Elisabet, and Helena follow them.

Later, as the hot summer sun beats relentlessly on them, Amalia, Marike, her children, and other immigrants from their ship wait in long lines for United States immigration officials to process them. One spokesman informs them in German that doctors will examine them for lice, eye diseases, and other health problems.

Amalia straightens her shoulders, lifts her chin, and whispers to Marike, "Who do they think we are? We Germans are a clean people. Lice, how disgusting!"

Marike worries that her children could have caught something. Fortunately, the doctor seems only interested in Marike's long hospital stay in Denmark. He listens to her lungs, which she knows still don't sound clear, and keeps asking, "TB?"

After all of this time, if he tells me I can't enter America, what will I do? I must make him understand. "Pleurisy, nicht TB," Marike repeats and shakes her head. Nearby, a German woman who speaks some English translates until the doctor comprehends. The harried doctor sends them to another line.

As she waits, Marike hears a scuffle and turns to see two uniformed men leading a boy away while his mother clutches his arm, pleading that they release her son.

"Mutti, are they Gestapo? Why are they taking him?" asks Elisabet.

"Policemen. I think they quarantine anyone with a contagious disease."

"I don't see how they can, after we've come so far," Amalia says.

"I suppose they're afraid and want to protect Americans," Marike says.

"They should know we are a hard-working, honest people." Amalia stomps off.

Soon they show their papers, answer many questions, and just as the sun is edging to the horizon, they are granted permission to enter the United States.

With perspiring foreheads, Amalia, Marike, and her four children lug their chest and suitcases and exit the immigration offices.

Everywhere Marike looks, she sees people—mostly immigrants. She wonders what they, like she and her family, have had to endure to earn their freedom.

"Isn't someone from the MCC supposed to meet us?" Amalia asks. "They will never find us in this crowd."

"Wait. In the distance, see that man? He holds a sign. It looks like, yes, it has WIENS printed on it," Marike exclaims.

When they frantically wave at him, the man joins them. In German, he introduces himself as Mr. Kornelson.

While he talks, they follow him toward his parked car, a late model Studebaker. The children stop and stare across New York's harbor at Manhattan's tall buildings. Marike can guess their thoughts—no bombed-out buildings, no sunken ships in the harbor, safe from harm.

"Hoboken, New Jersey, how strange it sounds. Almost Dutch," Marike says.

Mr. Kornelson says that it once was called New Netherland. From marshes and pastures, Hoboken, near New York Harbor, has grown to be a major transportation port.

After the family squeezes into his car, Mr. Kornelson points out the Hudson River. Heinz and Elisabet create a game, competing to see who can read the most street signs.

"W...a...s...h...i...n...g...t...o...n," Heinz calls out the letters.

"A...d...a...m...s," Elisabet says.

"Washington, Adams, if you could read all the signs, you'd know America's presidents. Washington was General Washington, fought for American independence from the British, first president," Mr. Kornelson explains.

"Mr. Kornelson, you are so kind to help us and take time from your work," Marike says.

He shrugs modestly, "It's nothing. When my family came from Germany, the MCC helped us."

"We might not have made it in those camps if we hadn't received those MCC packages," Marike looks out the car window at the distant past.

"I'm tired. When do we get there?" Edel demands.

Mr. Kornelson chuckles, "I imagine so, young fellow. You must be about the same age as my son. He's five." He takes his hand off the steering wheel to run his hand through Edel's unruly hair.

"I'm seven," Edel sits up to make himself look taller.

"Edel," Marike corrects him, "you're not seven yet. When you are, you will celebrate your birthday in your new American home. I always knew we'd make it to America—and a better life." Marike hums contentedly.

"You folks must be hungry." Mr. Kornelson glances in his rear view mirror at the children. "My wife packed some food for you. You can eat now or when you get on the Pennsy."

"What did you say? The what?" Heinz asks.

"The Pennsy we call it, the Pennsylvania Railroad. It'll take you to Akron, Pennsylvania, where you'll spend the night at the MCC. Somebody will meet you at that station."

"This Pennsy, as you call it, is it very big?" Heinz asks.

"Big? Why, it's one of the bigger railroads in the United States," Mr. Kornelson says. Then he carefully backs into a curbside parking space, behind a truck advertising Sunbeam bread. "You'll see their sign, a keystone in red with interlocking letters: RPR, for Pennsylvania Railroad."

"Will the Pennsy take us to Newton, Kansas?" Elisabet yells over the traffic noise as she opens the car door onto the street.

"Careful, New York cabbies will run you down. Now, you have everything—trunk, suitcase? I'll help you with your luggage and tickets. You'll have to change trains in Chicago." Mr. Kornelson carries their trunk. Marike clutches the suitcase in one hand and Edel's sweaty palm in the other. While Heinz helps his grandmother, Elisabet and Helena join him.

"Follow me," Mr. Kornelson yells as he uses their chest to part his way through the large throng squeezing into the railway station. They barely have time to look around before he guides them to the ticket counter and helps them purchase their tickets. Before he leaves, each of the girls curtsies. While Amalia and Marike mouth their thanks over the blaring loudspeaker, the boys bob their heads in modified bows.

Pointing at their tickets and the clock, Mr. Kornelson tells them their train will be arriving in two hours to take them to the MCC in Akron, Pennsylvania. He shows them the track where the train will arrive. Then they watch as he disappears into the crowd.

Marike wishes he could stay until their train arrives, but she understands he can't leave his automobile without getting a ticket. As people hurry by them, Marike expects to hear them speaking English, but is surprised to hear many foreign tongues. When she hears an elderly woman speaking German, she quickly follows her and asks her to point out the toilets.

Once they've washed off the city's grime, they return to their bench and unpack Mrs. Kornelson's sandwiches and apples.

"This must be Sunbeam bread. It's so white and soft. Look, I can squeeze it," Elisabet pinches her sandwich.

"What is this brown stuff with nuts?" Heinz pulls his bread apart, peering suspiciously inside.

"I'll bet it is peanut butter. Everybody says Americans love it," Elisabet says knowingly.

"Yeah, that and gum. See that sailor over there. You can tell he is an American, because he is chewing gum."

"Of course he is American. He has an American uniform. You don't know. He could be chewing tobacco."

"Elisabet, Americans don't chew tobacco. They smoke cigarettes or chew gum," says Heinz.

The loud speaker squawks.

"Quiet, I think they are announcing our train," Marike says.

"Who can understand such gibberish? I don't understand why anyone would ever want to learn English. Such an ugly language," Amalia complains.

Marike explains, "I heard our track number and Akron. See… our train is coming." *At least, the children won't be seasick on the train. They look tired. No wonder—they were too seasick to sleep. We still have so far to go to reach Kansas—across six states, Mr. Kornelson said. America must be enormous. I'm exhausted. When we arrive in Akron, we will be able to rest until we catch the next train.*

Chapter 41

Marike, Amalia, and the children have barely settled in their seats when the train begins to move away from the station.

"Mutti, what was the MCC service like?" Elisabet asks.

With a yawn, Marike covers her mouth and says, "I'm sorry to admit I kept dozing off."

Amalia sniffs, "No wonder. We arrived in Akron late last night. I'd barely fallen asleep when someone banged on the door, announcing services."

"At least the children were allowed to sleep. When I checked on them in the MCC's dormitory, they were sound asleep." Marike glances at Helena.

"I heard them wake you," Helena says. "When you told the lady we needed our sleep, I wanted to hug you. Instead, I shut my eyes tight, because I didn't want her to know I was awake."

"Fortunate child. I hardly had any sleep before they took us to the train station." Amalia's eyes begin closing as she mumbles, "No consideration. They should have let us rest after our long journey." Her head bobs as the train jerks forward.

Gazing out the train window at the receding city buildings, Marike doesn't notice Amalia is asleep. She says, "I was so tired I can't remember if I even properly thanked the director for all of their help." When she hears Amalia making a puffing noise, Marike turns her head to see Amalia dozing and her children's sleepy faces. Soon, their lack of sleep, the humid heat, and the train's clacking wheels lull them into a torpid state.

Exhausted, they barely notice the changing countryside as their train chugs from Pennsylvania through Ohio to Indiana and then to Illinois.

Finally, after many hours, they arrive at Chicago's Union Station. As Marike hurries the children and Amalia off their train, she is relieved to see a man waving his hat in their direction. Could this be someone the Mennonite Central Committee has sent to meet them?

Since there are other people calling to various passengers, she isn't certain. Although she decides he looks more European than American, as he wears a wool suit on this hot summer day. Removing his hat and bowing slightly, he uses a white handkerchief to wipe perspiration off his forehead.

"It's probably his only suit," Amalia whispers before he approaches them.

"Mrs. Wiens?" he asks in English, looking first at one woman than the other.

"Yes," Amalia and Marike answer, before Marike explains that they are both Mrs. Wiens.

Switching to German, he says he understands and that the MCC has sent him, Frederick Sawatzky, to assist them. "I'll direct you to your train on the Atchison Topeka and Santa Fe. I checked the schedule, and it's running late. We have plenty of time. Let's get your luggage first."

Marike introduces Amalia. Mr. Sawatzky takes Amalia's arm and leads them through Union Station to an area where luggage is being brought on large carts. While they wait with other passengers, Edel runs in the direction of a newspaper stand. Marike sends Heinz to retrieve his brother. As soon as Edel sees his brother approaching, he runs in the opposite direction. Soon a game of "catch me if you can" ensues.

"They could get lost," Amalia warns.

In the meantime, Elisabet and Helena look for signs of a *Toilette*. Sizing up the situation, Mr. Sawatzky calls the boys to him and then points the way to the Toilette for the girls. After Marike has provided him with their claim check and a description of their green trunk, he retrieves it from the large luggage pile. Once he has helped them purchase their train tickets and check their trunk, Mr. Sawatzky leaves. The family waits for their train.

"Mutti, I'm too hot," Edel says.

Elisabet pulls at her dress, "It sticks to me."

"I'm thirsty," Helena says.

"Please, Mutti, I'm thirsty too," says Edel.

"For goodness sakes, Edel," Amalia says, "you're too old to be whining like a baby. We're all hot. Take your sweater off. But don't lose it."

Looking around the large, noisy train station, Marike says, "I don't see a water fountain."

"Why can't I look for one? I'll bet I could find it." Heinz glances around. "I'm good at finding things."

"You'll get lost, miss the train, and then what will I do? No, better we stay together," Marike says.

"Aw Mutti, you forget I'm twelve now. I won't get lost. I promise." Heinz stands up and starts to walk away.

"Heinz, no, you might miss the train."

"Mutti, look, that funny looking lady is coming over here," Helena says.

"And she looks like she's covered in chocolate, why?" Edel asks.

"That's her skin color," Heinz replies. "Like ours is white."

"I'm not white. I'm pink," Elisabet says as she pinches her arm. "I've never seen anyone like her before, except at the play at our camp. Remember, when the actors put black stuff on their faces and sang?"

"Quiet, she's coming over here."

The woman, dressed in a brightly flowered dress and a matching wide-brimmed hat, strides towards them. Clutched in her hands are two sweaty bottles.

"Hi, you all, I'm Tizzy. That's short for Elizabeth Ann. All my friends call me Tizzy. Your children looked so hot; I thought they'd like a coke. Y'all look like you've been traveling a long time. Maybe you come from one of those foreign countries we hear about on the radio. I've got children, too—eight, all grown and scattered. I'm here visiting my oldest child." Tizzy stops, takes a deep breath, and grins.

As they stare in astonishment at Tizzy, Marike wonders what she has said.

"*Deutsch sprechen?*" Marike asks hopefully.

"No, nooo." Tizzy shouts, as if shouting will make it easier for Marike to understand.

"*Nein,* no," Marike repeats, disappointed.

"Coke—for the children," Tizzy says handing the dark bottles to Marike.

"Coke," they repeat.

Raising her hand as if holding an imaginary bottle, Tizzy pretends to drink, and then, she points at Edel.

Marike tentatively holds the glass bottles in front of her and peers at the strange liquid. "*Dankeschön,*" she says, with the children echoing her thanks.

"Y'all welcome. You have a safe journey, you hear. Bye now." Tizzy hurries away.

Amalia, who sat silently with her lips pressed tightly together, says "*Deutschfeindlich?*"

"What do you mean—German enemy?" Marike asks.

"She could try to poison us. After all, Americans bombed us.

You've forgotten Danzig? You're too trusting. You have no idea what she was saying. Throw that stuff away."

"It's too late." Marike watches as the children drink. As Helena tastes the Coke, her lips turn down in disgust. She hands the bottle to Edel, who takes large gulps, spilling some down his chin.

"Anyway," Amalia continues, "it's not proper to talk to those people. 'Coloreds,' I heard some Americans call them."

"She was being kind, that's all. I think she understands what it's like to be unwanted."

After they drink their cokes, the children question Marike about their trip. She recites what Mr. Sawatzky told her. They will travel south through Illinois, then turn west across Missouri until they reach the state of Kansas. She recalls the names of some of the cities: St. Louis, Kansas City, Topeka. Marike's restless children ignore her comments. Instead, they demand to know how much longer it will be until their journey is over.

They want to know how much farther we must travel until we reach our new home in Kansas. How wonderful it sounds when they say "our new home."

Many hours later, while the children doze fitfully, Marike studies the scenery as it evolves outside her window. She marvels at America's enormous vastness, although the prosperous metropolitan areas sadly remind her of Germany's once flourishing cities. Marike grimaces, especially as she recalls the piles of rubble of what was once the proud, treasured city of Danzig. Its history and architecture, like many of its citizens, are now buried forever.

In the distance, the farm houses seem like small dots on the horizon. When they were in Chicago, she could smell the slaughter yards. Now, their train car smells of stale cigar smoke, of bratwurst and cheese from their recent sandwiches, and of body smells she'd long ago learned to ignore.

In the bright sunlight, she recognizes the yellow wheat fields nodding in the wind. Soon, they will be harvested and feed many people. How peaceful they look as they stretch endlessly before her under the blue sky. Here, as in the cities, the war has left no traces.

Across the aisle, a father identifies landmarks for his young son. Even though Marike doesn't understand his words, his loving patience touches her. *It is the way he inclines his head in the direction of his son, as if he listens with his entire being—like my Horst would do. It has been five years since I read that terrible word—missing. Should I give up? If Horst came back, how would he find us?*

"Mutti?" Helena asks, concerned at her mother's silence.

Roused from her sad reverie, Marike touches her daughter's small face and redirects Helena's attention outside their window, where a farmer drives his tractor and baler.

"Newton, Newton, next stop Newton," the conductor calls loudly.

When she hears the brakes screeching and sees the train depot, Marike wakes her children. After the train has stopped, the conductor says something that Marike doesn't understand. She correctly guesses he is saying it will be a brief stop, and they must hurry to get off the train before it starts moving again.

"Amalia, children, you must hurry."

"What?" Awakened from her nap, Amalia appears confused.

"We're here...in Newton...the train will start again. We must get off now." Marike helps her mother-in-law stand while she urges the children to the train car's door. Amalia carefully descends the steps and takes the waiting porter's gloved hand as she steps off onto the platform.

Marike marvels at how gracefully her mother-in-law executes this small act. *If I didn't know differently, I'd believe she was a wealthy landowner.* Quickly, Marike and her children follow Amalia down the platform into the train station. Hardly have they entered, when a white-haired man, bent like a question mark over his cane, limps toward them. He stops, spreads his arms wide, and embraces them.

"*Willkommen*, Cousin Amalia."

"Cousin Albert."

As the children's grandmother and Cousin Albert exchange greetings, other train passengers walk around them. At last, Amalia introduces Marike and the children. Elisabet and Helena curtsy, and the boys bow and shake his hand.

"Such manners, like in old Prussia," says Albert.

"In these times," Amalia says, "It's not so easy to teach the young ones. Thank you for meeting us. I was afraid you wouldn't recognize us since we've never met."

"It was nothing. I just looked for two women and four children. But, I'm afraid my German is not too good."

"It's fine. You don't know how relieved we are to speak German," Amalia smiles gratefully.

They squeeze into Cousin Albert's car. He soon turns and drives on Kansas Highway 196. He tells them that they are headed in the direction of Meadowlark Road and Brainerd.

"Cousin Albert?"

"Yes, Helena, what is it?"

"Over there, those huge flowers, what are they?" Helena points.

Marike and the children gaze at the large flowers with their golden petals fingering the breeze.

"Sunflowers. Those are sunflowers, the state flower. There are lots in Kansas, growing in the ditches, everywhere. Some farmers think they're a nuisance."

Amalia says, "Sunflowers, the state flower, you say? Enormous is what I'd call them—like everything in America."

"I like them," Helena says. "Remember, Mutti, the daisies in Denmark?"

"I don't care about any stupid flowers," Heinz complains. "Tell us about Kansas."

"When you go to school," Albert says, "you will study Kansas history. The state animal is the buffalo, but there are not many left now. Over there, you see that clump of trees by the stream? Those are cottonwoods. The cottonwood is the state tree. And when you read about the tribulations of Kansas' early settlers, you will understand why the state motto is 'To the stars through difficulties.'"

"To the stars through difficulties, that's us," says Elisabet. "I can hardly wait to go to a regular school, but I'm scared. I don't know English. What if they put me with the little kids?"

Heinz blusters, "They'd better not put me with the babies."

To the children's cries, Marike reassures them, "All my children are smart. You will catch up."

As they drive past several farmhouses, Marike studies the clapboard houses with their abundant kitchen gardens surrounded by fences. One woman, kneeling in her garden, shakes dirt from recently pulled carrots. Clutching her wind-whipped scarf in one hand, she waves. Marike and the children return her greeting.

Amalia says to Albert, "When we were in the camps, your dear wife wrote to me about her flower garden. She said that before she got sick, it was her favorite place. We'd never met, but I love flowers too. She—you were our only hope. Our other relatives in Berlin were starving."

Everyone is quiet.

Albert says, "It's nothing—my duty to my poor wife and church."

"Still, to take in six virtual strangers is so much. I hope you have a big house?" Marike asks.

"When it's ready, you and the children will have your own house," Albert says. "For now, you can stay with me in my home."

With the car windows down and hot breezes blowing around them, Marike hears a meadowlark singing happy notes. She welcomes the country smells of newly harvested wheat, even fresh manure's pungent odor. The flat, treeless land seems bursting with life as insects dance over the freshly harvested fields. Even the sky's intense morning blue is washed out in the midday heat. To their far right, dust dances a death spiral upward.

An hour later, they enter the small town of Brainerd.

"Across Broadway from the Missouri Pacific Depot," Cousin Albert points and describes, "is Brainerd's largest building. Once it was a hand-operated grain elevator. Over there, we have a feed store."

Cousin Albert stops in front of a two-story stone schoolhouse and explains this will be their new school. Then he says that on Sundays, he will drive their family to the Emmaus Mennonite church, which is more than two miles from town.

Suddenly, the hot wind blasts dust in their faces.

"Cousin Albert, are all Kansas roads made of dirt?" asks Heinz.

"Smart boy. In the country and small towns like Brainerd, the roads are unpaved. Remember, America is a young country, not old like Europe. We're still developing."

Edel points to the depot. "I like trains. Will it stop here in Brainerd?"

"Children, stop bothering your Cousin Albert," Amalia warns.

"They're just excited. They have waited so long to come to America," Marike interjects, hugging her children.

"Edel, trains used to stop here daily, but now only once a week, which is why you had to go to Newton." Albert pulls into a drive-way beside a white, clapboard house. The children fling open the car doors and jump out. Marike follows, smoothing her wrinkled skirt as she mops her wet brow with her sleeve.

Noticing Marike's efforts, Amalia says, "It must be at least thirty-five degrees Celsius, and humid. I feel like a limp rag. I hope it isn't like this all the time."

Cousin Albert joins them, straining under the weight of their luggage. "You ladies get out of this heat. It's cooler in my house."

As they enter, Marike is surprised to find the parlor filled with smiling people. She turns to Cousin Albert, who explains they are church members who have come to welcome them. He grasps Amalia's and Marike's hands in his and leads them to the center of the simply furnished parlor. The children follow. As they enter, the people stop conversing and turn to look at them.

"Thank you for coming," Cousin Albert addresses the group. Then, he gestures to Amalia. "This is my wife's cousin, Amalia Wiens, and her daughter-in-law, Marike, and her four children: Heinz, Elisabet, Helena, and Edel. They've had a long journey. Their story is truly amazing. Near the end of the war, they and other Prussians barely escaped the brutal Russian Allies. They spent more than three years in Denmark's crowded refugee camps. How they ever survived is truly incredible. Unfortunately, Marike's parents, like many other Prussians, did not. Then, Amalia, Marike, and the children were sent to work on a farm in French Occupied Germany. We must give them a hearty *Willkommen*."

Everyone claps.

The children smile, and Edel joins in the clapping as they curtsy and bow. In German, Amalia thanks her cousin and the guests as Cousin Albert translates for her.

Overwhelmed, Marike mumbles her appreciation and sinks into an empty rocking chair.

One of Cousin Albert's sons approaches her, bends down, and says, "We couldn't wait to meet you. For years, mother talked of nothing else. If only she could have been here. We almost gave up when an official told us that they wouldn't permit you to come unless there were more sponsors. Fortunately, some church members, my brother, and I were allowed to be your sponsors."

"We're very *Dankbar*, grateful, I think is the word. I still can't believe we're really here," Marike smiles. "Three years—I thought the visas would never come. And your father was so generous to pay for everything. Please tell everyone thank you."

While their guests visit, Cousin Albert's daughter-in-law appears. She claps her hands, demanding everyone's attention.

"Thank you for your wonderful dishes in honor of our brave relatives from Germany. Besides traditional American dishes like fried chicken and berry pies, we have prepared some of our favorite German recipes. For instance, we have *Gurkensalat*, cucumber salad; *Schnitzel*, breaded veal; *Wurst*, sausage; *Sauerbraten*, braised beef; *Brotchen*, rolls; and *Schwarzwälder Kirschtorte*, Black Forest cake."

Mesmerized, Marike's children, with huge eyes, circle the table. Marike watches them, hoping they will resist the urge to touch anything.

Helena says, "Mutti, *Brotchen*, like the ones you used to make in the bakery."

Marike nods. She closes her eyes and breathes in their warm, yeasty smell.

Cousin Albert interrupts and says, "But first, our pastor will say a blessing."

"*Dank sagen wir alle Gott*," he begins.

After his blessing, he joins Marike, Amalia, and the children as they wait for their food.

"We're first!" Helena exclaims.

She is right, Marike thinks, as honored guests we're at the head of the line. Certainly, that never happened in the camps.

"Welcome, you've come a long way to join your ancestors," the pastor says in German and smiles knowingly at them.

"Thank you, but I'm not sure what you mean. Cousin Albert is my mother-in-law's cousin's husband. We're not related. We call him cousin. It's easier."

Waving his hand, he chuckles, "*Nein*, I meant our little church was founded in 1876 by West Prussian immigrant families—your mother-in-law's ancestors."

"Oh, now I understand," Marike says. *He's right; it is comforting to think of our Prussian ancestors coming to America. It makes America less strange.* The children rush past her, their plates piled high with food.

Amalia's sharp eyes also observe them. Before Marike can say anything, Amalia says, "Children, for shame, your manners please."

Marike closes her eyes. When she opens them, a woman wearing a faded cotton dress pats her arm. "*Kinder,*" she says, her eyes sparkling, and she shakes her toddler's chubby arm. Her son continues to poke bread into his mouth, while butter oozes down his chin. In short pants, his knees and ankles form soft, doughy creases. Marike notices the woman staring at Edel's skinny, bowed legs.

"*Alter,* how old is he?" She asks.

"*Sieben,*" Marike answers.

"Seven, really?" she points at Helena.

Before Marike can reply, Helena displays eight fingers.

When the woman's sunburned face registers disbelief, Marike tells her that Elisabet is eleven and Heinz is twelve. Suddenly, all conversation ceases as everyone stares at her children.

Marike sees pity on their faces as they look at her emaciated children in their too-small clothes. *I hurt for them. They probably think Helena and her siblings could be Vogelscheuches, scarecrows.*

Soon, after coffee and dessert, everyone leaves. While Marike and Amalia clean up the kitchen, Cousin Albert explains their sleeping arrangements.

Later that night, as Marike lies in bed, unable to sleep, she recalls her last night with Horst.

How he massaged her sore back. His unhurried moves always gave her pleasure, but this night especially, she treasured his touch. She inhaled his musky scent. Her senses, intensified by the danger, made their love-making seem as if it was their first. With her fingers, she tenderly touched his face, memorizing his fine features. If only she could erase war's ugly presence as easily as she brushed aside her tears. It wasn't the time to cry. Instead, she took courage and massaged his shoulders. She wanted her touch to protect him forever, just as she knew he had similar thoughts. When they finally united, she hoped it would be enough to sustain her. Afterwards, curled together, Marike couldn't sleep. Anxious thoughts of what might come disturbed her rest. When morning's grey light came and his hand sought her breast, Marike responded.

Oh, my darling, where are you? Her mind cries into the night's blackness. *Can you find us in this strange country? Are you even alive? Please, dear God, if only I knew something.*

Although her tired children fell asleep immediately, Marike continues to stare at the ceiling as if it held answers. She'd like to roll over, but with Helena on one side of her and Edel on the other, she doesn't dare, for fear she will wake them. Marike can feel heat rising from their small bodies. If only they had their own home and didn't have to sleep in their cousin's hot attic.

How can she complain, she asks herself, when her dear Horst could be sleeping on a dirt floor in a prison camp, or worse? It's been so long, too many years. Is it time?

The following Sunday morning, Marike hurries to ready the children for the Emmaus Church's Sunday school. Since adults also participate in the Sunday school, the entire household attends.

Hesitantly, Amalia, Marike, and the children enter the strange church. Cousin Albert, who is behind them, bumps into them.

"Look," Heinz says. "Men on one side and women on the other—not like our church in Germany."

"Mutter where do we sit?" Elisabet whispers.

Cousin Albert points to the front of the church, "Boys on the left, in front of the men and girls on the right, in front of the women. College-age students sit in the balcony."

The children and Marike look up.

"Look Mutter, some boys are sitting with girls," Elisabet nudges Marike.

Before Marike can answer, Cousin Albert explains, "One day they intend to marry."

Helena tugs at her mother's elbow. "But, Mutti, I don't want to sit way up front. What if I have to go to the bathroom?"

Cousin Albert motions to the window, and Helena looks outside and sees the outhouse.

After they're seated in the women's row, Amalia cups her hand around her mouth and whispers to Marike, "I heard American Mennonites are stricter than we Germans."

Marike whispers, "We'd best be quiet. The minister has begun."

In German, the pastor intones a lengthy prayer, which is followed by one of Marike's favorite German hymns. Marike closes her eyes and imagines she has been transported back to her Prussian church. Opening her eyes, the seating arrangement reminds her she is in Kansas. As the service ends, the pastor invites everyone to a housewarming for Amalia, Marike, and her children in a parishioner's nearby barn.

As they leave the church, Marike asks Cousin Albert to explain. She doesn't understand: What is a 'housewarming?' He coyly evades her questions. When Amalia and the children question him, he throws up his hands in mock despair and joins the men gathering outside. Several old timers look up at the cloudy sky and shake their heads. Marike is reminded of her father, worrying whether there would be enough rain for his Prussian crops. Instead, these American farmers repeat the word "tornadoes," a worry foreign to Marike.

Later, when Cousin Albert, Amalia, Marike, and the children arrive at the barn, they are surprised to learn their Mennonite friends have donated used furniture, bed linens, kitchen utensils, and even children's toys. One farmer presents Marike with a basket of corn cobs to use in her stove. Their community, Cousin Albert explains, has gathered all these things for her house. Around the corner from his home, they will live in another house he owns. Since he, at eighty, needs help, Amalia will live in his house as a housekeeper. Also, he promises them a cow, chickens, and enough feed for the animals.

Soon they will have fresh food. *Better yet,* Marike thinks, *we'll have a house of our very own—with six rooms.*

The four children wander around the barn. Each child examines their new possessions.

"The furniture is well used," Amalia comments loudly to Marike, as she wiggles the table's broken leg.

"It will do. We'll repair it," Marike replies quickly. *How I used to enjoy giving. Receiving can be hard. It must be especially hard for Amalia.* Turning to the group, she says, "*Dankeschön,*" and her mother-in-law adds her appreciation.

As Marike looks around the barn for the children, a woman whose eyes sparkle under a cloud of white hair approaches her. In German, she introduces herself.

"*Hallo,* I'm Martha, your neighbor. Have you seen your new home yet?"

"No, Cousin Albert has been busy, but he hopes to move us in a few days. It can't be too soon, I'm sure. It has to be hard for him, at his age, with so many children underfoot." Marike catches a glimpse of her youngest hiding behind a chair and motions for him to come. "Where are your brother and sisters?"

"Probably playing games with my grandchildren," Martha says. "Anyway, anytime you need anything, just ask us. Besides, we owe you, since we use your house—I mean your basement—as a shelter. Our house doesn't have a basement. I hope you don't mind."

Marike's children appear with excited looks on their faces.

"Mutti," Elisabet asks, "can we stay just a little longer, please?"

"The other children are going to teach us how to play baseball," Heinz states.

"I'm sorry, Cousin Albert is waiting. Another time." Turning back to Martha, Marike asks, "I don't understand. What do you mean shelter?"

"Tornadoes. Didn't they tell you? We get lots. I wish I could stay and visit, but my husband Henry is waiting for me, and he hates it when I'm late." Martha leaves.

To Martha's retreating back, Marike says, "Tornadoes, we never had those in Prussia. I wonder what one is like, but surely it can't be as awful as war."

Chapter 42

It has been a week now since we moved in, and time I scrubbed this kitchen floor. I can't put it off any longer. She studies the stained linoleum and calls Heinz and Elisabet. She has to yell a second time before they hear her and arrive, laughing.

"Mutti, you called?" Elisabet asks.

"Yes, I need a bucket of water to wash this dirty floor. I had to shout over all of your noise. What on earth are you children doing?"

Elisabet smiles proudly, "We're running up and down the stairs. We're trying to make lots of noise."

"I noticed, but why on earth are you doing that?"

"Remember," Heinz says, "that mean old farmer in Germany who always made us tiptoe up and down his crummy stairs? Well, now we don't have to."

"I understand, but could Elisabet and you go pump some water in the meantime? Don't bother with our well. The hand pump is rusted, and the water is green and slimy. Cousin Albert said we could use the well water from the empty house across the street."

Heinz makes a face. "Ugh, we have to carry water. I wish we had indoor plumbing like we did in Germany."

"I wish we had an ice box," Elisabet says.

"If wishes were fishes," Marike says.

"I know," Heinz says, "we would have a pond full."

Marike says, "As I was saying, we can store food in Cousin Albert's ice box. Now, I can't scrub the floor without water."

"Yes, Mutter," Elisabet takes the pail.

Heinz studies the floor. "That's a bad stain, probably the old kerosene stove leaked."

"You're probably right, but I still have to try."

As Marike watches the children leave, she notices dark clouds over their outhouse. Except for the barn door banging in the wind and causing the chickens to flutter, it's strangely quiet. Even the meadowlarks are silent.

Too quiet, Marike thinks, *I know something is wrong.* Despite the heat and the moisture that runs down the insides of her arms, she shivers.

As she glances at the sky, she is startled to see that the rampaging clouds have changed to a deep emerald color.

She watches as Heinz and Elisabet awkwardly hurry home. Water sloshes from the bucket they carry between them. The neighbors follow them, shouting.

"Our radio said tornado warning for two o'clock, Butler County," Martha yells over the noisy wind. "And it is one fifty now."

"Better get the children in the cellar," Henry, Martha's husband says. "By the way, where's your cow?"

"In the barn, but I forgot to fasten the barn doors," Marike points at the doors banging in the wind.

"Heinz, you and I will get the doors. The rest of you run for the cellar."

"Oh no, I forgot the flashlight. Just a minute, I'll be back," Martha retreats to her home.

"Elisabet, forget the water, get in the storm cellar. Go, now. I'll get Edel and Helena."

Marike runs inside the two-story frame house and finds Helena and Edel sitting on the stairs.

"Mutti, look, Edel and I are playing school. I'm teaching Edel to count in English," says Helena.

"Hurry, children, we have to go to the cellar," Marike grabs Edel's and Helena's hands.

Helena starts to cry, "I hate cellars. They're scary."

Marike half crouches with her face close to Helena's. "I understand, but a bad storm is coming. We'll be safer in the cellar. Come."

Helena holds her mother's hand as Marike hurries them outside and down the concrete steps. Martha joins them as Henry and Heinz fasten the cellar's flapping doors shut. Damp darkness sucks them in.

"Elisabet?"

"Yes, Mutti, I'm here."

"Is everyone okay?"

"Yes," they answer.

"I can't see, I'm scared," Edel complains.

"I know there's a light here," Marike feels along the clammy wall until something touches her face. Believing it's a cobweb, she starts to brush it away, until she realizes it's a cord. She yanks it. Suddenly, a single bulb dangling from the bare rafters lights the room. Dusty shelves, containing empty canning jars, line the cellar's walls. In the center of the cellar sit metal chairs and a cot, reminders of the cellar's other purpose.

With Helena and Edel, Marike sits on the cot facing Heinz, Elisabet, Martha, and Henry, who are seated on chairs.

The bare bulb casts shadows.

"My little chickadees, they'll be hurt," Edel cries as he jumps up.

"They're safe in the chicken house," Marike draws Edel to her.

Overhead, they hear a pinging sound.

"Mutti, are they bombing us?" Edel asks.

"No, Edel. No bombs." Marike draws him close.

"I'll bet this is a tornado. Cousin Albert warned us. He said they often happen in Kansas," Elisabet says.

"I don't remember any tornadoes in Germany or even Denmark. Do you?" Heinz asks.

Henry answers slowly, "Oh, I guess other countries have tornadoes, but most are in the U.S. Here in Butler County, we had one this past May. May 19 was the exact date. I remember, because it was my seventieth birthday."

"Was it bad?" Heinz asks.

"Was my birthday bad? Actually it was pretty good, even though we had to celebrate it in my daughter's cellar."

"I meant—" Heinz begins.

"I know, just kidding you. Naw, nobody got killed or anything." Henry shakes his head.

"Now Henry, hush, you'll scare these poor children," Martha says.

The children look up at the rafters shaking. Fine dust filters down. The light flicks off and on, until finally, there is blackness. The cellar doors rattle as wind, rain, and hail pummel them. When the temperature drops, the children huddle together for warmth.

Heinz gets up and walks in the direction of the slice of light between the doors, "I'm going to take a peek outside. How do we know what's happening?"

"No, Heinz, it's not safe. Wait," Marike yells over the shrieking wind.

"Your mother is right. Stay inside," Henry orders, his voice stern.

"Don't worry," Martha says, "I brought my trusty flashlight. In storms like this one, we often lose electricity." She clicks the flashlight. "See, light."

"Mutti," Elisabet says, "it's just like Danzig, when someone stuck a candle through the wall."

"It reminds me of a German prayer, *Gott liebt Dich und braucht Dich* by Trangott Giesen," says Marike.

"I think I heard it in church," Martha says. "What does it mean?"

"It says a candle is like God's gifts of hope and love when you live with and for others."

"I'm still scared," Edel says. "I wonder if tornadoes are bad like bombs."

"Maybe not as bad," Henry answers. "But tornadoes can still destroy."

"Oh, for goodness sakes," Martha says, "don't tell me you poor things were bombed?"

"Yes, we hid in a basement when we were bombed in Danzig. I'll never forget," Elisabet says.

Sitting down, Heinz says, "I remember watching the bombers and seeing the bombs fall. The noise, fire, earth shaking. It was scary."

Since she holds the flashlight, the children can't see her face, but Martha's voice softens. "It must have been pretty terrible—the bombing, the refugee camps, and all. During the war, Henry and I went to a movie theater, and before the feature started, they showed a newsreel of the Allies fire-bombing German cities. Some people cheered. It hurt to hear them, because we had relatives in Germany."

"We haven't been to a movie since," says Henry.

"For a long time, we didn't know if our German relatives were still alive. We just kept praying. Thank heavens, they survived. But Henry's uncle, we never heard from him. He is still missing."

"I'm so sorry," Marike says.

"Albert told us…about your husband. It must be awful for you, not knowing."

Marike nods. "For years, I hoped Horst survived, maybe in one of the Russian POW camps. When other German soldiers were released, Horst didn't come. The children and I talked. It's time. The German government gave me papers. When I fill them out, they'll give me a little widow's pension. I don't want to. It's like giving up—saying he's dead." Marike turns her face away and shudders.

"I 'member Vater and the bombs," Edel says, clinging to Marike's waist.

"You couldn't. You were only two," Heinz says.

"I do too," Edel yells. "I 'member the firecrackers and the house shaking."

"He does remember the bombs," Marike says softly.

"I liked Mutti's stories. All night long she told them—made me feel safe," Elisabet says.

"I liked her singing best of all," Helena says and begins to hum.

"And we're safe now. God always protects us. We found a home where we are welcome." Marike joins Helena, singing the children's favorite hymn.

The End

Acknowledgements

When a friend shared her Prussian Mennonite family's World War II experiences, I became interested in the little-known history of more than 200,000 Prussian refugees held from 1945 to 1949 in Danish refugee camps. Although I drew heavily on my friend's and her extended family's experiences, those of other Danish refugee camp survivors, and extensive research, the characters are entirely fictional. This is a work of fiction. Names, places, and some incidents have been changed. Any resemblance to people living or dead is not intended. The plot and characters are entirely my own. I am deeply grateful to my friend's family and to her, especially, for the history they shared and her assistance in translating the German texts. As she and her family prefer to remain anonymous, I have not included their names.

In April, 1940, German naval units, Luftwaffe squadrons and infantry divisions defeated and occupied Denmark. In early 1945, near the end of the war, 200,000 refugees from East and West Prussia and Germany fled to Denmark. The German military informed the Danish government that it would need to provide for the refugees. On May 4, 1945, British Commander Montgomery accepted the surrender of German forces in northwest Germany, Denmark, and Holland. In May and June of 1945, an estimated 10,000 refugees in Denmark died; approximately 6,000 of those were children. Most of the German refugees lived in camps surrounded by barbed wire and "protected" by Danish guards. By the time the Japanese surrendered in August 1945, millions of soldiers and civilians had died in World War II. Twelve million Germans were forced from their homes.

Now, almost seventy years later, much has been written about the victims of German aggression. Whether due to shame, guilt, or fear of retaliation, however, very little has been written about the ordinary German citizens' plight.

Others I would like to acknowledge are Teresa Funke, whose editing and guidance were invaluable. I appreciate the support of the Red Feather Lakes Writers Group and the Northern Colorado Writers Association, and the research of Sara Myers, former Red Feather Lakes Community librarian. I want to thank Judy and Tom Viola and Frances Feist for their help with the German phrases. I appreciate the editorial help of my daughter Michelle Riley, Copy Editor Saundie Weiss, and Editor Lisa Péré. To anyone that I may have failed to include, please accept my deep apologies and my sincere thanks for your assistance in making this book a reality.

Resources

Few fiction books include a resource list. However, the following sources were extremely helpful during the writing of this book. Readers who want more information about the real-life people, places, and times that I fictionalized in *Barbed Wire and Daisies* might find these sources interesting.

- Arne Gammelgaard. *Ungeladene Gäste, Ostdeutsche Flüchtlinge in Dänemark 1945-1949*, a German translation of the Danish title *Mennesker i Malstrøm*.
- Henrik Havrehed. *Die deutschen Flüchtlinge in Dänemark 1945-1949*.

These sources were especially helpful in comprehending the refugees' circumstances.

- John A. Lapp and C. Arnold Snyder, Editors. *Testing Faith and Tradition*.
- Harold S. Bender. "Gronau Mennonite Church (Gronau, Nordrhein-Westfalen, Germany)." Global Anabaptist Mennonite Encyclopedia Online. http://gameo.org/encyclopedia/contents/gronau_mennonite_church_gronau_nordrhein_westfalen.

- Christian Neff. "Ernstweiler (Rheinland-Pfalz, Germany)." Global Anabaptist Mennonite Encyclopedia Online. http://www.gameo.org/encyclopedia/contents/ernstweiler_rheinland_pfalz_germany.
- C. Henry Smith. *Smith's Story of the Mennonites* and *Early Russian Mennonite History, Part One, Excerpts from the Coming of the Russian Mennonites.*

I also consulted the following resources.

- Abram S. Benenson, Editor. *Control of Communicable Diseases Manual,* 16th edition.
- Rogers Brubaker. *Citizenship and Nationhood in France and Germany.*
- Douglas C. Dildy, illustrated by John White. *Denmark and Norway 1940: Hitler's Boldest Operation.*
- Manfred Ertel. *Denmark's Myths Shattered: A Legacy of Dead German Children.* http://www.spiegel.de/international/0,1518,355772,00.html.
- Kirsten Lylloff. *Barn eller fiende (Children or the Enemy)*
- Peter Darman, Editor. *World War II: A Day-by-Day History.*
- Friedrich Fiechtner, Editor. *Fateful Danube Journey: A True Account of an Emigration to Russia, 1816-1817.* Translated from the German by Theodore C. Wenzlaff.
- Stuart Fortey, Horst Kopleck, Helen Galloway, Veronika Schnorr, Editors. *HarperCollins German College Dictionary.*
- Martin Gilbert. *The Second World War: A Complete History,* Revised Edition.
- Jakob Grimm, Karl Ludwig, and Wilhelm Grimm. *Sixty Tales of the Brothers Grimm.*
- Bonnie Hamre. "The Mennonites of Paraguay." About.com

South America Travel. http://gosouthamerica.about.com/cs/southamerica/a/ParMennonites.htm.

- "History: Boom Town to Farm Town." Brainerd History. http://www.rootinaround.com/brainerd/history2.html.
- Anne Holm. *I Am David*. Translated from the Danish by L.W. Kingsland.
- Marianne Holmen. *Danish Practical Dictionary*.
- Ruth Hunt. *East Wind: A Survivor's True Story of Faith Inside the Gulag of WWII*.
- Jane Hutchings, Emily Hatchwell, and Brian Bell, Editors. *Denmark (Insight Guide Denmark)*.
- Eric Jensen. *Forever and a Day: The World War II Odyssey of an American Family*.
- Knud J.V. Jespersen. *A History of Denmark*. Translated by Ivan Hill.
- Marcus Job. *Our People: As Told by Survivors of Russian Labor Camps*.
- Kansas Tornadoes 1950-1995, Butler County Tornadoes. Tornadoes by State. http://www.tornadoproject.com/alltorns/kstorn1.htm.
- Maria Kreiser. *Meine Zeit in Gottes Händen. Though My Soul More Bent: Memoir of a Soviet German*. Translated and edited from the German by James T. Gessele.
- Dorothea von Schwanenflügel Lawson. *Laughter Wasn't Rationed: A Personal Journey Through Germany's World Wars and Postwar Years*. Previously published with the subtitle *Remembering the War Years in Germany*.
- Kirsten Lylloff. *Inter Arma Caritas: The Red Cross and the Administration of the German Refugees in Denmark 1945-1949*. http://www.historisktidsskrift.dk/summary/102_124.html.
- Charles Messenger, John Keegan (Editor). *The Second World War in Europe*.

- John Philipps. *The Tragedy of the Soviet Germans: A Story of Survival.*
- John Ries. "History's Greatest Naval Disasters." *Institute for Historical Review,* http://www.ihr.org/jhr/v12/v12.
- Wolfgang W.E. Samuel. *German Boy: A Refugee's Story.*
- Linda J. Schupp. *Assessing and Treating Trauma and PTSD.*
- Rudolf von Thadden. *Prussia: The History of a Lost State.* Originally published in German as *Fragen an Preussen.* Translated by Angi Rutter.
- Grabert Verlag. "The Nemmersdorf Massacre", *Directional Positions on Contemporary History, the Great Angle, Volume 2.* Translated by Duncan Edmister. http://www.kehrusker.net/index.php?option=com_content&view=article&id=250:das-massaker-von-nemmersdorf&catid=48:alliierte-greueltaten&Itemid=74.
- Peter H. Tveskov. *Conquered, Not Defeated: Growing Up in Denmark During the German Occupation of World War II.*
- U.S. Library of Congress. *Germany: Postwar Occupation and Division.* http://countrystudies.us/germany/44.htm.
- Joel Carl Welty. *The Hunger Year: In the French Zone of Divided Germany, 1946-1947.*
- Hamburger Abendblatt. *Why 7000 Children Had to Die; Second World War: The Cruel Fate of German Refugees in Denmark.* Translated by Arnim Johannis. http://groups.google.com/group/soc.history/browse_thread/thread/6bcebb2b169dddbf/bb2b.

CPSIA information can be obtained at www.ICGtesting.com
Printed in the USA
BVOW080954240912

01151BV00001B/9/P